The *Best* of

BOTH WORLDS

A NOVEL BY
Cher Jones

Life Changing Books

Published by Life Changing Books

P.O. Box 423

Brandywine, MD 20613

Library of Congress Cataloging-in-Publication Data;

www.lifechangingbooks.net

13 Digit: 9781943174140

Follow us:

Twitter: www.twitter.com/lcbooks

Facebook: Life Changing Books/lcbooks

Instagram: Lcbooks

Pinterest: Life Changing Books

Follow Cher:

Facebook https://www.facebook.com/BrandNewCher

Instagram https://www.instagram.com/brandnewcher/

Twitter https://twitter.com/BrandNewCher

Pintrest https://www.pinterest.com/BrandNewCher/

Blog http://brandnewcher.com/

Acknowledgements

It is with deepest gratitude that I acknowledge those that have helped make my life and my work a lot happier along the way. Please take this with all the love I am sending it out with, if I missed your name it was not intentional. I love you all.

First, I want to thank God, my Creator, and the lover of my soul. Thank You God for giving me the life, the support, and the talent to create. I pray that by using my talents, I honor and glorify you.

I would also like to thank my publisher, Life Changing Books, for giving this first time author a chance, and more importantly, a contract. You took my project and guided me through the process, and we have created magic. I am thankful for your belief in me and the opportunity to spread my words all around the world. This is a best-seller!

I am grateful to say a huge thank you to my family. You are my reason why. I love you each so very much, and I would never have had the reason to do any of this without you. To my daughters Toi, Kennedy, and Madison you are my world! I love and appreciate each of your different personalities. You make me happy and you keep our lives fun. You make me so proud, I hope I do the same for you. Mommy loves you like life. To my siblings Jermain, Willie, and Lavell, y'all created this diva that I am so I hope you are proud of what you created. All the adventures, all the antics, and all the memories are priceless. I love you all for real for real. To my beautiful nieces and handsome nephews, Aunty Cher loves you and always will, you will never have to wonder. To my daddy thanks for calling me your delight, for always loving me, for making me so pretty, and for passing on your gift of gab. I love you and Iris very much. And to my In-Laws, that are more like Out-Laws, I love how we get down. Y'all more than most, have taught me the true meaning of loyalty. I love you all. Aunties and Uncles thanks for loving me, I love you all. And finally, to the crazy original gangsters, also known as my cousins…we survived all the wild foolishness growing up, here's to more of the same. I couldn't love you more if I tried.

I also have to thank my friends. I am truly blessed to say that I have friends. Friends that love me, care for me when I'm grieving, take care of me when I'm in need, and celebrate all of the big and little things with me. Real friends. I love you all, and I will not even try to name all y'all on here. But there are a few names I would be remiss not to call. Elvira, Chaunda, and Dreame you all are crew! Whether I need a laugh, a cry, an ear, or a turn-up, y'all are always there for me. Thank you for adopting my family into your family and for sharing all the love you have with me and Team Jones. I love you all, your husbands, Kerry, Demi, and Corey and your children so much it's crazy.

Next, these last two people fit into too many categories, yet stand alone.

To my friend that became my sister, Adrienne D. Willis-Haynes, you embody truth, love, and respect. You and I have been through it all, and yet we still look good! I will always be grateful for your strength, support and trust. You always know what to say, and what not to say, and even if there's nothing to say, we're ok with that. Some people don't understand, but our love doesn't require them to. Thank you for always believing in me. I love you.

Finally, and most importantly, my husband, my best friend, my lover, my confidant, and my love, Tyrone S. Jones. Baby, without you none of this would be relevant. Without your support, and sometimes your push, I couldn't have finished this project. You always encourage me and our girls to be the leaders we were created to be. But isn't that what leaders do? They create other leaders. I am happy and grateful now that we are creating our legacy and we are doing it together. We create what we want. There will never be another you, and I wouldn't have it any other way. Thank you for loving me the way I deserve to be loved. Thank you for loving our girls so much that they will compare every future love to yours. You are our hero. You are our love. I am so grateful that you are mine. Here's to a future filled with wonder and joy, doing what we love to do. Now, let's get this money!

Team Jones
11/14/15

Dedication

This book is dedicated to the memory of my two angels

Quinnie Juanita Haynes

You are my heart, my rock, my mommy. I miss you more than words will ever express, and I hope you are proud of the woman I've become. Until we meet again, our love is never-ending.

Willie 'MJ' Marion Haynes, Jr

You let your light shine bright, and therefore, so will I
Until we meet again, I Love you to infinity baby boy,

Aunty Cher
#willz #missingmj #mylove
Instagram: Lcbooks

Pinterest: Life Changing Books

CHAPTER ONE

The club was packed tight. On the dance floor, bodies gyrated together to *Trap Queen* by Fetty Wap. Dakota's wrap dress clung to her curves for dear life as she squeezed through the crowd to rest her feet, but the music was way too enticing to stand still. Sweat rolled down her back, but that wasn't the only reason her panties were wet. She loved to dance; it turned her on being the center of attention.

Alexander came and stood next to her; she paid him no mind. Dakota plopped a juicy olive into her mouth and continued sipping her dry, vodka Martini, as if in her own little world. But she could feel his intense stare. Finally, she turned and looked at him. He was tall, dark, and handsome. He looked down at her with no expression on his face, and without saying a word.

"Yes?" Dakota inquired looking right back at him. She was used to being looked at by men, but could usually make a man blush. Not this man, though. He was enjoying the view and wasn't apologizing for looking either. They checked each other out. Neither said a word. He took her hand; intrigued, she allowed herself to be led to the dance floor. She began to sway her hips to *Can't Feel My Face*, by The Weeknd. Alexander watched her little show and she found herself enjoying his undivided attention.

She was really getting into the bold quiet type when he broke his silence.

"Why have you ignored me all night?"

The question caught her by surprise, but not as much as his baritone voice and his lack of an accent. She tried to come back with a snazzy reply, but he leaned in and kissed her. On the lips…no questions asked. No permission needed. This man was anything but ordinary; and Dakota was so tired of ordinary. She knew she should stop him, but she didn't. He leaned back and looked at her some more as if waiting for an answer to his question.

She was shocked by the kiss, and surprised by the softness of his lips.She managed to pull it together.

"I didn't see you," was all she could muster.

"I've been watching you all night playing with these little boys" he told her, motioning with his hand. "Are you brave enough to try a real man?" he asked.

She smiled, unable to help herself.

"Why? Are you a *real* man?" she teased.

He ignored the question and pulled her closer to him; she could feel that he was indeed a real man.

"I've wanted you since the moment I saw you." He told her.

All Dakota could think about was his baby smooth skin and "*damn he smelled good.*"

He had his hand casually on her ass, their eyes locked. Her body froze. His hand was down her pants and moving into her panties. His eyes never left hers. Her heart was racing but, she didn't dare move; someone might see. A sexy smile was spreading across his handsome face. She could tell he was used to getting what he wanted. Dakota dared to glance to her right and looked in the full length mirror to see if anyone could tell what he was doing. She couldn't see what he was doing in the dim night club light. She let him continue.

He was really pushing her outside her box, both figuratively and literally. She loved every exhilarating moment of it. Dakota quickly scanned the room to see if anyone was watching them; everyone was having too much fun to pay attention to them. Boldly, she swayed her hips widening her stance to allow him to find what he was looking for. They looked each other squarely in the eyes as his talented fingers gave her a preview of what was to come. Dakota closed her eyes and rocked her ass on his hand. Suddenly he stopped and licked his fingers as if that was the only reason he'd put them down there in the first place.

"You taste delicious. What's your name?" he asked seductively.

"Dakota" she murmured.

And when he leaned in to give her a luscious kiss, she could care less if anyone saw them. They kissed for a few moments and when he pulled back Dakota still had her eyes closed, "The lights are on," he whispered in her ear. She almost fainted.

Dakota's eyes flew open. Her heart was pounding until she realized it was just a dream. The same dream, almost every night

since that moment occurred. Sunlight streamed
Despite Dakota's best efforts to find the perfect
for her eastern facing bedroom, the sun always fou.
It was already after 7 am so, she didn't ever
her boyfriend, Brandon, knowing that he was well i,   ⌐⌐⌐⌐ut
by now. His body displayed his commitment to working out. Not
only was Brandon handsome with his smooth light-brown skin,
bedroom eyes, and luscious lips, he was fine. His chiseled features,
carved arms, slim waist, and powerful legs were partly natural, due
to good genes, but mainly from his dedicated workout routine. He
was a creature of habit and rarely veered from his schedule.

Dakota was no slouch herself. Although she was only
twenty-four years old, she carried herself like a woman. Her
caramel colored skin was flawless. Her hazel, almond shaped eyes
cast a spell on any man she looked at. She was beautiful by
anyone's standards, and she knew it. Dakota maintained her curves
through a healthy diet and yoga 4 days a week. She loved herself,
but wasn't conceited. If asked though, she'd tell you that her best
assets were her double D breasts, and her Tina Turner legs.

Yet, here she was all alone in the California styled king bed.
She lay awake, remembering the night she'd met Alexander. His
style was so different from any other man she had ever met. He
came into her life, like a storm. Taking charge of all of her senses.
Making her feel things she hadn't felt in such a long time. Her
pulse quickened at the thought of his touch; anywhere on her body.
His voice, his eyes, his lips, they all created a heat inside of her
that only he could quench.

The thoughts and emotions, she was feeling, made her wish
he was with her right now. *"But if wishes were horses, we all
would ride."* She heard her grandmother's voice in her head. This
thought only led her to think about riding Alexander like a horse.

"Yes, a big, black, strong horse…" Dakota had to laugh at
that last thought.

Sometimes her imagination carried her away, to far off
places, where there was no such thing as reality; no cares, or
worries, and definitely no boring ass responsibilities. But, she was
not in a far off place, she was home, and it was time to get up and
get the day started. She pulled the covers back as the dreamy grip
of sleep slowly released her.

since that moment occurred. Sunlight streamed into the room. Despite Dakota's best efforts to find the perfect black-out drapes for her eastern facing bedroom, the sun always found its way in.

It was already after 7 am so, she didn't even reach over for her boyfriend, Brandon, knowing that he was well into his workout by now. His body displayed his commitment to working out. Not only was Brandon handsome with his smooth light-brown skin, bedroom eyes, and luscious lips, he was fine. His chiseled features, carved arms, slim waist, and powerful legs were partly natural, due to good genes, but mainly from his dedicated workout routine. He was a creature of habit and rarely veered from his schedule.

Dakota was no slouch herself. Although she was only twenty-four years old, she carried herself like a woman. Her caramel colored skin was flawless. Her hazel, almond shaped eyes cast a spell on any man she looked at. She was beautiful by anyone's standards, and she knew it. Dakota maintained her curves through a healthy diet and yoga 4 days a week. She loved herself, but wasn't conceited. If asked though, she'd tell you that her best assets were her double D breasts, and her Tina Turner legs.

Yet, here she was all alone in the California styled king bed. She lay awake, remembering the night she'd met Alexander. His style was so different from any other man she had ever met. He came into her life, like a storm. Taking charge of all of her senses. Making her feel things she hadn't felt in such a long time. Her pulse quickened at the thought of his touch; anywhere on her body. His voice, his eyes, his lips, they all created a heat inside of her that only he could quench.

The thoughts and emotions, she was feeling, made her wish he was with her right now. *"But if wishes were horses, we all would ride."* She heard her grandmother's voice in her head. This thought only led her to think about riding Alexander like a horse.

"Yes, a big, black, strong horse..." Dakota had to laugh at that last thought.

Sometimes her imagination carried her away, to far off places, where there was no such thing as reality; no cares, or worries, and definitely no boring ass responsibilities. But, she was not in a far off place, she was home, and it was time to get up and get the day started. She pulled the covers back as the dreamy grip of sleep slowly released her.

Dakota lived by her planner on most days. But in general, she liked to let her day unfold as it may; following her whims. Today was her day off, and she was only going to do what she felt like doing. Maybe a facial and body scrub at home, followed by a fill-in and pedicure at Yakima's nail salon.

Even though Dakota owned a day spa, she still liked to support her best friend by dropping a few dollars at her place of business as well.

That sounds like a good plan, she thought to herself. *What about Alexander? Where does he fit in?* Ugghh…*I don't want to think about that right now.*

"Besides, he will fit in where he can get in, I'm sure he'll find a spot," she now spoke aloud to no one in particular.

She was nervous enough about creeping with Alexander and did not want to think about it right now.

"*Breathe,*" she reminded herself. "*You deserve some fun, remember?*"

It seemed she had to remind herself of that more and more these days. Especially now that her spa clientele was growing by leaps and bounds. It was a great problem to have, at her spa Tranquilité, but it was a problem none the less. Dakota had quality technicians working in her spa, but with such a demand for her exclusive packages, she had to start thinking about expansion. This meant, more techs, more room, more products, and more of her precious time.

She knew a hot shower would calm her nerves. Dakota always loved a body scrub in the morning; she really wanted to get a massage as well.

"*Maybe he'll give me one later,*" her thoughts crept into her mind as she stepped into the shower. The hot water flowed over her body. The sugar scrub she used kept her skin soft and glowing. Afterwards, she dressed in a two-piece, white, denim shorts set and some Steve Madden *Stecy* heels. She loved heels, and wore them with just about everything. She went for a natural look for her face and applied light makeup. She spritzed Daisy by Marc Jacobs, perfume into the air and walked through it. Now she was complete.

Feeling refreshed she headed downstairs to leave. She activated the alarm system, stepped out into the garage and hopped into her, white-on-white Escalade.

"What could be sweeter than the smell of a new truck?" She wondered.

The engine roared to life and XM Radio was playing one of her favorite songs. Warm sunshine greeted her and she inhaled the sweet smell of success.

She waved to a neighbor, and sang along as she rode to the nail salon hoping Yakima was not booked. Again, Alexander crossed her mind; she would have to deal with the plans they made sooner or later, so she chose to let her mind explore the possibilities. She could just picture him with his fine ass, looking all good and smelling like a man. Alexander was 6'3," dark brown, and built like a warrior. He was handsome, rich and most importantly confident. He carried himself like he was 'all of that' yet he wasn't cocky.

Confidence in a man turned Dakota on in a big way. She had never been attracted to a wimpy man. All of the male influences in her life had been confident in themselves; her grandfather, her father, and her man Brandon. Something about a man's confidence made Dakota feel safer with him. Some guys thought she was stuck up, but she knew they weren't self-assured enough to deal with a woman like her. She couldn't stand a cowering or apologetic man.

But, there was nothing that turned Dakota off about Alexander. Actually, everything about him made Dakota forget she was in a committed relationship, and this scared her.

She didn't want to lose Brandon, because she loved him. Brandon was always the man she saw herself married to. The man that she'd always envisioned having her children with, and growing old with. She knew in her heart that he was her true love, and she wasn't trying to mess that up. She just wanted her cake and eat it too.

It's just that her life had gotten into such a rut lately, it was ridiculous. Every day the same old shit; get up, run her business, come home, eat, watch TV, and sleep. Boring! She wanted to be swept off her feet every now and then, and not have to be so responsible all the damn time.

"What was so wrong with that?" She wondered.

Nothing, unless you considered Brandon might kill her for cheating on him. Brandon was Dakota's man of 6 years. She affectionately called him 'Don Juan' and true to his name, he used to be very romantic. He lovingly called her 'Coca' because, he said she was shaped like the old school Coca Cola bottles.

He was a great provider, but the excitement was gone from their relationship. Everything was predictable and safe; he even wanted to schedule when they had sex.

Brandon hadn't always been this way, but time changes things. Dakota could appreciate the fact that he wanted nothing but the best for them. She wanted the same things. She just wasn't ready to throw in the towel and except a life of hum-drum boredom to have it.

The whole time she was getting her pedicure, Alex was on her mind. Just remembering Alex's kiss made her body shiver. She wanted to call him, but she would wait a little longer. He said he would be free after 3 O'clock and it was only 12:30. So, she would wait.

The promise of this weekend brought the butterflies back to her stomach again. They'd had passionate sex a couple of times, but this would be the first time they would be together for a weekend trip. Oh, the things they could do, with a whole weekend of debauchery…

"What if things don't go as planned? What if someone recognizes me?" She worried.

This was risky business, but Dakota needed this exhilaration right now. She wasn't looking for a boyfriend, she already had one. She wasn't looking to lose her boyfriend either; she was just looking for some thrills and a feeling of freedom. Alex could provide that.

"Screw it, I'm going and whatever happens just happens!"

Dakota longed for spontaneity and surprises. Alexander was just the man to give her both. He kept her heart racing and her mind whirling from anticipation. With her mind made up, she left the nail salon in a hurry, on a mission home to pack her bags.

CHAPTER 2

She packed and repacked, a couple of times, before settling on just the right outfits for her trip. She didn't want to take too many things and arouse Brandon's suspicion. It had taken several days to convince Brandon that she needed to go on this trip, in the name of business, of course. And then it took even more convincing that she should go without him. That was literally the most nerve racking part of it all. She hardly ever traveled without Brandon in the past, and so he was more than a little shocked that he wasn't invited.

It was three thirty, in the afternoon, and Dakota was in traffic when her cell phone rang. Hoping it was Alexander, and fearing it was Brandon, she let it ring. OnStar announced that it was Brandon. Taking a deep breath she answered on the third ring.

"Hey babe, what's up?" She tried not to sound disappointed.

"Everything's good. "Did you leave yet?" He asked, as she knew he would.

"Yes I'm almost there; I've got about an hour to go."

Knowing he'd asked 20 questions if she didn't take charge of the call, she asked him what he was doing. But he wasn't falling for the side step. He ignored her question and asked,

"So what time is your class?"

She had told Brandon that she had training on franchising her business in Atlanta, GA, but she hadn't told him she wouldn't be alone. She knew his questioning routine, all too well.

"It's all day tomorrow starting at 7am, then a half day after that. I'll be home Sunday evening, why?" she asked out of frustration.

She knew better than to invite an argument but she couldn't resist. His predictability was getting on her nerves.

"I just wanted to know, damn is that a problem?" He asked, raising his voice a little.

"No honey, it is not a problem; I just thought you would be set after that session we had last night."She laughed… and finally he joined in with her.

After a couple more questions, they hung up and Dakota felt a little more confident with her decision.

She arrived at the hotel and found the most discreet parking space available. She looked around suspiciously a couple of times to see if anyone was paying her particular attention. Everyone seemed to be minding their own business today; no one looked suspect. After a couple of deep breaths, and a short self-pep talk, she opened the door.

She stepped out, trying as hard as possible to appear nonchalant. Dakota casually tossed her hair and grabbed her overnight bag from the back of the truck.

"Walk!"

She willed her legs.

Most of the time, she loved to be the center of attention and would welcome stares, but at the moment she felt an imaginary spotlight on her that she wanted no part of. Inside of the Hotel lobby, people moved about as if she were not there, so she relaxed a bit.

To her right was the check in desk and straight ahead was a bar.

"Perfect, I need a drink right about now."

She walked over and found a spot at the end of the bar where she sat down. From there, she could directly view the lobby doors and still not be immediately seen. Why was her heart racing so fast? Her nerves were all in a bundle ready to snap at any moment.

"What can I get you, honey?"

The bartender had walked up behind Dakota, scaring a couple years off her life.

"Damn you scared me!" Dakota exclaimed, feeling like a child stealing cookies out of the cookie jar.

The bartender gave her a knowing look that said "that's what you get for creepin'" but she didn't say anything out loud.

Pulling herself together, Dakota decided she wanted something strong.

"Give me a Jack on the rocks, please. Sorry. I'm in town on business and my mind was going 50mph when you walked up, I didn't see you." Dakota laughed nervously.

"No apologies necessary." The bartender replied. She could see right thru Dakota's flimsy "Business trip" lie, but she appreciated the apology.

"I'm Carrie and if you need anything, just give me a holler. Would you like to run a tab Miss?"

"I'd like to pay as I go thanks; by the way, my name's Karen." Dakota lied, "It's nice to meet you."

A couple of Jacks later, Dakota was quite relaxed and having fun flirting with some guys at the bar. One in particular, kept her on her toes. His name was Damon. He was from the mid-west on a business trip with some colleagues. He was light-skinned with green eyes and a baby face. They had started conversing over a couple of drinks, while they each waited for friends. He was obviously smitten with Dakota, and after building up the courage, he leaned in and whispered into Dakota's ear.

She giggled as the cutie on her left whispered naughty suggestions in her ear; she turned away, pretending to blush, when she caught sight of him. Alexander was here at last. The sight of him in his military uniform, took her breath for a moment. Alex was in the reserves and this was one of his weekends to 'be all that he could be'. He was having a conversation with a young woman who apparently wanted to be an 'Army of One' with him.

"Damn, that's all for me!" Dakota thought to herself. Cutie on the left was instantly forgotten. What she was planning to do to Alex might be illegal in some states, but then again who had to know? Dakota grinned to herself.

Alexander must have felt her stare and looked up at her across the lobby. Without hesitation, he walked over to her.

She slid off the bar seat as seductively as she could after three straight Jack Daniels, but lost her balance. His strong arms were around her waist before anyone could notice a thing. He held her tight, in his vice grip, like he would never let go.

"Feeling good, are we?" he teased. Staring into her beautiful, almond shaped eyes.

"Really good now" Dakota purred, admiring his luscious lips.

He leaned in and kissed her softly, then stepped back to admire her loveliness. The dress she wore accentuated all of her luscious curves.

"Damn! What am I going to do with all of this?" he asked the jealous men in the bar. All eyes were on Dakota, and each wished they were in his shoes that night. Not waiting for a reply, he picked up her bag and led her to the elevator. Dakota didn't even glance back. If someone saw her now, they'd know she didn't give a damn.

Dakota felt like a kid on Santa's lap, she was that excited. She had been in her share of hotel rooms in the past with lovers, and even with Brandon so she knew what to expect in general. But with Alexander, it was an open book; like one she had never read before.

Their room was located on the 3rd floor facing a busy street in downtown Atlanta. It was maybe a 3 star hotel, but Dakota could care less about ratings right now, the only stars she wanted to see tonight were the ones Alexander would take her to when he explored her universe. He unlocked the door and held it open for her.

"*Such a gentleman,*" Dakota thought to herself as she breezed into the safety of the room. She'd barely glanced around the room when he gently grabbed her by her arm. He spun her around to face him, and drew her close with one of her arms still behind her back. Dakota decided right then, that she liked this game.

"Is there a problem officer?" she asked pretending to be shocked.

He looked back and forth between her almond eyes and her voluptuous breasts, ignoring her question. He wasn't hurting her arm but she knew she couldn't get away even if she wanted; which she did not. She closed her eyes and waited for his kiss. Instead, he licked her softly on her earlobe and down her neck toward her breast. Her breast grew taught and her nipples hardened in anticipation of his tongue. She didn't have long to wait; he bit her nipple right through the sheer material of her dress. She arched her back to give him better access.

As he teased her body he loosened his grip on her arm and let it slip down by her side; only to quickly turn her away from him, toward the door. He leaned her up against the door as he pulled both her arms up, and now held both her wrists captive above her head in one of his strong hands. His other hand was seeking a very familiar spot.

His breath on her neck was slow and controlled, while Dakota's breathe was getting harder and harder to catch. Slowly his fingertips traced the outline of her body. His hand was up under her dress. She could feel his hands on her hot skin, his fingers knew exactly where to go, and what to do.At that moment his hand crept up and grasped her inner thigh firmly.

"Keep your hands up" his sexy voice whispered in her ear.

He was sucking her neck and shoulders while his fingers found their target inside her panties and danced inside her wetness.

"Don't move" Alexander whispered again.

She nodded her surrender. The metal door felt cool against her hot face. He knelt down behind her, to remove her panties and then slid her legs apart until she thought she might fall. Alexander positioned himself between her legs in a sitting position, with his back to the door, facing her private joy.

"Don't move" he reminded her, and then he buried his face in the softness between her legs and licked everything his talented tongue could reach.

"Ooo, you certainly know what you're doing, huh baby?" Dakota thought to herself. Sweet sensations flowed through her body, and all of her senses were alive.

He wasn't playing around anymore; he was on a mission to bring her to ecstasy. He eased his forefinger into her pussy and his thumb into her ass while his tongue worked her clit overtime. He was inside of her everywhere at once and still licking. Moans of pleasure escaped her throat as her legs began to tremble.

"Oh, shit, wait, wait!" she tried to say, but Alex ignored her pleas. He wanted everything she had to give; he planned to be inside of every orifice of her sweet little body so, he was going to make her *want* him there. His finger and thumb were rubbing together in circular motions on either side of her sugar walls giving her a sensation she had never felt before, and he was still licking and sucking her juicy pussy lips.

Her whole body shook and it was becoming harder, and harder to remain standing.

He knew she was on the edge; he was one of the rare men who actually knew where the G-spot was, and he could feel her G spot start to swell on the inside of her pussy.

"Alexander, I'm gonna cum!" she warned.

"I know you are," he thought to himself.

"I'm gonna cum so harrrrdd" she wailed. 'Don't stop…

"Don't worry I won't…"

"Please don't stop." She pleaded as her hips began to gyrate against his face.

"I won't baby, cum for me."

And he did not stop, even after she'd lost control and came twice in a powerful orgasm that brought her to her knees. He only stopped when she could no longer stand up, and even then he fingered her until he knew that she could not take anymore.

They sat together in a pile on the floor. Dakota fought to catch her breath as Alexander held her on his lap in his strong arms.

"How could a man be so demanding and so unselfish at the same time?" Dakota wondered. "What are you trying to do to me?" she asked breathlessly.

"Just trying to please you, beautiful" he grinned at her, "Are you pleased?" he asked.

All Dakota could do was nod in astonishment.

He smiled at that. "Are you hungry?" he asked after a while.

Dakota hadn't realized she was until then, "Yes, starving" she answered.

CHAPTER 3

The phone rang a third time and then a fourth until the voicemail picked up, again. Brandon wasn't going to play himself by leaving yet another message. He had already left three messages in an hour. He hoped nothing had happened to Dakota. But, knowing Dakota as he did, her cell was still in the car and she was probably in her room studying. Brandon wished he knew the name of her hotel and her room number. How had he let her leave without that vital information? He would have called her to make sure she had arrived ok.

"I know she's glad I don't have her room number, I would definitely call and she'd better pick up, too" he thought. *"Why does she need to go all the way to Atlanta, to learn how to franchise her business?"* He thought angrily to himself.

He brought home plenty of money with his business. Brandon knew he was starting to trip but he didn't care. He already knew she was going to say something like, 'my battery went dead' or 'I left the phone in the car by accident'.

"Accident my ass!" He said aloud to the empty room.

His mind was running on auto pilot now, and he let it roam all over. He thought she was at a happy hour somewhere letting men buy her drinks; getting tipsy and shaking her ass all over the place. Oh, how she loved to act like she was too tipsy to realize when a man was trying to holla at her.

Brandon was good and mad by now. His own infidelity fueled his paranoia. Voices were battling in his head.

"She'd better call with-in the hour or..."

"Or what?" he asked himself. *"Or I'll call her again, that's what!"* He shook his head out of frustration. He didn't want to think these thoughts about his Cocoa, his nick-name for Dakota.

"Look man, she's in Atlanta either studying trying to better herself or she is getting her groove on, either way you can't do shit about it," the reasonable voice in his head told him.

"Ok," he thought. Dakota wouldn't cheat on him, he knew that. He had to pull it together before she called, and he said something he didn't mean. He didn't want to lose Dakota; he had

plans to make her his wife. So, in his mind, there were certain things he wouldn't do with her sexually.

He had the 'freaky' kind of sex he wanted with other women. He never considered it cheating because he had no plans of letting Dakota ever find out. Besides, he would never let anyone come between him and Dakota. He never treated those women the way he treated her; no affection, no gifts, no hint at a chance to be in a relationship with him...just straight sex. And as far as he was concerned, that was ok. He stuck to his daily routine and Dakota never suspected a thing. What she didn't know wouldn't hurt her.

He decided to order a pizza and watch the fight that was coming on in an hour. He knew that would take his mind off of Dakota for a while. So, he called his favorite spot, ordered his favorite pie and jumped into the shower.

As the hot water streamed down his muscular body, from all angles, he suddenly remembered the last time he ordered pizza. It was a couple months back, but the girl that delivered was hot like fire. And, if he remembered correctly, she was outwardly flirting with him. The memory brought a smirk to his face.

"What would Coca think about me flirting the way she does sometimes?" He wondered. Then he found himself hoping that the same girl delivered again. She had a sweet rack and some juicy lips on her.

"I know she gets titty fucked by her man if she has one." He fantasized a little about sliding his dick between those tits and into her mouth. His dick started swelling in his hand when he thought about those big, juicy tits and the wetness of her mouth. He was pulling on it rhythmically when the doorbell rang.

"Shit!" he cursed as he got out the shower and grabbed a towel. He hadn't realized how fast the time passed while he was in the shower. Quickly he wrapped the towel around his waist and willed his dick to go down. He tapped the mirror, and the hidden security panel displayed those juicy lips he had just fantasized about. It was her! A sly smile slid across his face. His pulse quickened and his dick jumped back to attention. He gave the command to unlock the door, and told her, through the intercom, to step inside; he was on his way in just a moment.

She came in and closed the door behind her. She remembered this house from the last time she delivered here. The guy that lived here was sexy as hell. He was obviously rich and probably had a girl, "*but he could get it*" she thought to herself as she looked around. She secretly hoped they were there alone, so her little fantasy could play out.

Walking down the hall in his basketball shorts he could feel his dick swing from side to side. There wasn't time to put on draws or a shirt for that matter.

"Hey, sorry for the wait" he said walking up behind her.

She turned and gave him a once over and a sexy smile.

"No worries," she told him. "You're my last delivery tonight" she bit her bottom lip, still looking him up and down.

Brandon could clearly see the lust in her eyes.

He was giving her a good look too. She had a better rack than he even remembered. He caught himself staring, as her nipples hardened, so that he could see their outline through her shirt. His dick was coming to attention again.

Turning away he asked, "So, how much do I owe you?"

She didn't answer. He turned back around.

"Are we alone?" She asked. But the look on his face told her they were. She walked up to him, pressed her tits against his bare chest, and asked, "Where do you want it?"

Without hesitation, Brandon took the pizza out of her hands and said, "Follow me."

He led her into the game room and threw the pizza on the bar.

"What you drinking?" He asked reaching for two shot glasses.

"Whatever you're drinking," she replied.

With his back turned he poured two shots of Southern Comfort, one for each of them. But he drank both of them when he saw her beautiful, naked body before him. She had gotten out of those clothes faster than Houdini. She was ready. Her perky nipples were rock hard.

Brandon could feel his mouth watering. She knelt in front of him, and slid his shorts down. The temptation was too much. He cupped her tender breast in one hand and stroked his dick with the other. Crawling between his legs, she licked tentatively at his balls. Once in position, she sucked his balls slowly, one at a time, into her mouth. She took her time; suckling and licking his balls, and the base of his shaft while he jerked his cock.

"Put it in my mouth," she whispered.

That was it. He couldn't wait anymore. He pulled her over to the couch and laid her down. Straddling her stomach he laid his dick on her chest and squeezed her tits around his throbbing shaft. Slowly, he stroked until the head popped out near her open mouth.

She knew exactly what to do. Her juicy lips sucked his shaft in like a vacuum. Her mouth was hot and wet. And she was more than willing to please him.

Brandon rolled her taut nipple between his thumb and forefinger.

A moan escaped her throat. This motivated Brandon to pump harder. And in return she sucked harder. Her hands took hold of her own breasts freeing him to explore her open legs.

He quickly found her opening, and she was sopping wet. He slipped a finger into her tight little pussy. She frantically sucked the head of his dick each time he popped it into her eager mouth. Her mouth and her pussy were soaking wet.

Turned on, Brandon grabbed the back of her head, and pulled her up, so that he could stroke deeper into her mouth. Saliva seeped out the sides of her mouth and ran down her chin. Neither of them cared.

She squeezed her tits tighter around his dick and humped the two fingers he had inside of her. His balls began to tighten as the urge to come gripped him.

He stopped fingering her, so he could grip her head in both hands. He pulled her face closer and leaned forward. Now he was pumping faster and deeper than before. She began to sputter and choke a little on his cock. Brandon didn't care.

Her hands were busy on her clit. So her boobs were free, and bounced in rhythm with the pounding her face was taking. She felt her orgasm coming closer, and closer, each time his dick hit the back of her throat. Over and over he hit it.

Brandon's whole body tingled with sensation as he worked his dick in and out of her willing mouth. She gagged as he sloppily stuffed his full length into her throat. He paused, straining, at the end of each stroke; he was on the verge of cuming.

Her fingers worked feverishly jabbing in and out of her pussy.

His pubes scrubbed her face roughly. His body stiffened and his ass clenched. He held her head in place and pressed her face into his stomach, blocking her air supply for a few seconds, as the first spurts of his ejaculation jumped from his tip into her throat.

He held her so long, she thought she would pass out, but she didn't stop him.

Finally, he pulled out of her throat, and finished unloading on her big ass tits. She snatched air into her lungs and came so hard she was shaking.

She had never cum like that before. She liked it and wanted more. Luckily, he was still as hard as a rock.

"I want some more…" she told him. "I wanna ride you."

This time she wasn't timid, she was in charge.

"Lay back, I've got this." She told Brandon.

He happily followed her instructions. He lay back with his head on the arm of the couch. She straddled him sideways, keeping one foot on the floor, and she used the other as leverage on the sofa. The initial penetration told Brandon, that she was not used to his size. In fact, it took her several attempts to ease all the way down his full length.

She was so tight inside. But she was soaking wet, and that helped her slide down, until he was completely inside of her. Once she adjusted to his size, she rode him for damn near 30 minutes. Brandon enjoyed himself, and watched in amazement while she came over, and over again. Her muscle spasms giving him waves of pleasure, crashing in on top of one another.

She never seemed to tire or slow down. He couldn't hold back any longer, he wanted to put his weight on her. He picked her up, and laid her across the arm of the chair with her face on the cushions. He stood behind, and gently entered her. Once he hit bottom, he began to stroke longer, hard, and faster. He knew it felt good because of her moans, but he could tell he was hitting it hard too, because she was on her tiptoes.

"Yeah, there's nowhere to run…you gonna take this…um hmm, get all of it" he talked shit to her.

She gasped and squirmed underneath him when he leaned all of his weight on her, but she took it. He spread her legs wide and dug into her without mercy, he was about to nut and he wasn't holding back anymore.

"You wanted to get fucked, you getting it now," he chided and spanked her across her ass.

To his surprise, she yelled out "Give it to me harder!"

He gripped her waist, and pulled her back to him each time he thrust into her.

"Harder, harder....harder!' she screamed with each plunge he took, until she shook uncontrollably and came for him again. The sporadic squeezing and jerking of her body made Brandon cum hard as shit. He pulled out and shot his load on her back.

"Come on, let's take a shower." He told her, pulling her up. "What's your name, again?" they both laughed and headed for the shower.

CHAPTER 4

The restaurant overlooked the beautiful Atlanta skyline. It was quaint and cozy, yet it had an air of elegance. The tables were all covered in white linen and candles for ambiance. Soft instrumental music was playing throughout. Dakota was trying to decide what to order, everything on the menu looked delicious.

Alexander was looking at her as if she was the menu; this made her blush. She took a sip of her cabernet sauvignon and let the dry wine wash away all the worries in her mind.

"Why on earth am I thinking about Brandon now?" She wondered. No doubt he had called her by now; her class would be over and she should be at the hotel. *"Oh, well, I'll cross that bridge when I get there"* Dakota thought to herself.

Right now, all she wanted to do was enjoy the moment. Alexander probably knew what she was thinking, but he didn't ask. Dakota appreciated that. She hated when men asked obvious questions. But, there was absolutely nothing Dakota hated about Alexander. He made her feel so comfortable and beautiful. His eyes never left her; even when he ordered his food, he only looked at her.

After the waitress took their orders and left Alexander asked, "So what would you like to do after dinner, sweetness?"

"I'd like to do you" Dakota thought to herself but she just smiled.

"Maybe, dancing?" Alexander suggested and winked at her.

"Don't get me wrong," Dakota started "I like the way you dance, but if you don't mind I'd rather dance in our room..." She replied winking back at him.

Alexander was fun. His everyday norm was outside of her box. She loved being pushed the way he pushed her. It was almost as if she didn't have to take responsibility for her actions, she could blame it all on Alexander. But why not own up to her true self? If she really enjoyed these feelings so much, why not take the same attitude with Brandon?

She and Brandon used to have so much fun in the beginning. He was her 'Bad Boy' at first. But somewhere along the line, he became so obsessed with what other people thought. He wouldn't dare do anything that might embarrass either one of them; she was his "Wifey," and he constantly reminded her. She hated that dumb ass word, "Wifey." Brandon was controlling, but not in the way Dakota wanted. Dakota wanted to feel freedom in the control of another, not caged up. How could she express this to Brandon? She wanted so badly to feel this type of excitement with him again.

"There must be a way to get out of this rut we've fallen into," Dakota thought, *"all habits are learned and all habits can be broken."* She rationalized. *"I've got to learn how to break these bad habits,"* she thought to herself.

She tried to push the thoughts from her mind as the food arrived. They kept their conversation light. Both enjoyed their time together.

"Don't go getting all quiet on me now" Alexander said interrupting her thoughts on their way back to the hotel after a lovely meal.

Dakota turned away to look at her sexy 'tutor'. "Don't worry I'm fine, I was just thinking about some things," she spoke instead of saying what was really on her mind.

He smiled at her and squeezed her thigh. She smiled back before looking out of the window again *"Yeah,"* she thought, *"change is in the air,"* and Alexander was just the person to bring it out of her.

Back at the hotel, as she and Alexander exited the elevator to their room, Dakota vowed to herself that she would fully immerse herself into any and everything she did from this moment forth. Little did she know, that lesson number one was going to be one hell of a ride.

"Would you like to take a shower?" Alexander asked.

"Ok," Dakota replied. "Want to join me?" She offered.

"In a minute," he said, "you go ahead."

Eager to begin round two she quickly undressed and headed for the shower. As the hot water flowed over her caramel body, Dakota fantasized about things to come. If Alex made her cream with his mouth, she couldn't wait to get some of that good dick. She took her time and washed, but Alex never came into the shower. Wondering what could be keeping him; she dried off and went to see where he was.

He wasn't in the bedroom. She stepped out into the living area, and her breath caught in her throat for a moment. There was a man, in a leather face mask, standing with his back to her. Thinking she hadn't been noticed, she tried to quietly ease back into the bedroom.

"Be still!" A voice commanded.

Dakota was afraid, until she realized it was Alexander. But still her voice was shaky, "What?" She almost whispered.

"Come over here, and leave that towel over there." He said sternly.

Now Dakota laughed.

"Now…or suffer the consequences." Alex was so calm and assertive, that Dakota couldn't help but let out another nervous giggle.

She thought, "*Is he tripping or what?*"

Alexander turned to face her and she noticed the paddle in his hand. As soon as their eyes met, she knew he was not joking. He slapped his hand with the paddle and motioned for her to get down on her knees. She knelt down and forced herself to crawl toward him.

"That's a good girl," Alex told her "I have something for you." His body looked so delicious in those tight, leather pants and leather straps across his chest, she just wished he didn't have his handsome face covered.

"What do you have for me?" she asked.

"Shhh, don't talk unless I tell you to talk, understand?"

"Yes" she lied. But, Dakota didn't fully understand the role she was to play…yet.

As she came closer to him, he pulled a black silk scarf from his pocket; by this time, she was directly in front of him.

"What's that for?" she asked.

Before she knew what was happening, Alexander was behind her with the paddle in the air. The swift precision of the two licks he administered to her ass, let Dakota know that she had better cooperate. The sting of the paddle hurt, but she realized that it also made her pussy jump. She was surprised that she actually liked it.

She couldn't read his face, with that damn mask on, so when he circled around to stand in front of her, she flinched. This stopped him in his tracks. He waited a few seconds and approached her again; this time she didn't move as he knelt down in front of her.

"I'm going to put this blindfold on your eyes," he said patiently, "and you are going to do whatever I tell you to do. Understand?"

Dakota nodded yes; not daring to speak.

"Ok, can you see?" he asked after tying the scarf over her eyes.

She nodded no.

"Good, girl" he said.

Dakota heard a zipper and realized that Alexander had removed the mask. He

took her hand, pulled her into a standing position, and led her to the couch. Gently, he pushed her into a seated position. She heard him walk away. A few moments later music began to play and The Weeknd was singing *Earned It*, one of her favorites.

Alexander came back and placed a glass to her lips. He told her to open her mouth and tilt her head back.

She hesitated briefly.

At that point, Alexander put the glass down on the table beside her, took her face in both palms of his hands and said, "I am trying to open your mind to new and exciting possibilities. Don't fight me on this. In order to do this, you must trust me." He paused. "Do you trust me, Dakota?"

She nodded yes.

"Say it. I want to hear you say you trust me." He told her.

"Yes, I trust you Alex but..."

"That's all I need to know" he interrupted her. "And all you need to know is that this is the only time that I would put my hands on you like this; I would never hurt you in any way." He watched her closely as he talked. "You will have a 'safe word' that stops everything completely. If you want, or need me to stop for any reason say 'yellow' and I will stop. Ok?"

Relief rushed over Dakota. She smiled and nodded yes.

He could see the tension leave her pretty face and that made him happy. "So..." he continued in character, "when I tell you to open your hot, little mouth, just open it."

She smiled harder and tilted her head back with her mouth wide open. Alex poured the champagne into her mouth so fast that most of it overflowed and ran down her naked body.

The cool liquid tasted good and felt good, but not nearly as good as when Alex licked every drop off of her. He repeated this several more times. She had a good little buzz going on when he pulled her up from the couch and led her out to the balcony.

A gentle breeze caressed her body. Dakota briefly wondered if anyone could see her, but the thought left as quickly as it had come. Alex took her hands and put them on the stone balcony railing to let her balance herself. Dakota felt so free and sexy that she found herself wishing someone would see her. Well, kind of.

Her thoughts were interrupted by the now familiar sting of Alexander's paddle

Whack.

It was a solid swing that connected to both ass cheeks but, somehow, it felt good.

Whack.

Again and then again.

Chill bumps radiated up her back, and down her legs. Dakota knew her ass must be a pretty shade of pink by now, but she didn't care, she loved every ounce of pleasure and pain. She braced herself for the next swing.

Instead, Alex poured a warm liquid, which felt like baby oil, down her back. It ran over her hot cheeks into the crack of her ass. He proceeded to rub it down her thighs, legs, and back up to her ass. Here, he took great care in massaging her luscious cheeks. He even swirled his thumb in circular motions on her tight, little ass hole.

Sensations were flooding Dakota's senses. Her mind was completely open to everything Alex was doing to her. Her body ached for him to be inside of her.

When he was finished, he stood up very close behind Dakota. She could tell he was just as aroused as she was by now. His erection felt like steel even through the leather pants.

"*Good,*" she thought to herself "*I'm ready too, baby!*"

The next sound she heard made her pussy wet. It was his zipper going down, and she knew it was the zipper on his pants this time.

Alex didn't make her wait any longer; he entered her from behind. He slid into her, like a hot knife through soft butter. Deeper and deeper; he pushed deeper with each stroke.

Her wetness could not be contained. It flowed down her legs.

He wanted to last for her pleasure, but as he looked down upon her beautiful skin glistening in the moonlight, not to mention the two perfect mounds her ass formed, he could last no longer.

Dakota sensed that he was on the verge of exploding. His strokes were becoming more and more erratic. And when he pulled out to ejaculate, she surprised him by turning, and dropping into a squatting position, and catching everything he had to offer in her mouth.

She caressed his balls as she slurped up every drop and spit it back out on his long shaft. She was happy to feel that he was still hard, because she wanted more, much more.

So did Alexander. He scooped her up in his strong arms and whisked her away to the bed. He laid her down spread eagle and brought her to climax again and again with his talented tongue.

At long last, they had to take a break.

He was feeding her chocolate covered fruits when he whispered in her ear, "Can I have all of you Dakota?"

"You have all of me right now" she replied smiling.

"Not... everything," Alex continued.

Dakota wondered what he meant, but said, "Yes, you can have whatever you want" between bites of chocolate covered strawberries.

Pleased by her answer, Alex reached under the pillow and placed a small, silver, bullet shaped object in her hand; her blindfold had been temporarily removed.

She looked at it curiously. It had a little cord attached to it which was about 12 inches long; the cord was connected to a little control, which Dakota saw, was in Alex's hand.

"What's this?" Dakota asked.

"It's a vibrator. I'll have the remote control. Will you play with your pussy for me?" He asked.

She smiled. "Of course, anything for you, sexy."

Dakota placed the vibrator between her legs, keeping her eyes on Alex, and waited for it to vibrate.

On cue, Alex switched it on. The vibrator began to pulse and sent sweet sensations through her body. He asked her to lay on her side and he held her leg up in the air. He lay down behind her and positioned himself in the spoon position with her.

The vibrator was slippery in her hand, but she managed to keep it on, or near, her clit.

Her moans of pleasure had him fully aroused now, and she could feel him becoming hard again. He fingered her while she masturbated for him.

He took his dick and rubbed it back and forth from her pussy to her asshole. Everything was wet.

"Are you sure I can have everything?" he asked as he continued to tease her; rubbing back and forth.

Dakota couldn't speak, she was too aroused and on the verge of coming again. So, she just moaned and nodded yes.

"Are you getting ready to cum for me again?" he asked.

Another moan; Alex took that as a yes. "Good, this will only hurt a little bit" he promised.

Dakota barely heard what he said as she began to grind her hips. She felt him wrap his arms around her waist, in a tight embrace, as he waited for her to climax.

He felt her body begin to tremble and then shake. Just then, he thrust the head of his dick into her virgin ass.

Hot, pain shot up her back and mixed with the pleasure of her orgasm. Dakota let out a little scream. The oil he poured on her earlier helped. But she couldn't stop gyrating; she was in the throes of a climax when he broke thru.

He held on tight, because he knew her first time would hurt, but he also knew she would ultimately love this new sensation.

She bit back the pain as her body refused to be still. Alexander held back and waited for a moment, before he caught her rhythm, and began to stroke the rest of his shaft into her tight ass.

"*Damn, she feels so good*," he thought to himself. But her whole body was ridged and he could feel her instinctively trying to pull away from him.

"Play with your pussy, baby" he instructed her, as he switched the vibrator up a notch with the remote control. "You're gonna cum from this too, I promise you that!" he said, with his lips pressed against her ear. Tightening his arms around her tiny waist, he pulled her back to him.

Now, he long stroked her in her ass, until he felt her juices on him. She began to move in time with him. And, to her surprise, eventually the pain was replaced with desire for more. The pleasure was so good that they came at the same time. She couldn't believe it, but it was the best orgasm she had ever had.

CHAPTER 5

The next morning sunlight streamed across the room, in one thin line. The heavy drapery at the windows kept the rest of the room in darkness. Dakota had just awakened and wondered where Alex had disappeared to. She felt well rested. Actually, she felt wonderful; her body was more relaxed than it had been in a long time.

Alex had put it on her last night. As she lay awake in the dark, the memories came rushing back. There were so many new experiences in one night. He was so firm and commanding with her, and yet so gentle and patient. She loved how Alex knew what he wanted, how he took what he wanted, and how he gave her just what she wanted in return.

"How could he read her so well? Was he just that talented? Was she that easy to read? Did she give off signs that she was unaware of? So many questions swirled around in her head. *"Whatever it was,"* she concluded, *"he got it right."*

Dakota knew that she wanted to enjoy him for as long as possible; something this good couldn't possibly last too long. *"Shit, I don't even know where he is right now."* She pulled herself, from the warm embrace, of the bed, to go take a shower. The thought crossed her mind that she would get dressed once she ordered room service for breakfast.

The hot water ran down her body and awakened even more delicious memories. It seemed that every spot she touched held a secret. She could feel Alex's strong hands on her again and smell his manly scent; she even heard his voice calling her name.

"Dakota."

"Wait a minute that was his voice for real," she thought to herself.

"Dakota?" he called as he opened the door.

He was standing there with nothing on, but the sexiest smile she had ever seen, Dakota knew she could fall in love with a man like him. His eyes told her he probably felt the same way. His dick told her that it already loved her; it pointed its claims at her.

The temperature, in the room, seemed to increase as he took

the soap from her hand and caressed her body all over. She joyfully returned the favor. Afterwards, they ate the scrumptuous breakfast that Alex had delivered to the room.

He was the complete package as far as a lover was concerned. Dakota wondered briefly how good he was in other things. Aside from making her feel like a Goddess, could he keep her attention from day to day? She knew how easily she became bored with past lovers, but this felt so different from all of that. She felt a connection with Alex that she couldn't explain.

Then again, did she want to fall in love with him? What about the man she already loved? Could she really love them both? She wondered.

"What would you like to do today?" he asked her. "There is so much to do here in Atlanta."

Dakota pondered his question for a moment. She just wanted to be with him, but that seemed so childish to say. How could she express herself and not sound like a love sick little girl?

Alex sensed her hesitation and took the reins. "How about we order a movie and just talk? You know... get to know each other better" he paused, "on a non-sexual level."

They both laughed at that.

Alex grinned at her and she felt glad that he wanted to know more about her, the real Dakota. "Ok that sounds good, what kind of movies do you like?" she asked.

They spent the rest of the day laughing and talking about themselves and their lives. They were never at a loss for words. They had so much in common, and yet, were complete opposites on other things.

Dakota told him about her Day Spa and he told her about his practice as an attorney. They talked about their childhoods and siblings. They even talked about their friends and hobbies, but neither of them brought up significant others. And, Dakota was relieved. She wasn't ready to share that side of herself just yet.

Somehow, Alex knew that. He never made her feel uncomfortable or pressured.

She thought, *"He must be one hell of a lawyer if he is this tuned into his clients."*

"What's your sign?" She asked, curious to see if Astrology could explain some things.

"Virgo" he smiled confidently, seeming pleased with his

astrological sign.

"Ain't no way…" now she sounded like her best friend Yakima, who believed in signs and who used slang all the time.

"What?" he asked laughing.

"Are you kidding me right now?" she asked "Virgo is supposed to be my perfect match. Well, according to my bestie, Yakima. I'm a Scorpio!" she hoped she didn't sound too crazy to Alex right now; quoting Yakima of all people.

"That's what's up!" was all he said. To her surprise, he sounded almost as excited as she did.

The day went on and on like that. Each connecting with the other a little deeper. They were becoming real friends. This should have thrown up several warning flags for Dakota, but if it did, she ignored every single one.

They had more incredible sex that night. And in the morning Dakota packed her things and left for home. Back to reality and back to Brandon.

There were 17 missed calls on her phone, which she'd left in her truck, and the battery was on its last leg. So, she charged her phone as she drove home lost in thought. She had had so much fun with Alex and she didn't regret one minute of it. How could she? She learned so much about herself this weekend, and yet it scared her to think that maybe it was time to move on with her life.

"*Move on with my life?*" she thought to herself. "*My life has been Brandon for seven years now.*" They were best friends in High school and boyfriend and girlfriend ever since. They didn't have any children, and that was the plan until they were married, which seemed to have taken a back seat to their careers.

It wasn't like Dakota was ready to have children now, but eventually she did want to have some. She felt that her genes were too good to go to waste; meaning that she shouldn't leave this world without a little Dakota to replace her. She knew they would have beautiful children, and she knew Brandon would make a great father.

Brandon on the other hand was content with their life the way it was. He was not against having children, but he had been the oldest of seven kids, and his parents could never really afford a vacation of their own until all the kids were grown. He wasn't looking forward to a life of waiting on his piece of the pie.

He provided a good, albeit routine, life for himself and Dakota. They had everything anyone on their age level could want. Freedom to come and go as they pleased, vacations all over the world, and all of the material things they wanted. They even loved each other.

But the passion in their relationship had gone away and Dakota missed it terribly. She longed for the nights when they would talk for hours about the future and all of their dreams. She missed the love they made, at the drop of a dime, with disregard to location. It never used to matter to them who knew how much they adored each other; they wanted to shout it from the mountain top. Or in their case, kiss and show affection in public.

They used to be inseparable. Whenever you saw one, you saw the other. Brandon always put Dakota first and vice versa. And then slowly, but surely, things changed. It went from going to events separately, to making love once a week, to staying home and planning when they would make love.

No more talks about the future, no plans for a wedding or a honeymoon in Europe. No more anything. Only running their businesses and scheduled vacations. Anyone on the outside looking in would think they were the perfect "power couple."

That was Brandon's term for what they were. At first, Dakota liked to think of them as a "power couple," and then she realized that the image to the public was more important to Brandon than she was. Now, the term only got on her nerves.

Yakima thought they were the cutest couple ever, and longed for a relationship with the security of theirs. Yakima was quick to point out to Dakota that passion fades over time anyway, and that you'd better have a good man and an even better bank account to fall back on. Dakota knew that she had both, but *wasn't there more to life?"*

Her thoughts were interrupted as her cell phone rang. It had finally recharged and she knew it was Brandon before she even looked at the phone.

"What would she say? Why hadn't she called him first? Would he be angry with her for not calling all weekend?" She didn't want voicemail to catch the call, so she answered.

"Hello?" her voice sounded stronger than she felt and she was glad.

"Where the fuck are you?" Brandon demanded.

"What?" Dakota pretended to be shocked at his tone.

"You heard me D, where are you?"

"I'm in the truck on my way home, why?" She shot back.

"I know you didn't just ask me "why." I've been calling you all weekend and you haven't returned one fucking call, that's why!" He shouted.

"Well damn, thanks for asking if I'm ok."

"Oh, you're ok for now," he said sarcastically, "but when you get your ass home, it's on!" he yelled and hung up on her.

Dakota expected that. She knew he would be upset anyway; he never wanted her to do anything without his input. He was probably more upset that she didn't call to report in, than just the fact that she hadn't called. He wouldn't dare put his hands on her, he was twice her size and he didn't believe in hitting a woman. Dakota was glad of that now. Although, he'd snatched her up in the past, that was about all she could expect. Anyway, she had at least an hour before she would be home and now she was in no hurry.

CHAPTER 6

As Dakota turned down her street, her usual feeling of pride escaped her. She normally loved the beautiful trees that lined her street, but now she barely saw them as her 3200 square foot home loomed in the distance.

"Why do we need such a big house with no children?" she thought angrily.

There was no time to think about that now, she was home. Before she could push the remote control button, for the garage door opener, the garage door began to roll up. Brandon stood blocking her entrance. He gave her a menacing look and then moved so that she could pull into her side of the garage.

He was standing there in his boxers, a white tee shirt, socks, and slippers. This worried Dakota because normally Brandon was up and dressed, regardless of his plans for the day, by 9am. Dakota felt like the prodigal child returning home to angry parents. She couldn't look at him, but his eyes never left her.

He didn't rush her as she gathered her purse and keys, and took her time getting out of the vehicle. Instead, he went to the back of the truck and removed her designer bag containing her clothes from her trip. This prompted her to get out.

"I'll get it, Brandon." she said, but he was already heading into the house. *"Aw shit! Here we go,"* she thought and reluctantly followed him inside.

"The Look of Love" by Isaac Hayes was playing over the intercom system that ran throughout their home. She loved the whole *Dead Presidents* sound track, even though it was old, particularly this song, but now it seemed to have a chilling tone to it. *What was he doing before I got here?* she wondered. *And where was he anyway?*

She heard a noise come out of the game room and went in there. Brandon had plopped down in his favorite chair. He picked up a drink from the side table and took a sip. He was drinking his favorite cognac and she briefly wondered how long he had been sipping.

Neither of them spoke for a while. Dakota just stood next to their pool table as if she expected him to challenge her to a game of pool. They stared at each other across the room. Finally, Brandon spoke.

"Can I trust you, Coca?"

"Of course you can, Brandon."

There was silence as he sipped his drink some more and just looked her up and down.

"That's good to know." he said, putting his drink down and lighting a cigarette.

Dakota wanted a cigarette so bad, but she only smoked when she was either drinking or when she was nervous and Brandon knew it.

"Want a smoke?" he taunted her.

"No thanks" she replied trying to sound nonchalant. "I'm tired; do you want to talk about something?"

Brandon laughed at that. "Yeah, I want to talk about something. Don't you?"

"Like what?" she didn't like this.

"Let's talk about your weekend and then let's talk about mine."

Dakota could play this game better than he could, and he knew it. But, he'd started it. "Ok, mine was fine and yours?" she attempted a smile.

"Really? He fiend shock, "I thought maybe your weekend was hectic, since you couldn't find the time to call me."

"It was busier than I anticipated, I'm sorry that I didn't call you, baby."

"Oh, I'm still Baby? I thought I was just that nigga you lived with." Brandon sneered at her. He was losing the game already. But his comment struck a nerve.

"Well, you're not my husband, if that's what you mean." Dakota shot back. She hadn't wanted it to go this way, but it was too late.

"Humph, so I should marry you because you are so faithful to me, huh?" he asked. Dakota looked away and didn't respond.

"Well let's just see how faithful you are my sweet Coca" he said sarcastically as he grabbed her bag off the floor and emptied the contents onto the pool table. Dakota wasn't expecting this but she kept her cool. She turned away from him and walked over to the bar to pour herself a drink. She really needed a cigarette.

"How am I going to play this off?" She knew where he was going with this when he picked up a pair of her panties as if they were toxic. She forced herself to sit down, as if she didn't have a care in the world, and took a sip of her drink. The hot liquid did nothing to calm her nerves, but it gave her a reason to smoke. She took a cigarette and could barely light it, because her hands were shaking so bad.

Brandon apparently didn't notice, because he was sniffing her panties like a little dog. *"How stupid,"* Dakota thought to herself *"men think they know every damn thing and don't know shit!"*

"Why don't you just smell my pussy, instead." she offered, opening her legs.

This caught Brandon off guard, and she knew it. He looked up, from his investigation, and immediately noticed the cigarette in her hand.

"Why you smoking?" he threw back, "nervous?" he asked

"No, if you haven't noticed, Mr. Panty Sniffer, I always smoke when I drink" she said and shook her glass at him, so that the ice in the glass jingled.

"Yeah, well you also smoke when you're nervous," he paused; "I have noticed that." He watched her for a moment, and thought he noticed a slight tremble in her cigarette. So, he asked her, "Can I have a pull?"

Dakota knew he would notice the shake in her hand if she held out the cigarette, so instead she nodded towards the pack and said, "I didn't get the last one, pull away."

She hated when he was upset but pretended to be nice. She had fallen for that shit early on in their relationship, and it had bitten her in the ass more than once. She wasn't falling for it now.

"Aw, I can't have a pull off of your cigarette?" he pretended to be hurt. Dakota just rolled her eyes. "I want some of yours it tastes better." he whined.

"Really? I thought you wanted to smell my pussy, but maybe you'd rather taste it. She spread her legs, seductively. *"It* tastes better too."

"I know it does, but I don't like to eat behind other people, you know that D."

"So what are you saying, Brandon?"

"I'm just stating a fact." He said coyly.

"How can it be a fact, when you have no evidence?"

"The evidence is you. Look at you." He sneered.

"Yes, look at me Brandon. Look at me real good, because if you say something you don't mean, it may be the last time you get a close look."

"Oh, yeah, is that so?" he asked

"Yes it is. I mean it Brandon, think before you speak." She warned him.

He smiled an evil smile, nodding his head up and down, like a maniac. "I have been thinking, I've been thinking all weekend. Do you want to know what I think?"

"Yes." She said slowly.

"I think we should see other people." He said after a dramatic pause.

"What do you mean "see" other people?"

"Just that. I think we are too complacent in our relationship."

Dakota didn't have to pretend to be shocked this time. All kinds of thoughts ran through her mind. What the fuck? Was he high or something? This wasn't the Brandon she knew. He couldn't mean it, it must be a trap. Should she flip out? Should she show how shocked she was or agree? Her mind was reeling with questions that she couldn't answer.

Brandon could practically see the smoke coming out of her ears; "What's the matter, cat got your tongue? He asked. "Or did you leave it with that faggot you were with this weekend?"

"Brandon, listen…" she started.

"No, you listen, this is your only choice, either we both play fair and see other people or we can go our separate ways. That's it." He clapped his hands together, emphasizing the last two words. He wasn't pretending anymore.

Dakota couldn't get her mind to slow down enough to think clearly, so she blurted out "Either way is fine with me" she was lying and he knew it, "do what you want; I'm going to take a bath." She said turning to leave.

"Good, I'm tired of smelling that motherfucker on you anyway," he yelled as she walked out of the room. "And, when you're finished wash these fucking clothes!" he spat, throwing her bag against the wall.

She knew she had hurt him with her answer, but she was hurt too. "*Fuck him!*," she fumed. "*How dare he want to see someone else, after all this time? Was he already seeing someone?*" She wondered.

Dakota stormed through their master suite, into the walk-in closet, that led to the master bath. She had designed this suite herself and the bathroom was her haven. She started the water in the soaking tub, and when she reached for her Calgon, she had to laugh, because she really wanted Calgon to take her away. As she soaked, in the tub of whirling water, with lavender candles burning all around her due to their calming effect, her mind raced with questions and worries. Why did she feel like crying? Wasn't this what she wanted? Was she afraid that it was over with her and Brandon? She'd had flings before, how could she not have them?

She gave Brandon her virginity when she was 17, because she thought he would be her husband one day and the father of her children. But, after all, she was only 24 years old and she wanted to experiment, with other men, before she was married. None of them had ever meant anything to her. She didn't have proof that Brandon had ever been with anyone else, she was sure he had, but she never asked. In reality she didn't want to know. She wasn't one of those nagging ass women, which asked a bunch of stupid questions they really didn't want the answer to anyway. She prided herself on staying focused on her plans for her life. Her plan always included Brandon.

Whenever she'd stepped out on him in the past, it was just to experiment. She never wanted to hurt him in any way. She always thought that what you didn't know couldn't hurt you. Well, she was wrong, she realized. It did hurt, it hurt her so badly.

As she lay soaking, she put her head back and realized that the song playing on the intercom now was "I Miss You" by Harold Melvin & The Blue Notes. Brandon must have been playing the whole *Dead Presidents* soundtrack. As Melvin sang to her "Without you, I don't know what to do with myself, what to do with my time..." The pain in her chest hurt so bad, she didn't know what else to do, but close her eyes and let the tears flow.

CHAPTER 7

They spent the rest of the week sleeping in separate rooms. Dakota was in their bed, while Brandon slept in one of the guest rooms. They barely spoke a word to each other. "*How long will this last?*" She wondered.

And then, on Friday, Brandon announced that he had a date. He said it as if she were his sister instead of his woman of seven years. That hurt.

"Where are you going?" she asked.

"Why?"

"I don't want to run into you tonight." She meant to hurt his feelings.

"Oh, you have a date tonight, too?

"I sure do" she said smugly.

"Well, don't worry your pretty little head about that," he said and winked at her, "I won't be anyplace we normally go." He said, reaching into their Sub-Zero refrigerator.

His casualness infuriated Dakota.

"Good, have fun and don't forget to wrap it up." she threw at him. "If you need some condoms, there's some in my Coach bag."

Brandon looked irritated, for just a moment, then he laughed, grabbed his keys and headed for the garage. Just before he closed the door, he yelled, "Have fun with Yakima!"

Dakota wanted to say something, but he was gone. All she could do was watch him ride away in his new convertible Audi.

All alone, her thoughts turned to Brandon's date. Any woman would gladly take Brandon off her hands. He was handsome, street smart and rich. Not play, play rich either. He had stacks of money in the bank, and he knew how to wine and dine a chick. But, then again so did Alexander.

Shit, Dakota had it going on as well. She kept her long wavy hair colored a honey blond, which complimented her caramel skin perfectly. She was smart and business minded. Her spa was one of the most exclusive in the city, and she had her own stacks of money in the bank. She was the one who put together Brandon's business plan so that he could get the loan to open his business.

He owned a lucrative custom car shop where the average custom job ran $20,000 - $30,000. He could charge so much because once he customized a car, he guaranteed not to do another client's car the same way. Besides, a lot of his clients were professional athletes. She knew that Brandon earned all of his money, and she didn't take credit from him, he knew his business inside and out. But, they both brought money to the table so she wasn't with him just for what he could give her, and he knew that.

"I hope he doesn't think he can trust any of those gold digging bitches out there." she thought to herself as she got dressed to go out to dinner with Yakima. She knew she could talk to Yakima like a sister. She had been friends with Kima longer than she had been friends with Brandon. Yakima knew her inside and out, and sometimes understood her better than she understood herself. Yakima knew all about what was going on with her and Brandon. So she suggested going out to eat, at a fancy restaurant, and then to a movie afterwards. Dakota agreed because she needed to get out of the house; she was tired of not talking to Brandon.

She was putting the finishing touches on her makeup when Yakima's pretty face appeared on the security monitor, which was integrated into Dakota's bathroom, vanity mirror. Brandon decided that he didn't want to live in a gated community, but he had more security on the house than the law should allow.

Dakota smiled at the sight of her best friend. "Come on in!" she yelled into the intercom. "That's what you have a key for" Dakota joked.

Yakima had a key "for emergencies only" and she never used it without permission. Dakota respected that. A few moments later, Yakima came bursting into the bathroom, like she was out of breath.

"What y'all got this big ass house fo'? I know y'all get lost sometimes." she was trying to make Dakota laugh and it worked. Yakima always knew what to say. She had been in their house a million times and to ask why it was so big now, just seemed funny to Dakota.

"You so stupid, Kima. Give me a minute, girl. I'm almost ready."

"Hurry up chile, I'm starving. These fucking diet pills ain't working!" Yakima grabbed at her stomach, as if she were dying.

"So damn dramatic..." Dakota thought, shaking her head.

Yakima was always on a diet and Dakota didn't know why. Yakima had a perfect shape. They were the same age, both drop dead gorgeous, and had the same goals in life. But that was where the similarities ended. Yakima was half black and half Korean; she was proud of both of her heritages, but leaned hardest toward the black culture. She loved black men and slang.

Her mother, who is Korean, once asked Yakima if she wanted to have plastic surgery to make her eyes look more "American." Yakima told her that a crease in her eyelid only took away from her Korean pride, which made her mother happy and sad at the same time.

Yakima was her only child, and she gave her every luxury she could afford. Yakima's parents were very wealthy but Yakima wanted to make her own money. So, when she turned 21 they bought her a nail salon; and she worked hard at making her money. Even though she had plenty of nail techs in her salon, she still worked on clients personally; unlike Dakota.

"Dakota, come on, I been smelling funky ass feet all damn day, it's my turn to be served." she wined.

"Let's go then, with your hungry ass." Dakota chided.

"Shit, just 'cause you love sick and can't eat, don't mean I can't!"

"Who said I was love sick?"

"You did heifer. You losing your mind too?" Yakima asked.

"Let's just go." Dakota loved how Yakima always stated the obvious. "Where do you want to eat?"

"Anything, but Chinese." Yakima said, and they both laughed.

They rode in Yakima's car, a candy apple red, drop top, two-seater Lexus; Pure luxury.

"I think he has been seeing someone else all along," Dakota was saying. "I mean if not, how can he have a date already in one week?"

This surprised Yakima, "You playing right?" she turned to look at her friend.

"What do you mean?" Dakota asked.

"I mean this is Brandon we are talking about right?"

"Yeah, and?" Dakota rolled her eyes at this.

"And... if you wasn't my sista I'da scooped that up, a while ago,"

"Yakima, be serious, and please speak regular English."

"Ok. How about this? If Brandon wasn't your man, I would have been on a mission to get with him." She said, as properly as possible. "And since you decided to see other people; you just made it that much easier for the next bitch."

"I didn't decide anything!" Dakota interjected.

"Oh, no," Yakima agreed, "you just went to Atlanta, with what's his name, and didn't call your man all weekend, like it was all good. So, you're right, *you* didn't decide anything."

She was right and Dakota knew it. What could she say? She couldn't change the situation now. Yakima could see that she had struck a nerve, but she knew that if she didn't make Dakota see what she had, she might lose it to some other chick.

But that was enough for now.

"You know you never gave me the 411 on that weekend anyway…was it worth it?" Kima asked.

"Girl, it was." Dakota smiled just thinking about it.

"Damn, look at that smile, it was goooood!"

"Kima, he did things to me that was unreal."

"Well, does he have a name?"

"Alexander."

"Hmm, Alexander the Great, huh?"

"And then some! He made me feel like the only woman on earth."

"Only woman on earth, huh?" Yakima mused. "That's sweet. But, ummm, get to the details; the S-E-X!"

Dakota paused and then whispered, "He took my virginity."

"He took your what?" Yakima asked confused.

"My virginity, you know…" she patted her backside.

"Oh," it dawned on Yakima what she meant, "he got in that ass." Yakima laughed, "You and your damn experiments. Well, how was it?"

"Girl, I came so much, I lost count." Dakota screamed.

"Was it big?"

"Huge"

"Did you work it girl?"

"You know it!" they slapped five and laughed at that for a while.

Yakima pulled into the California Dreaming parking lot, she

found a spot, cut the ignition and turned to her friend.

"Well fuck it; it was worth it." She said matter-of-factly. "Besides, you and Brandon will be back to normal soon." She took Dakota's hand and continued. "Girl, take this break as permission to fuck whoever, whenever!" she said lightheartedly, in true Yakima fashion.

Dakota knew Yakima only had her best interest at heart, but now that she had "permission" she really didn't want to have sex, unless she could get with Alex. Only, he lived out of town. She mentioned this to Yakima.

Yakima's mouth dropped open and she had to look closely at her friend. "Wait a minute, what did he do to you? You've never gone back twice."

"Actually if I go back it would be the third time," she said shyly.

Yakima stared at her best friend, like she had three heads.

"I don't know Kima, he put it on me. But that's not all..." she trailed off, "I really can't put it into words."

"Can't put it into words?" Yakima asked, shocked. "Well can you draw it out? Yakima joked, "I need to know damn it!" They laughed at that. "But seriously, D, you never went back before, be careful Ma. When feelings get involved, feelings get hurt."

"I will, don't worry about me." Dakota promised. "Now, let's enjoy our date."

They enjoyed a fabulous meal of lobster and steak. And of course, plenty of drinks. Afterwards, they debated seeing *The Perfect Guy* or *Straight Outta Compton*. Dakota conceded, because Yakima really wanted to see *Straight Outta Compton,* and it really didn't matter to her. In the end, she was glad that they saw it, because it was way better than what she thought it would be.

When Yakima dropped her off at the end of the evening, around twelve-ish, her mind immediately went to Brandon. "*Was he home yet? Who had he gone out with? Did they hook up? Would he come home at all?*" This was driving Dakota crazy, how did he expect her to live like this?

She was tipsy, because she and Kima had watched the movie, at a theater that served alcoholic beverages. All she wanted to do was lie down and sleep it off. Dakota took off all of her clothes and slid into the empty bed. *"Satin sheets are a waste if you have to sleep on them alone."* That was her last thought as she drifted off to sleep.

The next morning when Dakota awoke, something told her to go see if Brandon was home. She never ignored her inner voice. She felt so childish spying on him this way, but she had to know if he was home. She eased the door to his new room open. The bed looked as if it hadn't been slept in all night. Dakota was instantly furious. It was really on now.

"Two can play this game." She thought. She hadn't spoken to Alexander since her return, but she felt it was time for a chat. She hoped that Alex wasn't too busy to talk to her. She found her cell phone and gave him a call. As the phone rang, she began to have doubts about calling him so early. What if he had a significant other? What if he was just with some other woman right now? How would he respond to a call out of the blue from her? She'd almost hung up, when he answered sounding out of breath.

"*Damn, he's busy,*" she thought. "Hello, Alex, can you talk?" she asked timidly.

"Of course beautiful, I can always talk to you." Relief flooded thru Dakota as he made her blush. "So, how are you sweetness?" he asked.

"I'm fine and you?"

"Much better now that you've called."

"I'd be much better if I could see you." She said waiting anxiously for his reply.

"Where and when?" Was all he said.

"Here, tonight if you can swing it." She held her breath.

"You're only two hours away; I'll be there in a flash."

Dakota couldn't help but smile as she said, "I can barely wait."

"Aaah, there's the smile I was waiting for, I can hear it in your voice." He continued. "I'm glad you called, I was beginning to miss you." He admitted.

"Well as soon as you get here I'm all yours." She promised.

"Umm, sounds like I better bring my appetite."

"The way I feel, you might need to eat your Wheaties this morning."

"I'll eat whatever you want me to eat," he teased. "I'll call you when I arrive."

"Perfect. Bye"

As Dakota hung up the phone, her mood immediately began to change. She walked into her closet to find her most "Fuck 'em girl!" dress, because Alex was on the way to the rescue, again.

CHAPTER 8

Alex got them a room right on the water. The sound of the ocean thru the open French doors, and the scent of the beautiful yellow roses, that he filled the room with, was enough to make Dakota want to stay forever. The sun setting on the water was the most beautiful Dakota had ever witnessed.

Alex ran a bubble bath for them in the Jacuzzi. Berry scented candles lined the tub. The Champagne was on ice. He had thought of everything. *Cake*, by Trey Songz was playing in the background. The mood was perfectly set.

Alex smelled delicious and looked so handsome, in a cream colored linen suit. His shirt was open displaying a chest that could have been carved by Zeus himself. Dakota felt like she was on an island in the tropics. All of her effort in finding the perfect dress was not wasted on Alex. He told her that the little black dress was almost as beautiful as she was.

She had to admit that the plunging neckline, which showed her navel, definitely accentuated her voluptuous breast. The back of the dress dipped all the way to the top of her ass; and two silk ribbons at the shoulders held it all together. The only other things she wore were a pair of black, open toe heels that strung up her calves, and a heart shaped diamond pendant around her neck. Her hair was up to show off her lovely neck. As she glanced around the luxurious hotel suite she was almost overwhelmed at his thoughtfulness. He seemed to read her thoughts.

"It sounded like you needed to escape the mundane today." That's all he said before he kissed her slowly and deliberately.

"I did, I really did." Was all she managed to say as he let her hair down and began to run his fingers thru it. Dakota wanted him so badly, her body ached. Trey serenaded them "They say you can't have cake and eat it too, but ain't that what you s'posed to do?"

His shoulders, arms and chest were so well defined she wanted to kiss every inch of his delicious body. His scent aroused her even more.

"I really like this dress," he began as he undid the ribbons on her shoulders and let the dress fall to the floor "but damn, it's only the wrapping on the present."

Alex took both her hands in his, and held her arms out to her side, and stepped back to admire her loveliness. As if he couldn't help himself, he dropped down to one knee and nuzzled his face in her stomach, inhaling her sweetness.

Dakota loved the feeling of his mustache on her bare skin.

"Such lovely shoes," he continued as he loosened the straps and helped her step out of them. By now, she was barefoot and he was on both of his knees, with his arms wrapped gently around her waist.

Dakota ran her hands across his chest and pushed his linen shirt off, exposing his chiseled back. In this position, his face came to her breast and Dakota caressed the top of his head, as they swayed to the music. She closed her eyes and let go. No worries, no cares, only her skin on his skin. As the song ended, Alex stood and carried Dakota with her legs wrapped around his waist to the Jacuzzi.

He placed her in the bubbles and quickly removed the rest of his clothes. He grabbed two glasses and the Champagne before he slid into the water behind her. He popped the top and as the Champaign overran the bottle, he let it pour down Dakota's back, which caused her to let out a scream.

"Let it out! That's right, let it all out." He told her and poured them both a drink as they laughed.

"Thank you for all of this." Dakota said as she lay back on his chest with the waters whirling all around them.

"This is only the beginning. I could give you this anytime you want or need it," he told her.

Dakota blushed. "Well, I definitely needed it today." She thought for a moment, and said, "You know what? I need something else too." She smiled at him seductively as she turned to straddle his lap.

"Please, help yourself to anything you want." He smiled back at her. Dakota could feel that he meant what he said, so she helped herself. She slid down his hard shaft, but he thrust himself in further than she anticipated. She gasped and tried to reposition herself, but Alex wasn't having any of that.

"No, no I've got you right where I want you baby. You are going to ride this entire dick," he let her know, as he thrust himself even deeper inside of her.

Dakota's legs were spread too wide to resist his deep penetration. She could only cry out as he went deeper with each stroke. The pain felt so good. His forearms were pressing down on her thighs and his hands gripped her ass. She couldn't get away.

Just as she began to feel the wonderful sensation of an orgasm coming, he began to suck her erect nipples, and to tell her how much he wanted her to call his name when she came.

"Say-my-name" he told her with each thrust of his throbbing dick.

"Ahhhh, don't stop baby, make me cum baby, make me cum!" Dakota pleaded.

"No," he corrected her "not baby, call my name. Say it. Say Alexander your good dick is making me cum."

He knew she couldn't possibly say all of that, but she had better try. He ran his hands up her back and grasped her shoulders to pull her down harder on his dick.

"Say it!" he demanded.

Dakota couldn't think straight. "Alex, I'm, I'm..." she stuttered.

He smiled; he was really enjoying this. "No that's not my name; say-my-fucking-name" he said as he began to pull her head back by her hair and bite her breast.

"Alexandaaaaaah," she said and then a screamed escaped her. "your di, di, dick," she gasped, "is sooooo, goooood!" Another, scream and Dakota could manage no more.

She was in a full-blown orgasm and words escaped her. Alex was satisfied, and besides that, her powerful muscle spasms on his dick caused him to cum just as hard as she did.

A few orgasms later, they lay in front of the fireplace on a beautiful white, fluffy rug. Dakota was thinking very hard and the crease, in her beautiful brow, concerned Alexander. He didn't want to pressure her or make her talk about anything that would make her feel uncomfortable; but he wanted to know why she was so quiet.

"Hey, beautiful, you're not thinking of leaving me tonight, are you?"

Dakota smiled and assured him that she was all his for as long as he wished. She had no intentions of leaving him, until she absolutely had to leave. She loved how he made her feel so secure and so precious. She had been fantasizing what it would be like if she were his woman, and she wondered if he ever thought about it at all.

The fire crackled and they lay with their limbs entwined around each other. What was his life like? She wondered. Did he have someone special in his life? Children maybe? She knew he had money and excellent taste, which made her wonder what his home looked like. Was it a bachelor pad, with lots of high tech toys, or very "grown & sexy."

"Where could she fit into his everyday life? Would it be like this most of the time?" She wanted so badly to ask him, but she didn't want to scare him off, by making him think she was in love or something. *"That would be silly, right? Or was it?"*

Was she falling in love with Alex? The thought scared her for some reason. Dakota pressed her face against his chest, and listened to the strong steady beat of his heart, and tried to stop thinking.

Alex pulled her body closer to his. She felt so small and soft in his arms that he instinctively wanted to protect her, from whatever it was that was worrying her.

"What could have her so tense?" He wondered. He thought to himself that if she were his woman, he wouldn't give her anything to worry about. He would treat a woman like Dakota like a Queen.

He wondered what her man was like. *"Was he a good provider? Did he put his hands on her?"* This last thought angered Alex, but he reasoned it away, with the fact that, there wasn't a single mark on Dakota's pretty little body. Besides, how could any man ever hurt her in any way? Whatever was going on with them had sent her running to Alex, and that was all that mattered to him.

She made him feel like a King. She should definitely be his Queen. Everything he did to her was like a new experience to him; it made him want to think of more exciting ways to make her smile. He loved the way she looked at him as if he couldn't fail. With a woman like her, on his side, he would be happy forever.

This made him wonder if she ever thought about being with him all the time, instead of whenever she needed to get away. He didn't want to scare her off and he definitely didn't want to ruin the mood, so he kept his thoughts to himself.

Her skin was so soft and her long thick hair smelled so good. She had curves, in all the right places, and the sex was off the hook. She was open to everything he wanted to do, and damn she could ride a dick! Especially, all the dick Alexander had to offer; he really hated when women made stupid comments like "that's too much dick" or they acted like he was killing them with the dick.

He knew he was well endowed but he prided himself, on how to handle himself, without just damaging the punani. He tried being gentle with Dakota, because he could feel that she wasn't used to his size, which secretly made him happy. But even when she got him caught up in the feeling and he went deeper than he had planned, she never stopped him or criticized him in any way. She was just as soft on the inside, and always wet, and so willing to please…by now these thoughts had his dick as hard as Chinese algebra.

Dakota was just beginning to wonder what Alex was thinking about, when she felt his manhood pressing into her stomach. She smiled to herself as her own juices began to flow. It seemed that she could never get enough of him. Just the thought of all of him inside of her made her body tingle.

She got on her knees to straddle him, but instead Alex pulled her up to his handsome face. No words were exchanged as his soft, talented lips began the fine art of cunnilingus. Her hips automatically whirled in rhythm, with the pleasure he gave her. He licked and sucked and probed until her body ached to have him inside.

Finally, he rolled over and pushed both her legs back. Dakota braced herself, for the deep penetration she knew he could reach in this position. He wasted no time making her wait. It felt like liquid lightening as he entered her and stroked long and deep into her love canal. Dakota closed her eyes and bit back a scream that was welling up in her throat.

He kissed her so intensely that she felt it in her toes. Dakota wrapped her arms around his neck and held on for dear life. Her body instinctively rocked with his, and they created a beautiful symphony of love. Alex caressed every inch of her body and didn't skimp on the lovin'. He never missed a beat or a stroke.

He was so talented and knew her body so well, that he

brought her to climax after climax. When they were both spent, it finally dawned on them both that they hadn't had anything to eat all day; other than each other. The thought of going anywhere didn't appeal to either of them so they ordered room service and made love all night.

CHAPTER 9

The next morning, they decided to get out and get some fresh air. Alex suggested a stroll down the beach to a quaint little seaside restaurant, where they could have breakfast outside. The day was absolutely beautiful. They laughed and talked as they walked hand in hand down the sandy white beach.

The restaurant was just opening when they arrived. They sat out on the deck and fed each other breakfast and sipped mimosas. Everything was so perfect, that Dakota forgot that she was in her hometown. Anyone that would have seen her at that moment would have seen a woman without a care in the world.

And that's exactly what Gina saw. Gina was never too fond of Dakota; in fact she was quite jealous of Dakota's looks, her money, and her man.

"Who is this fine specimen of a man that's feeding Dakota strawberries?" Gina wondered,

He was absolutely gorgeous and he, most certainly, was not Brandon. She knew that Dakota hadn't seen her, and so she watched them closely to try and tell if they were related. They certainly didn't look related; at least she hoped they weren't. Gina had always wanted Brandon and it looked like she finally had her chance.

She wondered if there was trouble in paradise with Brandon and Dakota. She had never seen Dakota with another man, other than Denver, Dakota's brother. Maybe, she was stepping out on Brandon.

"But out in public like this? Surely, not." Gina thought. But if she was on the down low, Gina wanted, more than anything, to be the person to burst Dakota's bubble.

Dakota never sensed that she was being watched so intently. All of her attention was on Alexander. He was her sole focus. She hadn't thought about Brandon, all day long. She was truly enjoying herself and all of the attention that Alexander paid her.

She loved how his eyes were always on her. When the waiter brought their ticket, Dakota excused herself to go to the ladies' room. She was smiling from ear to ear, as she seemingly, floated across the restaurant. But, as she returned to her table, expecting to see Alex, her smile faltered.

"*What the...?*" Was that Gina talking to Alex? *Her* Alex? Dakota saw red.

Gina was laughing, at something Alex had just said. Dakota attempted to compose herself enough to walk up to their table. So many thoughts ran thru her mind as she approached them. Gina saw her before Alexander did, because his back was to Dakota. Knowing that Dakota was approaching, Gina put her hand on Alexander's shoulder as she continued her fake laugh.

She wanted to watch Dakota's reaction to this, and it paid off in full. Gina knew, without a shadow of a doubt, that this was not a relative. This made her laugh even harder. And now, Dakota was furious.

"*Stay cool*" she repeated in her mind, but that wasn't working. Finally, she reached the table and Alex stood to pull out her chair. Both ladies eyes never left each other.

"Hey girl, how you?" Gina chirped as if they were old friends. It was all Dakota could do to keep her voice civil.

"Hey um, Gina right?" she replied with a cold smile on her face.

"Yep, that's right" Gina didn't hesitate. "I haven't seen you in a month of moons." Gina said happily. "I thought I knew your "friend" here but I was wrong," she lied. "I'm surprised you remembered me," she gushed on, not allowing Dakota to get a word in edgewise.

"I'm still friends with Brandon, but haven't seen you two together lately. How is he?" she asked, and waited as they exchanged icy glares.

Alex felt the tension and cleared his throat. "We need to go so that we aren't late Dakota" Alex said as he stood. "Nice to meet you..." he couldn't recall her name.

"Gina" Gina replied, as she reached to shake his hand. But, Alex ignored her hand and turned to take Dakota's hand instead. He side stepped Gina and escorted Dakota out of the restaurant.

Undeterred, Gina called out, "Bye girl!" in the sweetest voice she could muster. She was so happy, she could barely contain her excitement.

Gina's mind was running, a mile a minute, as she drove her sporty, two-door Infinity home.

"I knew they weren't related!" she declared out loud, and chopped her steering wheel.

Gina thought back to how close her and Brandon were growing up. They were always together, because their mothers were close friends. And she and Brandon were real friends that did everything together. Everyone knew, as kids they were as thick as thieves, and naturally everyone thought they'd become a young couple, as they grew older. Especially, Gina.

Brandon was the one that taught her how to throw a mean left hook, how to change oil in a car and he also showed her how to French kiss. However, before she could fully express herself with Brandon, Dakota moved to town.

Beautiful and charismatic, Dakota quickly became very popular. Even Gina wanted to be friends with Dakota. So, she invited Dakota to her sweet 16th birthday party. Little did she know, that she all but cut any chances, of ever having Brandon, on that fateful day.

Brandon and Dakota already knew each other from school, but never had much interaction, other than exchanging smiles, in the hallways, between classes. Neither shared any subjects or extracurricular classes. But, now they were sitting over in the corner of Gina's party looking a little too cozy for Gina's liking.

At first, Gina didn't even know that what she felt was jealousy. She'd never experienced the emotion, before then. Brandon was always available to her, whenever he wasn't working on a car, a hobby that would eventually make him a rich young man. Even then, Gina would hang-out with Brandon; handing him tools and talking about every topic they could imagine.

They enjoyed each other's company. There was a familiarity that only best friends or lover's share. Since they were too young, to be lovers, they just accepted the feelings as puppy love. And yet, all of that was, on the verge, of being a distant memory.

It seemed that all Brandon talked about, after the party, was Dakota. He wanted to invite her to everything. Gina hardly ever had time alone with him anymore. Yet, he and Dakota found plenty of alone time, without Gina.

Slowly, but surely, Gina realized she was losing her best friend. She was still the same Gina she'd always been, and so was Brandon, but now he was that with Dakota. Gina never stopped loving Brandon, but when he took Dakota to the Prom, it was the last straw in her book.

How many times had she dreamed of the day she and Brandon would go to the Sr. Prom together? She had imagined her dress, his tuxedo, and the jealous stares as everyone finally realized that they were a couple and deeply in love...now, that reality popped her bubble, Gina decided to love Brandon from afar. He was too painful to be around. Luckily, she was accepted to her first choice college, which was two states away.

Gina didn't think of herself as bitter. She knew that she would never be friends with Dakota, but the thought of not being friends with Brandon, all but broke her heart. She couldn't even bear the thought.

She figured Brandon just needed time to miss her. So, she rarely visited their hometown on breaks from school. And when she did visit, she made it a point to stay away from Brandon. It was hard. Harder than she anticipated, but it would be worth the wait when Brandon saw how she had grown up in all the right places.

Gina knew she was a beautiful young woman. She had curves for days. She could have her pick of any man, including professors at her college. She toyed with them and had plenty of fun. Yet somehow a fire still burned inside for Brandon. She knew that one day he would be hers and they would live happily ever after.

But it seemed as if Dakota had some sort of a spell on Brandon.

"How were they still so happy after all these years?" she wondered. *"What did Dakota have that she didn't? Nothing!"* She resolved to have Brandon one day. And now 'one day' was finally here.

"Yes, little miss perfect done fucked up now" she laughed to herself. Gina pressed the gas a little harder and the Infinity sped down the interstate. She had some plans to make. Smiling like a Cheshire cat, her speakers bumped to Nicki Minaj's *Beez in the Trap*, as she wasted no time getting home. Her time had finally come.

CHAPTER 10

Dakota knew how much Gina wanted Brandon. Gina had never tried to hide her feelings for Brandon. Until now, Dakota never let it worry her. But now she was worrying. She knew that even if Brandon got with Gina to spite her, Gina wouldn't see it that way. And what if it started out as spite and turned into something else? They were friends way before she and Brandon were. They practically grew up together. Everyone expected them to be a couple... the questions were whirling around in Dakota's head.

"Pull it together!" a voice in her head snapped at her. *"Who has Brandon's heart?"* it asked. *"You do"* the voice answered.

"True." Dakota thought, feeling the tension ease a little. *"I have his heart and no one has ever even turned his head,"* she thought to herself with pride. Feeling better she relaxed a bit. *"So, why are you here with Alex right now?"* a smaller voice asked.

She turned and looked Alex. His chiseled features were so handsome, and he was so considerate...but he was not Brandon. She knew this had to end. It was delicious and fun, but not worth losing Brandon. Especially if he was willing to change.

They were leaving the hotel, after checkout. And Dakota knew she had to make a decision on what to do. She didn't want to give Alex up, but she didn't want to hurt him by stringing him along. As if he sensed her decision, Alex placed his hand over hers without saying a word.

They rode that way, without a sound, just the music playing, until they reached Dakota's truck. Neither knew what to say, yet they both felt what wasn't being said. When they got out of his Mercedes, Alex wished he could do or say anything to change what felt like impending doom, but he wanted it to be Dakota's choice to be with him. She smiled at him and hugged him tightly for a long while.

"I know what we have it something special..." Dakota began.

"Just bad timing?" Alex finished.

"Maybe, or maybe it just wasn't meant to be."

"Well, if anything changes, you know how to reach me."
Alex kissed her forehead gently.

She stared into his eyes, until her own started to well up with
tears, then she just held him for a long while. Soaking in his feel,
his taste, his scent. Eventually, she got into her truck and was
gone. Alexander watched her drive off, knowing how hard it
would be to forget about her.

Dakota couldn't look back. It was already going to be hard
to forget about Alexander. For the sake of her relationship with
Brandon, she would have to do it. So, she just drove. Without
looking back. Finally, she turned the music up and let the tears
flow. *"Brandon, you had better be ready to make a change…"* she
thought to herself.

The next day, Brandon stayed out from work. Brandon never
missed a day at the shop. His business was booming to say the
least. He worked hard, in the beginning, to make sure his custom
detailing was cutting edge. His work had caught the attention of
some professional ball players, and his shop stayed booked ever
since. He always felt a sense of pride when he thought of all he and
Dakota had built together. He loved his work and so did she.

So, when he told his right hand man, Kev that he was taking
some time off, Kev was surprised. He assured Kev that everything
was all good, he just needed a minute to himself. Kev knew it had
to be more to it than that, but he also knew how Brandon valued
his privacy, so he didn't press him. Brandon trusted Kev as his
manager. He knew Kev would handle the business while he was
away. He was grateful to have one less thing to think about. Today
he wanted to be alone with his thoughts. There was so much he
needed to sort out. His mind kept going over and over how things
had taken a left turn with his relationship.

Everything was on point in his mind. So he couldn't figure
out why he and the love of his life were sleeping apart. Why was
she acting like she had something to hide. And why the hell did he
say they should see other people? He knew damn well that he
didn't want to "see" anyone else. And he sure as hell didn't want
his Coca to see anyone else either. However, there was a nagging

within him that said "this is what she wants," but he didn't really want to believe that voice.

What he wanted was his woman and his life to return to normal.

"*Shit, I'm a good man*" he thought to himself. Was being predictable a bad thing in Dakota's eyes? What did she want from him? And why now? He had recently purchased the rock, of all rocks, and was planning to ask Dakota to marry him. Now, it seemed like forever wasn't as long as it seemed, before all of this.

"Ah, to hell with it!" he said out loud. "*Time to get with the program, two can play this game*" he thought as he smirked at himself in the mirror, he reminded himself that he really was a handsome guy. Not a pretty boy, but handsome in a GQ kinda way.

He stayed fly and his clothing was the latest fashion. He had that "good" hair and those "bedroom" eyes, not to mention his physique. Besides, women were always flirting with him when he was not with Dakota. He loved the attention just as much as Dakota did. And, yeah he fucked a chick or two here and there, but that's just because he didn't want to ask his Coca to do certain things in the bedroom. He didn't love those hoes.

"Yep, tonight the turn up is going to be real."

CHAPTER 11

The doorbell rang for the second time, but Gina was in no hurry. In fact, she wanted to make him wait. She loved being in control and wanted to build the anticipation in Paul's mind. Her mind had been doing 100mph ever since her chance meeting with Dakota this morning. All kinds of thoughts ran through her mind. She plotted all day long. But, now her plans were set. She had already contacted Mama J, the nick-name she always called Brandon's mother, Joan. Gina knew for a fact that Brandon still ate dinner with his mother on the 1st Sunday of every month. So, she secured an invitation to dinner for tomorrow, the 1st Sunday.

Her plans were to invite Brandon out to catch up on old times, but in actuality she wanted to pick up where they left off all those years ago. So, tonight she wanted to get her mind right. She wanted a "release" so to speak. Gina knew that being around Brandon always made her feel like an out of control school girl. Giddy, and silly was not how she intended to be tomorrow. No, she would be confident and in control of herself.

She had stumbled upon this calming technique her last year of college. At the time, she wanted to graduate with a certain g.p.a. but her grade was borderline failing. However, the professor of that class never looked her in her eyes, because he was too busy looking at her tits and ass. She was desperate for an "A" and decided to be the last to leave class the next day.

As the other students fled the room after class, she slowly shuffled her papers and deliberately dropped a few on the floor. Her heart was beating a mile a minute, but she got down on her hands and knees reaching for the errant papers. She held her breath, as well as her pose, until she was sure the professor had his eyes on her. She dared to sneak a peek over her shoulder and he was staring directly at her ass. She shifted a little and slid one leg to the side, ever so slightly arching her back so that her short skirt revealed her bare bottom. Then at that exact moment, she made eye contact with her professor and held his gaze briefly. Her heart leapt at her boldness, but she knew the "A" was hers, if she could just follow thru. Slowly, she backed out from under the desk and walked straight over to ask if there was anything she could do, for a little extra credit tonight, before the final tomorrow.

Two hours later he was on his hands and knees begging her to tell him what to do. So, she did. And it was the most fun she'd had all year. She realized he would do anything to fuck her in her ass. She wasn't worried about the anal, because his dick was rather small, but she made him work for it.

First, he had to make her a drink.

"And, if you see the ice in my glass, you'd better be up making another one" she told him.

To which he happily agreed. She sipped her cocktail as he massaged, then licked and sucked each of her toes. Next, he gave her the sloppiest "head" she had ever received. He had skills too. He actually made her cum on his fingers.

Finally, he rolled her over onto her stomach, but she could see the glazed look in his eyes as she watched him in the dresser mirror. It almost turned her stomach. So she clinked the ice in her glass and he reluctantly hopped up to make her another drink.

She watched in amusement as he hurried to return to his task. He handed her the drink and grabbed the baby oil from the bedside table. As the cool liquid cascaded over her backside she smiled to herself at how easily she would exceed her g.p.a.He rubbed the oil all over the top of her juicy ass and down her thighs. Then he parted her ass open and stuck his tongue as far in her asshole as he could get it. His fingers were fanned out on her cheeks, keeping her ass open, but his thumbs were inside of her pussy making her wetter and wetter. She craved a climax but he kept right on sucking and rubbing. Gina dropped her drink onto the carpeted floor and arched her back to entice him to enter her.

And it worked! He swooped up and jammed himself inside of her wet little tunnel. Pumping furiously in and out, and squeezing her ass cheeks rhythmically made her cum hard. She creamed inside, all over his shaft. He cried out as he ejaculated all over her back.

Needless to say, she got the g.p.a. she wanted. Although, surprisingly it was because of her calm and confidence during the exam not the automatic "A." Yet she always accredited it to getting "right" the night before.

So, tonight she would get "right" to build her confidence before her big reunion with Brandon tomorrow. As the doorbell rang for the third time, she sashayed to the door in a Kimono styled mini dress. Paul was Partner at the law firm she worked for upon graduation. He was a no-nonsense kind of guy that kept everyone on their toes in the office. He wasn't mean, but he wasn't there to make friends either.

Gina knew that if anyone found out, about what they did every now and then, there would be consequences. So, did Tom. Even though they were both single, office romance was frowned upon by the firm. Gina worked late almost as often as Tom did. As fate would have it one night they literally bumped into each other in the elevator and the electricity between them was undeniable. Right after, they were given a case to work together and the rest is history.

Now, here he was at her door with a single pink rose in one hand and a bottle of merlot in the other.

"Sorry to bother you miss, but I followed the rainbow to the end, and I'd like my pot of gold please" Tom joked.

Gina, grabbed his tie and pulled him inside the door. "I've got your gold, sir, but you're gonna have to dig for it!" she teased as she pulled him in closer for a sensual kiss.

Unlike Gina, Tom wanted someone else to take control in the bedroom. He made a lot of decisions in his high profile career, so he welcomed relinquishing the reigns to Gina. She wasted no time giving him a corkscrew, because she knew after a couple of drinks Tom would do whatever she directed him to do. And she was ready to get "right".

CHAPTER 12

After catching Yakima up, on everything that happened with Gina, Dakota was mad all over again. Kima could see that little vein popping up on the side of her forehead and decided enough was e-damn-nough. She jumped up off the plush couch in Dakota's game room. Marched over to the bar, grabbed two shot glasses and a bottle of Patron.

"Fuck it," she laughed, "I've done my fair share of best-friend listening, now we're at the part in the movie, where we get drunk, and do things we'll regret tomorrow. You down?" Kima lifted the glasses and bottle into the air waiting for Dakota to turn her down.

"Why the hell, not?" Dakota shot back, grinning like a mad woman. "Hurry up before I come to my senses" she yelled as Kima sloshed Patron into the two shot glasses.

"Bottoms up" Kima said as they downed the first of many.

"Oooo, that burns!" Dakota whined.

"Well, here take another to cool your throat," Kima said, pouring another round.

They took the next shot. This time both were gasping for air as the hot liquid burned all the way down their throats. Looking at each other's expressions, they both fell out laughing. Deciding to chase the shots with beer seemed to be the solution to their problem. Dakota got up to open a Heineken for them to share, but wobbled to the left. This made them laugh even harder.

Three shots and two beers later, they were dancing and singing at the top of their lungs. In the excitement, Yakima took her tank top off and started swinging it around in a circle over her head as she danced to the hype beat of Beyonce's 7/11.

Not to be out done, Dakota followed suit, but flashed Yakima her breasts as if she were in a girls gone wild video. Peals of laughter filled the room. Yakima mooned Dakota, and soon, they were both as naked as the day they were born. Dakota wobbled again and as Kima laughed she was hit, in the head, with her own shorts.

"Bullseye!" Dakota screamed and dove onto the huge couch. Grabbing a pillow and expecting retaliation she peeked over at Kima who was suddenly quiet.

Kima stood there, with a joint in her hand, which fell out of her shorts, and a smirk on her face. Dakota started shaking her head back and forth no.

"Girl, you know I don't smoke" she slurred as she eyed Kima coming towards her after lighting the joint.

"I know" Kima said soothingly, "so I'mma blow you a shotgun" she said trying to keep a serious look on her face.

This made both of them crack up. "Come on girl, it ain't like the boss gonna piss test you....oh yeah, *you* the boss!"

Even more laughter. Kima flipped the little joint around and motioned for Dakota to lean in closer. She did, and Kima began to blow the smoke into Dakota's mouth, and then her nose, when she closed her mouth.

Dakota tried to hold the smoke, like she'd seen in so many movies, but coughed like she was dying instead. When she caught her breath, Kima handed her the rest of a beer. They were each laying at opposite ends on the arms of the couch. After a little while, Dakota remarked that she was not high and she didn't know why people wasted their time smoking weed. Kima leaned toward her staring.

"What?" Dakota asked.

"Wait a minute," Kima said moving closer.

She crawled across the long couch. Now they were inches apart, but Kima was leaning over Dakota's face, staring at her forehead.

"Yep, I thought so!" Kima laughed.

"What?" Dakota asked seriously, not daring to move.

"That damn veinis g-o-n-e!" She stated happily.

It took Dakota a minute to spell out the word because she was indeed high. When she finally caught on, Dakota began to laugh.

Then Kima kissed her forehead and said, "See, I made it all better."

It was surprising, but she definitely felt better.

Kima kissed her again, this time on her nose. She paused, and looked into Dakota's eyes and waited. Dakota tilted her chin and closed her eyes, but Yakima licked her neck instead.

She knew that was Dakota's spot, because of all of the sex talks they'd had over the years. As Yakima's tongue gently flitted over her skin, Dakota felt like she was on cloud nine; yes, she was definitely lifted. Yakima's silky hair fell across Dakota's stomach as she moved lower and lower towards Dakota's open legs.

Dakota knew that Kima was bi-sexual. She also knew how many men were whipped by the head Kima gave. Now she realized that Kima knew exactly what to do with a pussy too. All of Dakota's inhibitions were out the window…g-o-n-e!

Kima spread Dakota's legs even wider and gently licked her thighs. She licked her finger and lightly rubbed the skin that separated Dakota's pussy from her ass; her taint. Kima licked up and down Dakota's clit, until it began to stiffen and swell. Still rubbing her taint rapidly, she began to lightly suck Dakota's juicy clit. Little moans of pleasure escaped Dakota's mouth and her moistness glistened on Kima's talented fingers.

Kima stretched Dakota's pussy wide with her thumb and forefinger, then gently she began to finger fuck her with the first two fingers of her other hand. Slow and gentle, at first, making Dakota arch her back, because she wanted Kima to go deeper. She knew what Dakota wanted, but Yakima kept her fingers where they were and started sucking Dakota's clit again.

She could feel Dakota's g-spot beginning to swell against her fingers. She rubbed a little faster, a little harder all the while sucking and licking her clit. Dakota's nipples were erect and she started squeezing them herself, with one hand while playing in Kima's hair, with the other hand. Dakota was lost in ecstasy when Kima pulled her clit back and began pounding inside her pussy with her two stiff fingers.

"Push…" Yakima whispered. Dakota felt the orgasm coming down on her quickly.

"I'm gonna cccummmm," she stammered.

"I know you are, now push my fingers out" Kima instructed as she pounded at her soaking pussy.

"PUSH, NOW" Yakima demanded right before she began sucking her clit again. And Dakota pushed, with her vaginal muscles, as those slippery fingers slid in and out of her quivering snatch, until she exploded just as Kima spread her fingers wide inside of her.

Dakota's orgasm was so strong, it squirted ejaculation across the coffee table. Three, very distinct squirts, each shooting past the table. She was shocked by her own ejaculation; which she'd never seen before. Dakota threw her head back and screamed with delight when Kima slid her fingers out of her pussy, and up her ass and finished eating her until she couldn't take anymore and begged Kima to stop.

Dakota's head was spinning from her extended orgasm. Her heart was pounding and her legs quivered. She never dreamed a woman could make her feel so good. She wanted nothing more than to return the favor. She wanted to make Yakima feel like she felt. Only, she had never been with a woman before.

But the tequila said "girl you got this!" And she was more than willing to try.

Yakima was already up pouring two more shots. Which Dakota gladly accepted. She was looking at Yakima with new eyes. Her body was flawless. She had an athletic shape with perky breasts. Her skin was a creamy caramel color from head to toe.

Dakota wondered what she tasted like. She didn't have to wait long as Kima leaned in for a delicious kiss. It was soft and sensual. Dakota was getting wet all over again.

"Sit on the bar with your sexy ass," Dakota told her. Yakima smiled from ear to ear as she hopped up on the bar.

"What you gone do with all this?" Kima teased as she spread her legs wide.

"I'mma eat you up!" Dakota said with confidence. This made Kima laugh.

"Oh really?" she mused "well get to it" she demanded as she stroked her clit. She dipped her finger inside her wetness, as she leaned back on her elbows. Dakota timidly began to kiss her breasts and lick her nipples. Kima poured a little patron into her navel and waited for Dakota to slurp it out. Which she did, but had a look like a deer caught in headlights.

Kima knew she had to guide her along.

"Hey, hand me that joint out of the ashtray" she told Dakota, pointing to the coffee table. Dakota did as she was told, hoping that Kima would blow her another shotgun to calm her nerves. Kima popped it into her mouth.

"Light my fire, sexy" she said and waited for Dakota to fire it up. She inhaled deeply all the while keeping eye contact with her pretty little student.

"Come closer. I won't bite" Kima told her.

Kima leaned forward and Dakota was on her tip-toes to get her lips close enough for an effective shotgun. This time she inhaled as much as she could take. Closing her eyes, Dakota let the sensation overtake her.

Yakima watched her closely, as she fingered herself. She couldn't wait to have that hot little mouth on her pussy. When Dakota started giggling, Yakima knew it was time. Kima rubbed her wet fingers across Dakota's lips, and Dakota licked and sucked them enthusiastically.

"There you go" Kima cooed "Now lick this pussy just like that" she said as she guided Dakota's head to her hot spot. Dakota's mouth was open, hot and wet as she suckled Kima's clit. "Ummm" Yakima moaned as she began to grind against Dakota's face.

Dakota gained confidence when she heard how she was pleasuring Yakima. She moved her face side to side while pressing into Kima's wetness. She couldn't believe how good Kima tasted. She saw that Yakima had a finger in her mouth, which prompted Dakota to slide her finger into Yakima's tight, little snatch. Yakima's g-spot was already swelling. Dakota could feel it close to her pussy's opening. She wanted to make Kima cum as hard as she had cum.

"I want you to turn around for me" she said. Dakota slid two of the bar stools on either side of her. "Kneel down and lean across the bar" she told Kima.

Yakima did as she was told as Dakota knelt between her open legs. Dipping her finger into Yakima, she continued rubbing her spot as she sucked her clit from beneath. Kima was fucking her face. And Dakota was loving every minute of it. Her face glistened from Kima's juices. But she wanted to do more. She stood up.

Standing up behind Kima gave Dakota more leverage as she pumped her fingers in and out. She slapped Yakima's gyrating ass.

"Ohh, yeah! Spank it harder" Yakima cried o

"Yeeesss…harder, harder!" Kima screamed.

By now, Dakota was pumping her whole arm as she rammed Kima's pussy, with her two fingers. She spanked her ass until it turned red.

"I'm gonna cum all over you" Kima warned.

"*Yes you are*" Dakota thought as she pressed her thumb firmly against Yakima's asshole, never stopping with her other hand.

"Push, baby" she reminded Kima. And as Kima pushed, Dakota's thumb slipped into her ass. Yakima bucked wildly and ejaculated her orgasm, in a stream, that made Dakota's look mild. Her body went stiff as another stronger stream shot from her pussy.

Dakota was amazed.

Suddenly, Yakima reached swiftly back and grabbed Dakota's head. She forced Dakota's face between her legs, "Lick it, lick it, lick iiiittt!" she demanded over and over again. She had a vice grip on Dakota's hair, grinding her pussy against any part of Dakota's face she could reach.

Dakota stuck out her tongue as firmly as she could, trying to breath between Kima's gyrating. She could barely breathe, but she was so turned on, she didn't care.

Yakima was using Dakota's hair to move her face up and down in a rapid nodding motion. When Dakota's tongue brushed across her asshole Yakima went crazy. Yakima was furiously rubbing her clit with one hand and holding Dakota's head hostage with the other.

"Oh shit, I'm cuming agaaaaiinn!" Yakima screamed as her body locked into place. Dakota could feel Kima's asshole pulsating right before her pussy squirted.

Finally, Yakima released her grip on Dakota's hair and collapsed onto her side.

High and drunk, Dakota staggered over to the couch.

"Damn, girl! You sure you never ate pussy before?" Kima teased, walking over to join Dakota on the couch. "Shit, I need a cigarette!" she joked.

Dakota smiled to herself, leaned her head back and closed her eyes.

CHAPTER 13

"What the hell is she talking about?" Brandon wondered to himself.

He had been at the club, for about 45 minutes, and was already on drink number four. The music was cool. He hadn't asked anyone to dance, even though there were some sexy women there. He noticed that he was the topic of conversation at a table of ladies. He could tell by the extra-long stares and all the high-fiving going on.

Eventually, the babbling woman, seated next to him found her nerve and broke free from the pack. Now, he was wondering how he was ever going to escape. She had just asked him if he was tender.

"What the hell?" he thought. His face must have given him away.

"Do you Tinder?" she repeated. "Because you can check out my profile if you do. If you don't, I'm on Instagram and Facebook," she rambled on.

He looked her up and down. She was pretty, nicely dressed, and sitting on a fat ass. Brandon started thinking about what else she could do, with that mouth, besides talk a mile a minute. He wondered what she would do if he just cut to the chase, and invited her back to his room. Maybe she'd go. At the very least, she'd be offended and leave him alone.

He caught the bar tender's eye and waved him over for another drink.

"Would you like another drink?" he offered.

She just nodded and raised her glass to the bartender; never missing a beat.

Brandon had had enough.

"I'd love to take you to my room, get you out of that sexy dress, and see if you can take dick as well as you can hold a conversation." he interrupted.

She stared at him with wide eyes.

"Well, at least she shut up" he thought.

"Sure. I can take dick" she said calmly. "Just let me tell my girls I'm leaving" and she slid off of the bar stool.

"Check please!" was all Brandon said.

They walked up the block to his hotel. Once in his room, they wasted no time getting down to business. The slinky dress that she was wearing came off in a flash. Her lingerie was on point too.

She knew when to shut up and use those sexy lips to make Brandon forget all his worries. Her mouth was really quite talented. She had full luscious lips, and her kisses were enticing Brandon to find out more about that mouth.

He walked her over to the bed and pushed her into a sitting position. She waited as he removed his clothes, giving him direct eye contact the whole time. This was different from Dakota, who usually closed her eyes or made minimal eye contact during sex acts.

"Damn, why am I thinking about Coca right now?" he thought as she began to take him into her mouth. The hot juiciness of her mouth got his full attention. She was good! Brandon figured he would push his luck and see how far he could go with her.

He began stroking into her mouth. She was taking it all. So, he pumped harder and further into her mouth. Now he was hitting the back of her throat, she was still taking it, but started to pull back slightly.

"Oh, no you don't," Brandon mumbled.

And leaned with her as she lay back on the bed. Her mouth was so good he felt the urge to cum. He decided to pull back. After all, he didn't want to scare her.

As soon as he pulled out, she wiped her mouth, with the back of her hand.

"Now, let's see what your mouth can do." She said.

Brandon was confident in his skills and didn't hesitate. He let her get comfortable on the bed as he slid into position to kiss her 'other' lips. He grabbed her legs and began to kiss her thighs lightly. He was slowly moving towards her opening, kissing and licking every inch of her skin.

"Come on" she moaned, grabbing at his head.

But Brandon had a certain way he liked to do things; he didn't like being rushed and he definitely didn't need any instructions. He ignored her pleas and continued at his pace, in fact he slowed down even more. Finally, he reached his destination. She quickly began grinding on his face, yelling out directions.

"Lick it faster! Suck my pussy…suck it!" she demanded.

Her legs were wrapped tight around his neck.

"Damn she strong," he thought.

Brandon wasn't no punk, but he was getting a little nervous about his access to air. If she held on any tighter his air supply would be completely cut off. He hoped she was close to cuming. She was rocking from side to side, and before he knew it, she had rolled over on top of him! She rode his face like a pony. His entire face was wet; at one point she farted and he almost choked. She was like an octopus that he couldn't get away from. When he eventually got free of her grip, all he wanted to do was make her pay for that sneaky shit.

"So, you like that sneaky, freaky shit huh?" he asked her.

"Yeah, I do."

"Cool, I got you. Turn around and get that ass up in the air."

She did as she was told, getting on her knees and arching her back to get her ass up high for his pleasure. He smacked her hard across the ass.

'Higher! Poke that ass out, got dammit. You better act like you want this dick."

He pulled her ass open wide, intentionally trying to hurt her, but she moaned as if she liked the pain.

"You like that?"

"Hell yeah. Fuck me hard, I want it right now!" she instructed.

Fucking her doggy-style he thrust deeper and deeper into her pussy. But she was still barking orders at him.

"Faster! Harder! Deeper!"

"Ok, I can go harder and deeper" he thought. Brandon pumped faster and harder.

"Spank it! Slap my ass!"

He slapped it over and over as her ass turned red. He pushed her face down, into the bed, trying to shut her up. He was putting all his weight on her, and she had her ass pushed up for more punishment.

Reaching back with both hands, she spread her ass cheeks wide. She wanted to tell him to get in her ass, but her face was pushed into the mattress. She grabbed his dick and pushed it up to her ass.

He pushed deep into her hole, not caring if it was wet or not. She wanted it rough, and that's how she was gonna get it. She tensed up only for a moment, then caught his rhythm. It didn't take long for her to get wet inside her ass, and as she did, he could feel her pushing back onto his shaft. She had both hands firmly planted on the head board, forcefully pushing back and taking him deeper into herself. When she came her entire body began shaking, Brandon couldn't hold back any more. He slid out and came all over her back.

CHAPTER 14

A couple hours later he was alone in his room. Things had gotten pretty wild with ole girl. It was fun, but she talked too damn much Brandon mused as he drifted off into a fitful sleep. Dreams of Dakota racked his mind all night.

In his dream, he and Dakota were at a movie laughing, and having a good time. She asked him why they didn't have any popcorn, so he went to get them some. When he came back she was sitting with someone else. When he confronted her, she acted like she didn't even know him. She got up to leave and Brandon tried to follow her, but his feet were stuck to the floor and he couldn't move. He struggled for what seemed like hours.

He woke up feeling like hadn't slept at all. He wanted to sleep the day away. And if he didn't have dinner plans, with his mom, he would have. Especially since he'd checked into this hotel room to relax. But he loved his mother's cooking and wasn't going to miss out. Besides, he remembered her saying that she had a surprise for him. So, he jumped into the shower to get ready.

As he pulled into his mother's driveway, his stomach started to rumble. He smiled thinking of the good food he was about to eat.

"Hello, beautiful," he greeted his mother as she came out on the porch.

"Hey, baby" she said kissing his cheek and dragging him into the house.

She was so excited he asked, "What's going on, mom?"

"See for yourself!" she said spreading her arms wide.

Brandon's mouth dropped as he saw Gina, his childhood best friend, standing right behind him. She was all grown up; in all the right places. Composing himself as quickly as he could, he smiled and gave Gina an awkward hug.

"*Damn, she looked good*" he thought as she turned to walk into the kitchen.

His eyes followed her curves and stopped on her juicy ass. The leggings she wore left little to the imagination, but Brandon was imagining some things he could do on those dangerous curves.

Gina smiled to herself as she added a little extra sway to her walk. She knew he was watching. She looked back quickly and caught him adjusting himself. She gave him her sexiest smile; inside she was doing cartwheels!

Dinner was delicious as usual. They all laughed and reminisced over good memories. Joan pulled out some old photo albums. Before anyone knew it, it was dusk dark. Gina knew she would have to make her move soon before Brandon decided to leave.

"Well, I don't want to wear out my welcome" she announced, drawing the protests she'd hoped for, but waving them off.

"I really enjoyed myself and would love to continue to catch up, but I know you have plans tomorrow Mama J, and you've gotta get home to Dakota, Brandon."

Joan pulled Gina into a big, bear hug.

"Well it was so good seeing you Gina" Mama J said. "We have to do it again."

"Of course" Gina replied, hugging her lovingly. She turned to Brandon and pretended to give him a goodbye hug. And just as she'd hoped, he held on a few seconds too long. Little did he know that she could have held on all night, but she had a game plan to stick to.

"Leave him wanting more…" she reminded herself.

She pulled away from him and began collecting her belongings. Brandon couldn't take his eyes off of this 'new' Gina, especially all the junk in her trunk. He had to force himself to look away.

"Well, Ma, I'm going too. I love you, dinner was delicious as usual." He said giving her a juicy kiss on the cheek.

"Thanks Brandon, you know I love cooking for you. Be safe, son."

"I will."

"Goodnight and thanks again." Gina said to Mama J.

"You're more than welcome, sweetie. Goodnight."

Brandon walked Gina out onto the porch.

"Wait, how about we go grab a couple drinks and finish catching up?" he offered.

Gina smiled shaking her head no.

"Ok, I'll buy!" he said, not wanting the night to end.

Gina pretended to think it over.

"Well, ok you've twisted my arm" she teased. "Where to?"

"I know a great little bar, it's in a hotel, but that's not why I'm suggesting it."

"Um, hmm!" She pretended to be insulted.

"I swear!" Brandon couldn't help but laugh, as he opened the car door for her.

If Brandon could have read her mind, he would have skipped all the foreplay and taken her straight to the room, but he had no idea of the plans she had for him. He was genuinely happy to see her and to reminisce and if that led to a little more, then so be it. He was more than a little curious to see how many ways Gina had changed. Getting her away from his mom, and all the polite conversation, she could be herself and really keep it one hundred.

An hour later, Gina was so wet, that she could have slid off of the secluded booth she and Brandon shared. Her plan to get Brandon, was working. She made sure to lean her body on his every chance she got. She'd laugh and touch him on his chest, or thigh. She rubbed her breast against him and used every trick in the bag to see a rise in his pants.

Brandon felt the attraction between them. How could he ignore it? Every other minute she was touching him, rubbing him or pressing those soft titties on him. It took all of his self-control to keep his dick from getting hard; he didn't wanna play himself if all this shit was really just in his mind. But, the more they drank, and the more she pressed up against him, the more he started to think with his 'other' head.

Four drinks later, Gina finally saw the rise she'd been looking for all night long. It was time to go in for the kill. She shivered all over.

"Is it cold in here to you?" She asked snuggling up against Brandon.

"No, I'm good" he replied.

"Well let me sit in the corner of the booth" she said and slid closer.

Brandon was closest to the wall and had nowhere to go. She slid across his lap, bouncing her ass on his dick in the process. She giggled as she apologized for her ample bottom.

"Sorry if I just molested you by mistake" she lied.

"I do feel violated, that's a lot of junk in the trunk" he was teasing, but he couldn't hide the admiration in his voice.

That's exactly, what Gina wanted to hear.

"Don't make me put it on you for real, I'll have you trapped under all this ass begging for mercy!" she said seductively.

Brandon looked her over from head to toe.

"How come she didn't look like this when we hung together all the time?" he wondered.

He was shaking his head, and she could tell he was trying to keep her in the 'friend' zone, in his mind.

Boldly she whispered "But, wouldn't that be fun?" and licked his ear.

Brandon was trying his best not to play himself, but that was an obvious invitation. He couldn't resist any longer.

"Yes it would." was all he said as he slid out of the booth. Taking her hand, he led her to the elevator, never taking his eyes off of her stunning figure.

CHAPTER 15

By the time Dakota awoke, a few hours later, Yakima was gone home. She showered, ate a slice of toast, with butter and jelly, her favorite, and fell into the bed exhausted; sleeping most of the day away.

Dakota was starving when she woke up. Walking into the kitchen; her mind ran across Brandon. She knew he had not been home last night, and there were no signs of him having come home today, while she slept. *Where was he? And who the fuck was he with? How was this bitch more important than coming home*?

Pushing the thoughts from her mind she made herself a quick dinner. Nothing fancy; her guilty pleasure, Ramen noodles. She only ate them every now and then, because Brandon would always trip about how bad they were for her health and shit. He always had something to say about every damned thing.

"They taste de-damn-licious to me. Boom! In your face B!" she said, slurping an extra-long noodle into her mouth.

She tried watching a movie, but couldn't concentrate on it for love nor money. Brandon was all she could think about.

"Where was he? Who was he with right now? What was he doing? Was he fucking? Why wasn't he home?" Dakota was losing her mind.

She had to get out of the house. She wanted someone, or something, to take her mind off of all the thoughts running through her mind. She remembered hearing some of the ladies, at her spa talking about a new spot they kept going to. It was in the lobby of a hotel, but it was a really nice bar. She figured it couldn't hurt, and at the very least it would get her out of the house, and give her something to think about other than Brandon's ass.

Dakota finished her noodles and headed upstairs to get ready to have some fun. She popped her iPod into the surround sound system that ran through the whole house. She started her 'party mix' playlist, and the first song up was *3005* by Childish Gambino. Dakota loved music, it always put her in a better place emotionally. She had the music bumping like she was already at the club. Once she was dressed and on fleek she headed downtown.

Twenty minutes later, the valet handed her the ticket for her car. Strolling into the bar she was aware of all eyes on her. She never shied away from attention. Just the opposite; she loved it. Although, it wasn't packed, she knew she'd still get her mind off of Brandon. She always enjoyed live music, and there was a cover band playing some 90's hits. The bar wasn't what she expected, it was dimly lit and very cozy; she liked it.

Dakota found a seat at the bar, and ordered a drink. The bartender was very attentive to her; Dakota thought it was charming. She ordered a Mai Tai and began to casually survey the room, but before she could, the bartender was back with her drink. And he felt the need to formally introduce himself to Dakota.

"Hello gorgeous. My name is Henry, and I am at your service. Please allow me to give you this Mai Tai on the house."

His smile was contagious. Dakota knew he got lots of tips with that smile and charming personality. She figured a couple free drinks wouldn't hurt, so she accepted. Besides, Henry was distracting her from thinking about Brandon.

"Thanks, Henry. I'm Dakota. Not too much going on in here tonight, huh?" she asked. He agreed that it was a slow weekend night.

"But, that gives me more time to talk to you," he flirted with her.

Dakota smiled at his efforts and sipped her Mai Tai. He did indeed, seem to have a lot of time to keep Dakota occupied. Henry told her that he was an aspiring comedian. He was pretty funny too, he kept her laughing for over an hour. But eventually, he got busy with customers. So, Dakota turned to look out at the rest of the bar.

Her heart skipped a beat. She couldn't believe her eyes. She thought she saw Brandon. She didn't have a clear line of sight, and almost sprained her neck trying to see. He and a woman had just entered the elevator, which led to the hotel upstairs, and the door was closing. Dakota jumped off the barstool, and almost ran, but she caught herself.

The doors closed, right before she could get a good look. She slapped the elevator door and pressed the elevator button like a mad woman. She knew that she was tripping but she couldn't help herself. She watched the numbers going up and waited to see which floor the elevator stopped at. She realized that even when the elevator returned she wouldn't know which room he was using. She thought about knocking on every door on the floor, but figured she'd get put out, and Brandon wouldn't open the door even if she did find the right room.

All she could do now was go home, and wait. Thankfully, Henry had put her purse behind the bar. She thanked him, gave an excuse and left a tip for Henry and left for home again. She knew she was in for a long night.

So many thoughts raced through Gina's mind. She was going to put it on him like he'd never had sex before. She was horny and having waited so long, she was ready to have Brandon inside of her.

Her smile faltered when she saw Dakota sitting at the bar. *"What is she doing here?"*

Gina was not about to let Dakota interfere with what was about to go down. Instinctively, she walked faster towards the elevator; damn near dragging Brandon. Out the side of her eye, she saw Dakota looking around the room. As if magic, the doors to the elevator opened, as soon as she pressed the button. Gina pulled Brandon into the elevator and quickly pressed the close button repeatedly.

"Damn, slow down shorty. We've got all night!" Brandon thought to himself; completely unaware.

At last the doors closed and the elevator started moving. Heart pounding, and adrenalin flowing, Gina kissed Brandon passionately showing him how much she wanted him.

It was on as soon as they hit the room. They disrobed at the door. Brandon scooped her up, cave man style, and threw her over his shoulder.

She loved how strong and fit he was. She nibbled on his back, right before he threw her onto the bed. She bounced once, and he was on her. Pouncing, as if she were his prey.

He paused briefly, looking into her eyes, for any sign that she may have changed her mind. For an instant, neither moved; until she wrapped her legs around his back. He felt her wetness and pushed into it.

He was instantly surrounded by her velvety softness. She moved with him catching his thrusts and giving as good as she took. Their bodies rocked. He lifted her leg and turned her onto her side, with one leg on his shoulder. Each thrust digging deeper into her.

A cry, of surprise, escaped her as the first stroke invaded new territory. But Gina still gave her all to him. She felt him hitting something that had never been hit before. Stroke after stroke he dug all up in her box, until she exploded. He pulled back a little, and allowed her orgasm to pass; he intended to keep going.

When she stopped shaking he turned her over, and hit it from the back. Squeezing her ass and her tits. He wanted to touch her all over.

Gina couldn't get enough of his hands all over her. But, she wanted to give him something she knew Dakota wasn't giving him. She wanted to stand out in Brandon's mind, whenever he thought about the two of them. Reaching back she put her middle finger and her ring finger in her ass stroking in all the wetness there.

"I want you in here," she moaned.

"Oh yeah?" he asked, and slapped her hard across her ass.

"Yes! Yes, daddy in here" she emphasized and slapped her own ass.

Brandon didn't need convincing. He slid out of her and was positioning himself to enter her ass, when she got up.

"No. I wanna ride it" she said and pushed him back on the bed.

"Time to take control…" she thought to herself.

She slowly straddled him; maintaining eye contact the whole time. She grabbed his dick. She rubbed it, teasingly, against her asshole. She was on her knees, and deliberately kept her ass up high enough, that he couldn't push into her.

"Not just… yet." She stroked his shaft, with her hand, and lowered herself just enough to let his tip, press into her asshole, a couple of times. She relished being in total control.

But Brandon was not waiting any longer. She was driving him crazy. He pressed his forearms down on her thighs, forcing her down lower and lower.

She struggled at first, wanting to maintain control. But finally, was overcome by his strength. She let go, all at once, impaling herself onto his manhood.

The time for holding back was over. Brandon pulverized her juicy asshole. He could feel it clinching, around his dick sporadically. He knew she was cuming, when she started grinding on his dick.

And so was he. He pulled her ass cheeks apart, so hard, as he spent his load she thought she might tear. But, the pain was worth the look on his face when he climaxed inside of her.

They had both used up their lustful energy. They lay next to each other, trying to catch their breath. Neither believing what just occurred. Gina recovered first and suggested he join her in the shower.

Twenty minutes later, she was riding him again; except this time it was his face. She took pleasure in rubbing her pussy all over his face. Gina made sure not a spot was missed! When she climaxed, they switched positions.

Now that Brandon was on top, his mind flashed back to the previous night. He had pulled back, because he didn't want to scare the woman, that was giving him head. Before he could even wonder about if Gina could take it, she grabbed his dick and said "Jam it down my throat."

She leaned back on the pillows and licked her lips. Brandon could not believe his luck. He fucked her mouth, but not too roughly at first. Then he felt her pulling him harder into her face. So he pumped a little harder.

The back of her throat seemed to open up. He felt like he could slide down her throat if he wanted.

"*Gotdamn that shit feels good*" Brandon thought. He stroked longer, harder; leaning his weight into it. He closed his eyes and leaned his head back.

But Gina wasn't having that. She wanted him focused on fucking her mouth. She slapped his ass rapidly, prompting him to look at her. She wanted him to fuck her mouth like it was her pussy.

"So you like it rough huh?" He grabbed the headboard. He fucked her good and long. She loved it; fingering herself the whole time.

He wanted to be where those fingers were.

He pulled both of her legs up into the air, and let them drape over his shoulders. Pumping into her sweet pussy again. She moaned and squeezed her nipples; rolling them between her fingers. She took his dick so well.

"I wanna cum hard" she told him.

He nodded his agreement.

"Choke me…" she whispered.

Brandon thought she was kidding and didn't respond to her request.

"Do it. Choke me. I wanna cum hard baby" she asked again.

She pulled one of his hands to her neck.

"*Fuck it*" Brandon thought "*Why not, if she likes it?*" and he let his hand close around her neck, not really choking her at all.

She smiled at that.

"Choke me till I cum all over this delicious dick. I wanna cum all over you" she pulled at his other hand.

As soon as it closed, around her neck, she started bucking underneath him. Amazed, he closed his fingers tighter around her throat.

Her hips were swiveling figure eights on his dick. He could feel an orgasm coming from his toes up his legs. He pounded harder, deeper and chocked her a little more. Her body convulsed under his as she came; causing him to cum too. Impulsively, he pulled her up, by her neck, and came all over her face.

CHAPTER 16

Brandon slept harder than he had in a while. No dreams. No tossing and turning. Just sleep. His body needed the rest. But, as soon as he awoke, he thought of Dakota. He really missed her. He was glad that Gina hadn't spent the night. It was a great night. He still couldn't believe it happened, but right now all he wanted to do was get home and see Dakota.

The bathroom was steamed up like a sauna as Brandon washed the night before away. Thoughts of Dakota, not Gina, filled his mind. He wanted to see her, hold her, and kiss her.

Driving home he thought about what he would say to her if she were there. He wanted to get back to normal; to get their lives back on track. He was 'feeling' himself, and had really showed his ass the last couple of weeks.

He knew he could pull any woman he wanted, but the only one he wanted was his Coca.

"*Does she still want me?*" he wondered.

The thought of losing her scared him. He realized that, no matter what, he had to trust her. Besides, she was a good girl. He knew, in his heart, that she loved him and would make a great wife and mother.

"*I'm gonna make it right between us.*" He decided.

Dakota was actually afraid, for the first time, in her life, of losing Brandon. She wasn't 100% sure that it was him last night, but it was an eye opener. All kinds of crazy thoughts bombarded her mind. Nothing would ever be the same again, unless she made it right between them.

She figured Brandon wouldn't change his ways, but now it seemed, it wasn't worth breaking up over.

"*Consistency in a man is not a bad trait*." She thought to herself.

"It will probably make him a better husband and father." She said to the empty room. She wished he would come home; she really missed him.

As if on cue, she heard the garage door going up. Her heart skipped a beat. It was Brandon returning home.

"*What now? Will he be happy to see me? Or is he still acting brand new?*" New thoughts flooded her mind.

No matter what, Dakota was going to let him know, that they were *not* seeing other people anymore, so he could just get that through his head. She waited for him to come into the house.

Brandon opened the door and called out for Dakota. No answer, but he knew she was there, because her car was in the garage, and the alarm wasn't set. So, he called again.

"I'm in here" she called back grateful that her voice didn't break.

She had been crying all night and didn't want Brandon to know.

"*Please don't let her be trippin.*" Brandon silently prayed. "*It's time for this to be over. Time to get right...*" he thought as he headed up the stairs.

Finally, he opened the bedroom door and their eyes locked.

"What's up" he asked not knowing what else to say.

"Just chilling." She lied

He walked over and sat on the edge of the bed next to her. He could tell she'd been crying, but didn't mention it. Instead he rubbed her hair back, off of her face, and kissed her cheek. She smiled a little at that.

"So, can we talk?" he asked.

"Sure"

"I've missed you"

She paused, not saying anything for a moment, but decided to be honest.

"Me too"

"I want you back"

"Yeah?"

"Yeah, I do. Don't you?"

Tears were brimming up in her eyes and she didn't trust her voice, so she just nodded yes. He pulled her into his strong arms, and held her like he would never let go.

The tears flowed, and she didn't attempt to stop them. Her man was home. Finally she was in his arms where she belonged. In that moment, all was forgiven.

Dakota felt like new money in his arms, and there was nothing Brandon loved more than money; except Dakota. He realized this now. He knew that he would never let her go, again.

They both believed they could move forward. Neither wanted to let the other go.

He pulled back, and wiped the tears from her beautiful face. He hated to see his Coca like this. He knew in his heart that he was the reason she was crying. Partly from the cold shoulder he'd given her lately, and partly from relief that now it was all over.

Brandon vowed to himself, to never hurt her like that again.

"I love you baby. Let's put all of this behind us and get our shit together. I don't want nobody but you Coca." He told her.

Hearing his pet name for her, brought fresh tears to her eyes.

"I love you too babe." She cried. And she meant it too.

They talked for a long time. Neither confessed anything, but they cleared the air. By the end of the day, they were laughing. That night they slept together. No love making, only sleep. But it was the best sleep either had in a long time. Everything felt new and exciting again.

The next day, to Dakota's surprise, Brandon was still in the bed when she awoke. It was after 8am. He wasn't asleep though, he was watching her sleep. She smiled; happy he was there.

"Want to play hooky with me today?" he asked.

"Absolutely. What do you wanna do?"

"Just get dressed and let's see where the day takes us."

Dakota smiled. She didn't want to say anything to ruin the moment.

"Alright, let's do it."

The day was beautiful. It was sunny and bright. Brandon dropped the top on his car. He looked at Dakota, as if for the first time. He loved the way her hair blew in the wind. She was gorgeous. And she was his.

They laughed and talked. Conversation came easier than it had in a long time. Both were truly enjoying each other. Dakota couldn't remember the last time they had so much fun together. She hoped this was a new start for their relationship.

Soon, the smell of the ocean was in the air. They were almost to the beach. Brandon knew that Dakota loved to walk along the beach. They left their shoes in the car and headed, hand-in-hand, towards the sound of the crashing waves. It brought back memories of when they would walk for miles and dream out loud.

"Remember, how we would come down here and talk about our dreams, Coca?"

"Of course! We would talk about everything we were going to do with our careers…"

"Yeah, all the money we would have." He laughed

"We definitely had high goals. Weren't we supposed to be millionaires by now?" she joked.

"Shit! I don't know 'bout you, but I'm on track like a mofo!" and they both laughed.

"Yeah, we've come a long way baby." Dakota said after a pause.

"Look," he said seriously, "I know we both thought we'd be married by now, but"

"Brandon.." she interrupted.

"No. Let me say this." He insisted. He stopped walking and took her face in his hands. "I love you Dakota. Plain and simple. I really wanted to give you the life of your dreams."

He thought for a moment, looking for the right words. "I wanted everything to be perfect, but I had to realize that being happy is more important."

Brandon seemed to be struggling with what he wanted to say. Dakota smiled and kissed him.

"Don't kiss me just yet." He hesitated, searching for the words. "I have a confession." He said, letting his hands drop down, to hold her hands in his.

Dakota's heart dropped.

"Was he breaking up with her? Is that why he didn't even try to make love to her last night? Did he want someone else?" Too many thoughts were running through Dakota's head.

"I put you up on a pedestal. Which eventually became a prison for you. I always knew that I wanted to make you my wife. And I had it in my mind, that my wife shouldn't do certain things… things I like to do." He looked at her, trying to tell if she understood what he was saying. "You get what I'm saying Coca?"

She didn't get what he was saying, but she didn't say anything. Her head and heart were conflicted.

After a moment, he continued. "I never thought to ask you if you were satisfied with our love life. I enjoy our sex. I do!" he assured her. But, I do want to do more …things."

That was it! Dakota couldn't take anymore. The tears were back, and fell one by one down her cheeks.

"So, this is how it ends?" her voice was barely audible above the waves.

"What?" he laughed. "How what ends? Are you crazy?" he asked disbelievingly.

She couldn't believe he was actually laughing.

"Well what are you saying?" she asked folding her arms.

"*This woman of mine…*" he thought to himself. He wrapped his arms around her and squeezed her tight; shaking his head.

"I'm saying I wanna try some new shit."

"With who?" she asked suspiciously, and pushed his arms off of her.

Brandon relished the jealousy he saw in her eyes.

"With you!" he barely managed before laughter overtook him again. Relief flooded Dakota and she realized that she had been ready to knock his lights out.

Finally, she joined in with Brandon laughing, until both their faces hurt.

"You shoulda seen the look on your face…wow! I thought you were gonna stroke out just now" he chided her.

"Shit I thought I was too. I was like, 'what the fuck?' in my head." She confessed.

"I know how that crazy ass mind of yours works." He threw his arm around her shoulder.

"Come on let's get you something to eat…crazy."

"I ain't hardly crazy…but I am starving." She said, trying not to smile. "Let's head back to the car, but don't think you're off the hook that easily. What kinda shit you wanna try?"

She was giving him the side-eye, but secretly she hoped it would be something, like the new things, she'd recently experienced.

"I was thinking we could *both* contribute new suggestions."

"Um hmm, you ain't slick, but you think I'm slow. Well, I'm not falling for the okey doke." She thought to herself

"Ok. You first." She wanted to see where his mind was before she blurted out anal or squirting or whatever.

"Can't out fox the fox, huh?" he thought to himself. Dakota had always been sharp, so he didn't want to start out with anal or choking. She'd know something was up. No, he had to start light.

"How about we get a couple of videos to get some ideas?" He suggested.

Grateful for the out, Dakota jumped on the suggestion. This way neither had to wonder where the other got their ideas from.

"Sure! We could go to the Triple X store today and watch when we get home." She smiled deviously at him. He agreed and returned the smile.

CHAPTER 17

Dakota had butterflies, in her stomach, as the first Blue-Ray disc started playing. She really wanted Brandon to be open to change. They were eating Chinese take-out, straight from the boxes.

Brandon fed her some boneless spare-ribs, and she gave him a bite of her eggroll. It felt like old times. Only, now she really appreciated what they had. She hoped that Brandon felt the same. They laughed and talked about which scenes they wanted to recreate. Everything was good.

Then Brandon's phone rang.

"What up? Who dis?" He answered, thinking it was one of his boys. Not many people had his personal cell number.

"Hey sexy, it's me!" Gina replied. "What you gettin' into tonight? Hopefully, me…"

Brandon froze for a second. *"How the fuck…?"* He had no time to wonder how she got the number.

"Oh, hey man. How you?" he stammered.

His face looked strange, to Dakota, and his voice sounded like he was choking; all wrong.

She stopped watching the movie and paid attention to Brandon's conversation. Her "spidey-senses" were tingling, and she prayed she was wrong.

She looked at him and tried to keep a straight face.

Brandon could feel Dakota's eyes on him. He tried not to panic. But Gina wasn't catching on quickly enough.

"I wanna see you tonight." She continued. "I must confess, I was trying to wait for you to call me first, but I thought why not call you instead. I mean it's not the 1950s or anything, right?" she laughed.

"Yeah, I'd love to go with y'all, but I'm spending some Q.T. with my lady, so…." His voice trailed off and he prayed Gina would buy a vowel, and solve the puzzle.

Dakota muted the movie, and turned towards Brandon.

"Some Q.T….what? Like some quality time with Dakota?" her voice was rising.

For some reason she sounded upset. Brandon wanted to end the call, before shit went all the way left.

"Yeah, you understand man. I'll catch you next time."

When he pressed end on his phone he could hear Gina asking more questions, but he prayed that Dakota didn't hear her.

"So where were we?" he smiled grabbing the remote to unmute the movie.

But, Dakota had heard her.

"Who was that?" Dakota tried her best to sound casual.

"One of my boy's in town and he wanted to hook up and play some pool." He lied

"Which one?"

"Huh?"

"Which boy?" she persisted.

Brandon's brain was in overdrive. He really wanted the night to go smoothly, but he knew Dakota wouldn't let this go. And all though he knew he was digging the hole deeper, he kept lying.

"Dick. You remember him, right?"

"Yeah. I never did like his ass." She snapped at him.

She wanted the night to keep going in the right direction, so she didn't press the issue. Besides, she thought to herself, she really didn't want to know, who had the nerve to call him out the blue like that.

"I'm glad you turned him down. Niggas need to *know* not to just call out the blue like that." She said calmly.

Brandon caught the hint loud and clear.

To his surprise, Dakota let it go. He definitely had to check Gina, for that shit, though. But for now, he was relieved to dodge the bullet. He pulled her close, and kissed her all over her face.

She loved when he did that. She began to giggle, and he knew they would have a good night. And they did.

The sex was amazing for both of them. They made love all night long. Dakota was more aggressive than usual. Brandon appreciated that she took the initiative and gave as good as she took.

Dakota loved how Brandon didn't do any of the 'usual' stuff. He was actually receptive to her taking the lead. They came over and over again clinging to each other as if their lives depended on it. Finally, falling asleep in each other's arms.

The next morning crept up on them, like a thief in the night. Brandon awoke first. He jumped in the shower, and threw on his workout gear. He started his workout playlist, and began stretching.

No sooner than he got on the treadmill, in their home-gym, his phone rang. It was 7:30 a.m. Caller i.d. showed a blocked number. But, Brandon knew exactly who it was.

"Yeah?" he answered.

"Hey Brandon. Is this a better time to call?" Gina asked sweetly.

"Yo, how you get this number, Gina?" he half whispered.

"Oh, I called my cell from both of your phones, the other night, while you were in the shower." She said matter of factly. "Can you talk?"

"Yeah, but…"

"So, when can I see you again?" she cut him off.

He didn't want to hurt her feelings, but he thought she understood, it was only a fuck for him. He wasn't sure how to say that to her. This was his best friend, once upon a time, and he couldn't just talk to her, any old kind of way.

"Gina…" he hesitated. "I mean, what's up?" He asked, hoping he didn't have to state the obvious.

"What do you mean?" she asked.

"You know I'm with Dakota. That's not gonna change. Period."

Silence.

"I mean, what happened was all good, but…" he continued.

"But your precious Dakota comes first." She finished for him.

"Yeah." Then, he tried to soften the blow. "I mean… me and you are still good, but you can't just be blowing up my phone, Dakota won't understand. You feel me?" He hoped she did.

"I get it." She said. "I just thought y'all weren't together anymore."

"What made you think that?' He asked.

Gina thought about telling him that she saw Dakota with Alexander, but decided not to play her trump card, yet.

Instead, she replied, "Well, just because of what we did the other night."

"True. That was fun, but I'm in a situation. You know?"

"Yeah, I do." She paused. "I enjoyed it though, didn't you?" she asked.

"For, sure" he whispered, again.

"So can we keep it on the low?" she asked hopefully.

"Yeah" he lied. "But let me call you. I got your number; I'll lock it in my phone and hit you up. Ok?" he asked.

Gina knew he was brushing her off, and she was pissed, but she played it off. She didn't want Brandon to see that side of her.

"Ok, cool. Just don't make me wait too long." She warned. "I mean, we are friends from way back, right?" she said trying to lighten the mood.

"Of course; way back." He agreed.

"Aight then, call me…soon, Brandon."

"I will," he lied again, "but I gotta go." He said and hung up.

He cut the treadmill off, and just looked at the phone for a while.

"This shit can't go right…" he thought to himself.

Gina, looked at the phone for a long while, after hanging up.

"How the fuck, he gonna try and play me?" She thought angrily.

She paced the room, back and forth. Trying to get herself together.

"Why is he acting like this?" she wondered. *"He know he wants me!"*

They had so much fun the other day. And now he was acting brand new, all for his precious Dakota.

He was choosing Dakota over her, once again. But what he failed to realize, was that Gina wasn't a love sick little girl anymore. She was a grown ass woman; used to getting her way.

"And, I'll be damned if she keeps him from me now. We will be together." She vowed to herself, as she flipped through the pictures in her phone. Brandon still looked sexy, even when he was asleep…

CHAPTER 18

It had been almost 3 weeks of blissful reunion. Dakota was happier than ever, with her relationship. She and Yakima had gotten past their initial awkwardness, after their little rendezvous. Business was booming. Everything was going Dakota's way.

"Brandon, on line 2, Dakota." Her assistant notified her.

"Ok, thanks, Kim."

She picked up the phone.

"Hey babe. What's up?"

"You." Brandon replied. "How about we shoot down to Hilton Head Island tonight, and stay for the weekend?"

"Absolutely. Sounds like fun. What's the occasion?" she asked.

"Just feel like getting away with my favorite girl."

"Cool. I'll get out of here early so that I can pack, and we can get on the road."

"No need to pack." He told her. "Just wear that lil sexy thing I like."

"I thought we were staying for the weekend?"

"Yes, we are."

Now she was intrigued. But, she knew Brandon probably wasn't going to tell her any more than that. So, she let it go.

"Ok, Mr. Mystery, what time should I be ready?"

"Be ready to roll by 4, since it takes about 3 hours to get there. I love you."

"I love you too, baby."

After hanging up, Dakota smiled to herself. In the past, every time Brandon took her out, she was looking for a ring. But since their reunion, she was content to just be together. Well, not really, but she wasn't looking for the ring, with a flashlight, in the day time anymore.

When Brandon and Dakota arrived on Hilton Head Island, he still hadn't given her anymore clues. She was beginning to enjoy the mystique of it all. They arrived at a beautiful home. Lanterns lined the gravel, circular driveway. The trees and the home were breathtakingly beautiful. Brandon parked and opened her door.

"Come on baby." He said, taking her hand.

Dakota's intuition told her something was up. She had a million questions, but she just went along with the program and let Brandon do his thing. But why did it feel like his hand was shaking?

They walked up to the door and were greeted by a man dressed as a butler.

"Welcome Mr. West., Ms. Morgan is looking exceptional tonight." He complimented Dakota. She smiled at this and leaned into Brandon.

"Yes, she does." Brandon replied admiring his Coca.

"I am, at your service. Follow me, please."

He opened the doors and led the couple to a romantic dining room.

Dakota was extremely impressed. It was so lovely, and secluded, that she had goose bumps all over. There was a beautiful chandelier hanging in the center of the room, over the table, which was covered in crisp, white linen and fine china.

David uncorked a bottle of Dom Perignon champagne, and poured them each a glass.

Dakota couldn't remain silent anymore.

"What are we celebrating?" she asked.

"We are celebrating us, baby. To us…" he said lifting his glass to toast.

"I'll drink to that!" Dakota clinked her glass to Brandon's and sipped the champagne.

"I love you, more than anything in the world, Dakota Morgan…" Brandon began. "I love everything about you, except…." He paused, as if deep in thought.

"*Except what?*" Dakota thought to herself.

Brandon had his hands clasped together, as if he was about to pray. Dakota couldn't help but notice that his pinky finger, seemed to sparkle.

Her breath caught in her throat when she realized what was happening.

Brandon smiled watching her eyes grow wider, and wider.

Finally, he continued.

"Everything except your last name. I'd like to change that, if you don't mind."

Dakota looked at him in disbelief, but she was already nodding her head yes.

"Coca, will you marry me?"

"Yes, baby, yes I'll marry you!" She screamed as he slid the 3 carat, canary yellow, princess cut, diamond ring onto her finger.

It fit perfectly. Dakota let out a scream and hugged Brandon, with all her might. They kissed. They laughed. They relished the moment.

A minute later, David was back. He congratulated the couple on their engagement and handed Dakota a small black box. She looked at Brandon for confirmation. He nodded his approval. So, she opened the box.

Inside was a gold bracelet with diamonds in the shape of the infinity symbol.

"I don't know what to say"

"Well, we'll be together for the rest of our lives, so I'm sure you'll think of something sooner or later" he teased her.

"Shall I serve the food, sir?" David asked.

"Yes, indeed."

Dinner was amazing, they had steak and lobster and shrimp, but Dakota could barely eat. She couldn't stop looking at her ring. It was so beautiful. It fit so perfectly. She absolutely adored it; and she adored Brandon for going all out for her.

"So, did your mother know that you were proposing?" she asked.

"Oh, yeah. Mine, yours, and of course Yakima, too." he said between chewing. Brandon was having no trouble eating his food.

Dakota screamed again. "Kima knew and didn't tell me? Wait till I see her again!"

"I'm gonna call my mom and let her know you said yes." Brandon announced.

"Ok, put her on speaker phone." Dakota suggested.

Brandon called and put the phone on the table between them. It rang twice, and Joan picked up.

"Hello?"

"Hey, Ma! Guess what?"

"She said yes?"

"And you know it!"

"I did know it!" Joan screamed and shared the news with someone in the background.

"Who you telling already, Ma?" Brandon asked jokingly.

"I was just telling Gina, she's over here visiting. She says congratulations." Joan shared.

Brandon looked at the phone like it had slapped him, in his face.

Dakota actually felt her blood run cold.

"*What was Gina doing over there?*" They were both thinking it, but neither said a word. Actually, neither knew, that the other had seen Gina recently.

"Brandon? You still there?" his mother asked.

"Yeah, Ma. Tell her thanks for us. We've gotta go. Love you much!"

"Love you both!"

Joan was still screaming when they hung up and luckily David came in with a desert cart. Both were grateful for the diversion. There was an odd silence, which was only filled by David serving their deserts. Both Brandon and Dakota were lost in thought.

"*Why the fuck is this bitch back in town? And why does she keep popping up in my life?*" Dakota wondered to herself. "*Is she spying on me? Or...is she after Brandon? Either way she ain't getting shit for her efforts. She'd better back the hell up and play her fucking role.*"

Brandon was lost in his own thoughts.

"*Gina is straight trippin', why the hell is she hanging out with my moms? Is she trying to get at me, for not returning her calls? Or is she trying to catch Dakota over there and snitch?*" he wondered.

But between the champagne and the sweet, decadent dessert all thoughts of Gina were soon a distant memory.

"Baby, I love you. I love my ring, and I appreciate all of this." She gestured to the room.

"You deserve it Coca. You're going to be my wife, and that means the best of everything for the rest of your life."

"I know you had to do some planning to pull this off without letting me find out. I mean, I had no clue."

"Yeah, well you know how I do." He bragged.

"Yeah?" Dakota looked him up and down seductively. "Well you know how I do, so uh… let's get to it."

"What? You want some of this?" Brandon leaned back in his chair so she could get a full view of what he was offering.

"No, I want *all* of that." She said leaning towards him.

They kissed passionately. Moving closer and closer almost pulling the table cloth off of the table. A glass fell over and broke the spell they had on each other. Realizing that they needed to get to their room, quickly, they left to continue celebrating their engagement.

Brandon picked Dakota up in his arms, cradling her like a precious treasure. David met them at the entrance of their private dining room and led the way to their exclusive suite. When they arrived David opened the double doors, revealing a room straight out of a fairytale.

The suite was filled with fire & ice roses, the kind he had given her on their very first valentine's day as a couple. Although, back then, he could only afford a half dozen, she loved them. Now, her room was filled with them, and the scent was amazing. There was more champagne on ice, in a silver bucket, next to the huge bed. There were more pillows on the bed than the law should allow.

Off to the left was a gorgeous, luxurious bathroom. David started the water in the Jacuzzi styled tub and lit the fire place. Dakota took in the majesty of it all, as Brandon and David talked privately, off to the side. She noticed that David was showing Brandon how to work, what looked like a remote control. Then Brandon handed David a device, and walked over to where she was looking out of the bay windows onto the moonlit ocean.

"You like it?" he asked wrapping his arms around her waist.

"I do." She leaned her head back on to his chest.

Just Right for Me by Monica began to play. It was one of her favorite songs. They swayed to the beat. Dakota felt like she was on top of the world, and nothing could bring her down. No one and nothing could pull her from Brandon's strong, loving arms.

"Is there anything else, sir?" David inquired.

"No, we're good, man. Thanks" Brandon replied.

"In that case, I'll retire and see you in the morning for breakfast. Sir. Madam." He bowed and left, closing the double doors behind him.

"I've got a little surprise for you in the bathroom."

"What's that?" she asked

"Go check it out..." he motioned for her to go.

She went into the bathroom; her heels clicked as she walked across the marble floor. In the center of the room was a chaise lounge with a beautiful lingerie outfit on it. The fireplace crackled and popped, and the Jacuzzi bubbled away, as she changed into the sexy lingerie Brandon had chosen for her. It fit perfectly and the red accentuated her honey blond tresses to a tee.

She realized that the music playing was not random. It was a playlist of their favorites, created just for tonight. She walked out in the sheer material, that seemed to be made for her body, and began a sensual dance for her man. Selena Gomez was singing *Good For You* and the words were perfect for her strip tease.

"...cause I just wanna look good for ya..." she sang along as she removed her clothing seductively.

Brandon lay back on the bed, completely naked, enjoying the show. He poured them both another glass of champagne when she finished her dance and led her to the Jacuzzi.

Some serious love making went down that night. All night. Somehow they managed to put Gina out of their thoughts and completely immersed themselves into each other.

They truly made love that night. They caressed and kissed. They confessed their love for each other over and over again. Their passion could not be contained. They laughed and cried reminiscing about the past. It was a perfect night.

The next morning, they ate a delicious, lobster, brunch and laid out on the beach. Dakota admired the way the sunlight danced through her diamond. She was so happy.

But a nagging thought kept popping up.

"*Gina is gonna be a problem.*" She thought over and over again.

She tried to push the thought away, but it persisted. She hated the fact that this bitch had something on her. But would she really tell Brandon? Dakota couldn't leave it to chance. She wasn't about to get this close to getting what she wanted, only to have it snatched away again. She would just have to go see Ms. Gina.

Brandon dozed next to Dakota on the beach. He couldn't shake the thought of Gina at his mom's house. He knew she was up to something. He just couldn't figure out why she would want to hurt him. They had been so close.

As he dozed he dreamt of a happier time with Gina. When they were still best friends in school. They were always together, but on this particular day, they were all alone at Gina's house. They were watching TV when Gina asked if he knew how to French kiss.

He didn't know for sure because he had never done it before, but he figured it couldn't be too hard. Besides, he'd seen it done lots of times in movies and stuff.

"Yeah, sure. Why?" he asked her.

"Just asking," she said

Now his curiosity got the best of him, and he became acutely aware that they were home alone. He also noticed that the dress Gina was wearing, was hitched up exposing her thigh. He'd never noticed how smooth her legs were before. Actually, he'd never noticed anything girly about Gina; she was just Gina. But now, in the absence of adult supervision, and sitting on the couch with her leg almost touching his, he noticed a lot.

"Do you know how?" he asked her; unconsciously licking his lips.

"Well…no." she admitted, "but I want to."

"Want me to show you how?" he offered.

"Yeah, I guess."

Brandon's heart was beating hard, and he didn't want her to feel it and know that he was nervous. So, he just sat there for a few minutes pretending to really care about what they were watching on TV. He calmed himself and turned to look at her. She looked nervous, too.

"I guess we can do it right here." He said shrugging his shoulders.

"Ok" Gina said. Turning towards him. She closed her eyes.

But his eyes were fixated between her legs; as she'd turned towards him, her dress twisted more and revealed the edge of her panties. Brandon had a strong urge to touch her there.

She opened her eyes to see what was taking him so long, and she caught him looking. But she only closed her eyes again and leaned closer to him so, he leaned in and kissed her softly. Then he kissed her again and she parted her lips in anticipation of his tongue; the French part of the kiss.

Brandon closed his eyes and let the kiss happen naturally. And it was great. She licked at his tongue and kissed him with a yearning he had never felt before. A slight moan escaped her throat and she pulled his hand to her bare thigh. They kissed and kissed some more while his hand slowly crept up her thigh.

"Damn, she's so soft and smooth." Brandon thought.

At long last, his fingers touched the edge of her panties. He expected her to stop him, instead she kissed him with more urgency. Brandon decided to go for it.

He pressed his forefinger against her smooth skin and slid it under the elastic edge of her panties. His heartbeat sped up. Thoughts whizzed through his mind. Still no resistance from Gina. Relief flooded through him, because the thought of stopping, without touching her "there" was unbearable to him now. He was past all stopping points; there was no turning back.

Was it his imagination, or did Gina just spread her legs a little more? He waited to see what else she was going to do to help him out. Nothing else happened. So, he inched his finger down, past her clitoris, down some more to the jackpot. It was warm and moist; and the softest thing he'd ever touched in his life. As if by instinct, his finger flicked back and forth, just inside of her opening.

Gina gasped and he immediately removed his hand, thinking he had hurt her. Her eyes flew open, but instead of anger, he saw lust. She grabbed his hand to put it back where it had been, when the front door opened. They jumped as they heard both their mother's laughter preceding them down the hallway.

Neither of their mothers had a clue what had just happened.

All day long, Brandon couldn't stop smelling his finger. Every time he thought about what happened, he smelled it. It smelled sweet and musty at the same time. Like some exotic perfume he'd never smelled before. He couldn't wait to get Gina alone again.

And every time they were alone after that, they did everything they could think of with the exception of him penetrating her vaginally.

Brandon awoke from the dream, still remembering some of him and Gina's escapades before he met Dakota. He looked over at Dakota, admiring her ring. He knew she was very happy, and he couldn't let anything change that.

"I shouldn't have tapped that…" he thought remorsefully.

But he wasn't going to lose Dakota over one damned mistake. He was going to get to the bottom of this shit. There was absolutely no reason, in his mind, that Gina should want to hurt him or Dakota. Gina was gonna have to tell him her intentions.

CHAPTER 19

It was all Gina could do, not to throw up, when she heard the news. And, Mama J would not shut up about it. She fumed inside of her head, but smiled and laughed with Mama J. She couldn't wait to get out of there. She had some more plans to make. She was not going to let Dakota pull this shit off.

"Oh, wow! Look at the time…I've gotta get going Mama J." Gina lied

"Aww, really?"

"Yeah, I have to get started on something I'm planning" This was true enough.

"Well, you go do what you gotta do. You are welcome anytime, so don't be a stranger ok?"

"You know I won't. Love you."

"Love you too."

Gina gave Joan a big squeeze goodbye, and trotted down the porch stairs to her car. How could Mama J be happy about this? *If she's so close to Dakota, then why isn't Dakota ever over there when I am?*

"*She knows I'm supposed to be her daughter-on-law, not that simple bitch.*"

Then her thoughts turned towards Brandon's shady ass.

"*So, now you wanna marry this bitch, huh? So, I was just a fling? Well, I've got news for you Brandon, I'm not gonna go away so easily.*"

She'd stop this wedding, and get Brandon back, if it was the last thing she did.

Speeding down the interstate, dodging cars, switching lanes, Gina's mind was focused on one thing, and one thing only. Brandon.

She reminisced on the times they were intimate. She remembered their early teen years like it was yesterday. How they played in each other's underwear like other kids played video games. Every time they were left alone, which was a lot, they were trying something new. Always doing different things to make each other cum without having 'actual sex'.

The no sex rule was Brandon's. He wanted to be responsible and not have a baby that could change their whole lives. So, Gina went along with it, because she loved the intimacy they shared. They had masturbated together, they'd given each other oral, and they'd dry humped like crazy. Each of them had hickeys all over from each other.

Once Gina pretended to be drunker than she was, in an attempt to get Brandon to penetrate her and take her virginity. She straddled his lap, without any panties on, and only ended up wrestling him, trying to remove his underwear. Frustrated, she even pretended to pass out, hoping he would take the bait, as she lay spread eagle in front of him. But he never did.

She was persistent though, especially once Dakota moved to town, and their time together became few and far in between. She was determined to have him be her 'first'. Desperate times called for desperate measures. She baked some special brownies just for Brandon. And the next time they had a few hours together, she made her move. She fed him the marijuana laced brownies, knowing that Brandon didn't smoke, and he had never had weed before. She also knew, it would take longer for the weed to kick in since he had eaten it, versus smoking it.

As she waited to see any change in his demeanor, she was up to her usual antics. She was on his lap with no panties on, and he was down to his drawers, when the weed kicked in. She could feel his manhood rising between her legs, and the familiar ache, of wanting him inside of her. She knew this was her best chance. He was gripping her ass, with both hands as she kissed him deeply, grinding on his lap. She felt his fingers enter her wetness, but she wanted more this time. She reached down and took him into her hand, stroking the length of him. He was so hard, and completely into fingering and kissing her, she decided now was the time.

She lifted up, off of his lap, high enough for his full length to stand straight up. She swiftly pulled his dick forward and sat down on the tip. His eyes opened, but he didn't stop her. She smiled at him and pushed herself farther down his shaft. His fullness hurt more than she anticipated. Slowly, she slid up and down until he was completely inside of her. The pain was exquisite, and she loved every minute of it. Suddenly, he lifted her up off of him, laid her down and fucked her like she'd always dreamed he would.

She wrapped her legs around his young waist and locked her feet together on his strong back. He plunged into her again and again; kissing her all over her face and neck. She arched her body up to take him deeper. It felt like he hit something deep inside of her, which triggered her orgasm. She convulsed underneath Brandon, throwing his rhythm off. This triggered his orgasm; his body went completely stiff. He began to pull out of her, but Gina locked her legs and wouldn't let him draw back far enough to actually pullout.

His resistance was futile, and they came together in a strong orgasm. But when the passion faded, Brandon was pissed with her.

"How could you do that?"

"Do what?" she asked innocently.

"Make me cum in you like that?" he accused.

"Did you cum in me?"

"Hell yeah" he said shaking his head.

"I didn't think you came. I know I did, and it was good. Let's do it again." she tried to entice him some more.

"What?"

"Come on, let's do it some more." She reached for him.

"What if you're pregnant?"

"I'm not! But let me be on top this time to make sure all the sperm falls out"

"Do think that would work?" he asked, unsure if he should trust   her.
"Yeah, because your dick would be blocking the way and dragging the sperm back out at the same time. So… we sorta have to do it again." she lied.

She looked at him with wide eyes, as if she were afraid of what would happen if they didn't have sex again, with her on top. Brandon felt weird, he couldn't shake off this disconnected feeling. He'd only had a shot of brandy, and only because Gina had dared him to drink it. But, for some reason, he felt like he couldn't think straight.

"Aight, come on. Get up here." He agree semi-reluctantly.

He couldn't deny his attraction to her. He wanted to be back inside of her; urgently. And he couldn't understand why he couldn't resist her tonight. He normally would have been able to resist penetrating her, and then go home and jack off, with no worries of having an unwanted pregnancy.

Now, as she mounted him, Gina was glad that she had drugged Brandon. His defenses were completely down, and he confirmed what she already knew; he wanted her.

When he entered her the second time, he wasted no time pushing all the way into her. There was no gentleness in any of his movements. He was on a mission. And although, it hurt a little more, Gina realized she liked it better. He thrust up into her and applied pressure to her thighs, to bring her further down his shaft, at the same time. She watched his face closely, she wanted to see his desire for her, in his eyes. But his eyes were closed. He was digging into her with long, deep, strong thrusts. She felt her orgasm coming and wanted to make him cum as well. She leaned over and tried to kiss him, but his mouth latched onto her nipple instead, and he sucked it so hard, the pain shot down her back.

This triggered her orgasm, and her muscles writhed up and down his hard, young dick. His teeth clamped down on her nipple, and his hand grasped her other breast in a vice grip. She tried to pull back, but he was going wild; lifting up off the couch jamming himself in between her wide open legs. His mouth opened to gasp in air and she was freed.

"Get up, get up, get up....I'm cuming." He urged her, slapping her ass frantically.

But it felt so good to Gina, that all she could do was push down harder on his throbbing manhood. She knew he would cum inside of her again, and he would be furious, but she could not get up. It was worth the risk, in her eyes.

Brandon's body was rigid. His movements were jerking her about, but he couldn't fight against nature. He finally exploded inside of her, as her own orgasm swept over her as well. They came together, sweating and moaning and grinding for several minutes.

When it was all over, the look he gave her almost broke her heart. And after that, they never hooked up again. Obviously, she wasn't pregnant, but it didn't help that Dakota was a part of the picture either. Gina tried everything to get Brandon back in her bed, to no avail. He even acted as if he didn't remember that they'd had sex.

"*Maybe he didn't recall the actual event. I mean, he was high for the first time.*" She thought to herself. The memory hurt, but it brought forth an idea. One that would help her plan, of getting Brandon back for good.

Gina laughed to herself as the idea blossomed into a plan, and the plan was as devious as she had ever been.

"*Yeah, boo-boo, you will be mine…*" she thought.

She picked up her cell to make a call…this plan would need some back-up, and she had some favors to call in.

CHAPTER 20

Alexander went to sleep and woke up thinking about Dakota. He had just about anything a man could want in life. He had a successful law firm and he was a millionaire by the age of 35. He lived in a luxurious, sprawling 4 bedroom, 4 bath home on an exclusive, beachside golf course. He had a Mercedes and a Range Rover, a maid, a part time chef, and a nanny for his 5 year old twin boys. What he didn't have was a woman he loved to share it all with.

Once upon a time, he did have the love of his life. His soul mate was tall, slender, and beautiful in every sense of the word. She was Nigerian born and raised until she was 16 and then moved to the states. Her parents were very wealthy and afforded her all the luxuries in life. She wore the finest jewelry, and clothing and attended the best schools. In fact that's where Alexander met her, at Princeton. The very first time Alexander laid eyes on her, he couldn't turn away. She radiated confidence and her aura was welcoming.

He asked his friends if any of them knew her name. One friend did, but he couldn't pronounce it, and she walked by while he was trying.

"It's Falilatu." She corrected him.

"It's beautiful. And so are you." Alexander commented.

"Thank you. What is your name?"

"Alexander."

She looked at him for a long while, then she smiled, the prettiest smile Alex had ever seen.

"You're beautiful too, Alexander." She said and laughed.

And so it started. They became fast friends and soon they were inseparable; where you saw one, you usually saw the other. They were both law students and very competitive. They pushed each other in ways no one else could. They were young and in love and thought they could and would conquer the world.

When they graduated they were married and honeymooned in Nigeria. Falilatu's parents loved Alexander very much and gave them the money to start their law firm. Business came slowly at first, but when they won a case that garnered them national attention, their phones rang off the hook. The business took off quickly and escalated very quickly. Soon they were working 70 hour weeks with very little down time together.

They decided to bring in partners in their firm. This allowed for Falilatu, or Lila, as Alex called her, to work part time. And Alex could work a regular 40 hour week, most weeks. The romance was immediately reignited in their relationship. That's when Lila shared the good news; they were going to be parents. Life could not be any sweeter.

Both were very excited to be parents. They would talk all night about names, and which schools the child would attend. They moved out of their loft and into a real home with a nursery and a yard. They decorated and planned for the future.

But it was to be short lived. There was a complication during the birth of the twins that was fatal for Lila. Alexander was crushed. His whole world turned upside down. He was a new father and a widow at the same time. His and Lila's parents helped for a long time with the babies and helping him through his grief. And eventually, Alexander found the will to carry on for his two little warriors.

So this was the life that he had lived for the last 5 years. It was just him and his sons Alex and Xander. He missed Lila more than words could describe, and never thought that he would love again. But his body missed the touch of a woman. He missed holding someone soft and sweet in his arms. He missed kisses, and intimate conversations, and laughing at things that only the other person understood. Everyone told him it was time for him to get back into the field.

So he did; with no intentions of falling in love at all. He only wanted to fulfill the urges his body craved. And maybe, just maybe, a friend that he could be himself with. But absolutely no love involved. He couldn't imagine loving anyone the way he loved Falilatu, and quite honestly, he couldn't bear the hurt of losing another love again. This was how he kept his heart guarded for so long. That is, until he met Dakota. Her beauty attracted him to her initially, but her confidence turned him on even more. He also loved the way she was so open to trying new things and how she gave herself to him.

And even though she seemed to be perfect for him, there was a catch. She was involved with another man. At first that was a part of the pros list for Alexander, since he didn't want a commitment anyway. Except, the more time he spent with her, the more he wanted her all to himself. He wanted her to want him the same way; all for herself. He realized that he missed being in love.

He didn't want anything that was forced, he wanted it to be natural and reciprocated. This was the main reason he didn't pressure Dakota with questions that he wasn't even sure he wanted the answer to. Yes he wanted more, but what if she didn't. On one hand, he would rather wonder, than to know for sure that she didn't want that with him, but on the other hand, he couldn't live the rest of his life wondering what could have been. It was a catch 22 for sure. But in the end he decided to go see her one more time, and ask the question that's been on his mind since the last time he saw her. Did she miss him at all?

CHAPTER 21

It was Monday morning; back to normal life. Dakota pulled into her reserved parking space at her spa. She walked in on cloud nine and couldn't wait for the staff to see her new ring. Kim, her assistant, was the first to notice.

"O-M-G! Is that what I think it is?" Kim screamed

"Yesss hunty!!" Dakota screamed back.

This drew everyone else over to see what all the commotion was about. They all ooooed and awwwed over her engagement and her fabulous ring. There were hugs and tears; most of them had been with Dakota since the beginning of her spa, and knew how she felt about getting married.

"Ok, ok, ok, now everyone back to work. We've got clients arriving soon." Dakota shooed her employees back to work.

"So, that's why your office looks like a florist shop..." Kim started, but clamped her hand over her own mouth.

"What?" Dakota was at a loss for words as she opened the door to her office.

It was filled with yellow roses. Every flat surface had a vase of yellow roses on it.

"*How thoughtful*" she thought, but then another thought overlapped the first. "*Why would Brandon send me yellow roses like...?*" Dakota almost couldn't finish the thought.

It couldn't be. Maybe Brandon was just changing it up a little with the color of roses he sent. But she knew this wasn't from him. He was changing, yes, but some things never changed. She didn't remember ever telling him the name of her spa...but this had Alexander's name all over it.

"*But why? Why now?*" she wondered.

"Surprise!" Kim yelled, directly behind her. "Isn't this romantic?" she gushed.

"Oh, uh, yes...yes it is, Kim. When did they arrive?"

"Just this morning. The van was waiting when I got here."

"Well, help me clear my desk, please. How am I going to work in here?" she laughed.

"I wish I had these kind of problems." Kim said, as she helped clear Dakota's desk.

"Aww, thanks. Here, put some on your desk." She said handing Kim two vases.

"I guess it's the only way I'll get some." Kim pouted.

"Girl, please, they're just flowers."

But as soon as Kim closed her door, Dakota dropped into her chair.

"*What the hell is going on here?*" she picked up the phone and dialed a very familiar number.

"The Newly Weds are back!" Yakima screamed into her phone.

"We're not married yet, Kima."

"Whatever, chic, you will be soon. I saw the rock he gave you!"

"I know, right? I love it!"

"You should, girl. You got a good one in Brandon."

"I know...but girl, I got a situation on my hands."

"What you mean?" Yakima got serious.

"Well, my office is filled with yellow roses."

"Are you seriously complaining about having an office full of roses right now?"

"No. Listen, Yakima. I said *yellow* roses."

"So, he switched up the color, big deal."

"Kima!"

Yakima thought for a moment. And it dawned on her that Alex had filled their hotel suite with yellow roses.

"Oh, shit! What you need me to do?" she asked.

"I don't know, but we gotta do something. Brandon can't see these."

"Chile, he don't even come to see you there, how would he see them?

"Just because they're here, he'll come."

"You've got a point there. I'll be over as soon as I can get clear. Alright?"

"Cool. Thanks, girl."

They hung up and Dakota leaned back in her chair and took a deep breath. Everything was going to be ok. Nothing to worry about. Crisis averted. Back to work, she thought.

The morning flew by quickly as Dakota immersed herself into her work. She trusted all of her employees, but she kept her own books. She trusted her accountant, only after going through the numbers herself first. Everything looked good. She decided to take a much needed break. She ended up staying in the break room longer than planned, because some employees had come in and heard the news of her engagement. They all wanted to congratulate her personally.

Dakota was still smiling as she walked down the hall to her plush office. She loved the design of her spa. It was European in style; she'd always wanted to go to Europe. She had a designer come in and decorate it for her. But, her office was the jewel in the crown. She wanted a place that beckoned her to come in each day. Her designer hit the nail on the head.

Her desk was sleek and modern with an oversized plush chair. Her desktop computer display was 27" and boasted 14 million pixels. Her wireless keyboard was ergonomically fitted to her hands. There was a chandelier, a tufted couch, a wall mounted flat screen TV, and a Bose surround sound system. She loved everything about it.

"You've come a long way, baby." She thought to herself and admired her ring.

She returned her attention to her work. Strolling down the list of clients for the day, her eyes locked on a particular name.

"What the hell?" she thought.

She couldn't believe the name of the 12:30 appointment.

She picked up the phone.

"Kim, when was this 12:30, full body massage, scheduled?"

"Which one?"

"The one with Olivia."

"It was scheduled last week, when we had a cancelation. Why? Is everything ok?" she asked.

"Oh, yeah. Everything's fine. No worries." Dakota lied.

She was worried. It was 12 O'clock, and in less than 30 minutes, Alexander would be naked laying on a table less than 20 feet from her office.

What was she going to do? How did he know this was her spa? She didn't remember, telling him the name. Was this just a coincidence or was he trying to see her? Her mind was reeling. If it weren't for the flowers, she would have thought it was a coincidence, but now…

"*Should I leave? Or maybe I'll just stay in my office.*" Her heart was speeding up. It had been so hard to put Alex out of her mind. Now, here he was again. "*Why?*" She wondered.

Something told her to leave, and Dakota always followed her intuition. She quickly gathered her things and rushed towards her door. There was a knock on the door, as soon as she reached it. She snatched it open, thinking it was Yakima.

Standing there in nothing but a spa robe and some slippers was Alexander. Dakota was speechless.

"Looks like I caught you just in time." He smiled that gorgeous smile at her.

"Alex!" she said, a little too loudly. "What, what…I mean, uh…why are you here?" she managed to get the question out.

"Well, I'm glad to see you too." he joked.

"I am too." She blushed. "I just wasn't expecting…" she had no words.

"Not expecting to see me?" he finished for her.

She nodded.

"May I come in?" he asked, poking his head into her office.

"*Damn you smell good.*" She thought. "Uh, sure, come in please."

Alexander walked in and closed the door behind him.

Dakota just stood there with her belongings in her arms.

"Am I keeping you from something?" he asked.

"Oh, it can wait. So…why are you here?

"I'm getting a much needed massage."

"I mean, why here? Did you know this was my spot?"

"Yes, I did. And it's very nice, I might add."

"So, are you here to see me, Alex?"

"Of course. I haven't heard from you in a while. I missed you." He came closer to her.

Dakota backed away, until she hit the edge of her desk and could retreat no further.

"Well, I…I don't think that's a good idea." She said weakly.

He leaned down and nuzzled his face in her hair; breathing in her scent.

"I miss everything about you. Don't you miss me?" he looked into her upturned face.

She shook her head no, not trusting her voice.

"Come on now, not even a little bit?" he kissed her forehead. Then he kissed her cheek, and finally her lips.

Dakota didn't resist.

Another knock at the door, jarred her back to reality.

Not waiting for an answer, Yakima swung the door wide as she entered.

Alex leaned back, but didn't move from where he was standing.

"Well, excuse me for barging in, but it's an emergency, so if you'll excuse us please." She said.

No one made a sound, and no one moved. They just looked at her.

"Uh, Yakima, this is …."

Yakima took one good look at her best friend, and knew what was up.

"Shhh! No, no, let me guess." She said with her hands on her hips. "This here is Alexander the great." She finished. Looking him up and down.

"Yakima!" Dakota started

"Wow!" Alex laughed, looking directly at Dakota, as usual.

"Oh, yeah. I heard about you, Mr. Man. What you doing here?" Yakima continued.

"Well, I'm here to get a massage, which I'm running late for, so I'd better go. If you'll excuse me?" he gave Dakota a meaningful look.

"Umm, hmm. You probably need to take some of these roses with you. This ain't a good look, all up in her place of business and stuff."

"I would never do anything to embarrass or hurt you Dakota. You know that right?" he turned to look at her.

"I know Alex, but some things have changed since the last time I saw you…" she looked down at her ring.

Alex's eyes followed her gaze.

"He's a lucky man. Congratulations."

He turned to walk out.

"What about all these roses…" Yakima stepped in his way.

"Kima! Let him go!" Dakota pleaded.

Yakima pumped her brakes and backed off. Alexander paused in the doorway, and held his hand up to his face, with his thumb and pinky extended in the universal 'call me' position, and turned and walked out.

Yakima closed the door behind him.

"See that shit? What you need to call him for?" she ranted.

Dakota knew Yakima's heart was in the right place, but sometimes she was a little extra.

"I can't believe he's here." Dakota shook her head, trying to clear her mind.

"I can't believe he's that damn fine!" Yakima exclaimed.

Dakota looked at her; she looked so serious. They both burst out laughing.

"Girl, you be having those soap opera problems."

"Tell me about it…"

Yakima stood up, and started gathering up vases.

"What's the plan?" Dakota asked.

"We bout to decorate my salon with all these damn roses. So, pick up some vases and come on outside. I got my homeboy's van for an hour."

Dakota shook her head as she put her stuff down, and picked up three vases, Kima never ceased to amaze her.

CHAPTER 22

"Thanks for all your help." Gina said to Tim.

He had just finished installing surveillance cameras in her apartment. He had already walked her through how to start and stop the recording on a discreet remote control.

"I don't know who's about to fly into this trap, but I pity him…or her." He said, looking her up and down.

He didn't trust Gina. Ever since, she caught him in the act with another male student in college, she'd held it over his head. Now, that he was able to do her this favor, he felt a flood of relief. Now he didn't have to worry about her saying anything to his wife-to-be about his college escapades. He was happy to do the favor, but Tim wasn't slow, he'd also linked her surveillance to his lap top, and would now be in control of any future blackmailing.

"Now, you know I'm not like that, Tim. I wouldn't hold anything over anyone's head…unnecessarily."

"No, of course not, Gina. Enjoy."

She couldn't wait for him to leave. All of her plans were coming together, just the way she envisioned them. All of the cameras were installed, and another friend was on his way over with the most important ingredient in her plan. Just as she was thinking about him, Dexter rang her doorbell.

"Hey buddy!" she greeted him warmly.

"Hey Gina. How's it going?"

"Going great, come on in."

He came in and looked quickly around. He was tense and jumpy. Gina noticed and offered him a drink.

"No thank you." He said sharply.

But Gina just shrugged it off. She wasn't going to let anything ruin her mood, or get in her way, so she pretended not to notice his rudeness.

"Well, let's get down to business. What do you have for me and how does it work?"

"It's a, uh, drug that allows a person to be aware of what's going on, but have no control over their motor functions." He explained.

"So, in other words, they know what's happening but can't do anything about it. Is that right?"

"Well, sort of. They would be able to feel sensations, but otherwise they are essentially paralyzed for approximately an hour and a half, depending on dosage. And for some reason, their eyes can move."

"Oh, like blink and stuff?"

"Not only blink, but can move and watch what's going on around them."

"Ok. I see. So, say a man became aroused on this drug, would his gears still shift?" she asked.

"Well he could have an erection, if that's what you're asking me. If he were properly aroused, I mean, because he would be aware of what's going on, and he could feel different sensations." He said looking at her from the corner of his eye.

"Yes, that's exactly what I need to know. How much is too much?"

"For an average sized man, good health, young…I'd say 3 drops into an 8oz drink, would hold him still for 90 minutes. But not much more than that, it may have adverse long lasting effects if overdosed." He warned her.

"Like what?"

"Stroke like symptoms, such as, one side of the face permanently frozen, and loss of use in some of his limbs. Just don't overdose! Is that clear?" his voice was high pitched and shrill.

"Yes, of course, 3 drops only. We wouldn't want to permanently damage him…" she replied calmly.

Gina was already lost in thought. Dexter could tell that his words were falling onto deaf ears. Secretly he hated Gina, but didn't want to cross her. He'd seen some of her dirty work, when she interned at the lab with him, and he wanted no parts of it. He was ready to get away from her as quickly as possible.

"So, here is the drug. There's about 9 drops all together. Please be careful, Gina."

"I will, Dexter. I always am." She smiled a wicked smile at him. "What do I owe you?"

"Nothing." He said a little too loudly again.

"Well, then you'd better be on your way, Dex. Thanks for stopping by."

She ushered him to the door, and closed it in his face, as he turned to say something. Her printer had just stopped printing. She walked over, picked up the picture it had printed out, and roared with laughter.

"*This is just too easy.*" She thought to herself.

She slipped the picture into an envelope. Wrote a cute note, and slid it inside before sealing it up tight. She googled the address she needed and printed the postage. Then she drove to the nearest post office and dropped it off for an early delivery.

"Now, let's see how fast you can get over to my place." She said to a picture on her phone.

"Listen to me, Yakima, you're not hearing what I'm telling you." Dakota whined.

They were at Yakima's house after moving all the flowers into her salon. Dakota was on her fourth glass of wine. Yakima was cooking something from a recipe book, and only half listening to Dakota.

"Ok, what?" she put the food on low and turned to face Dakota, with her hand on her hip.

"She's trying to steal my man."

"Who is, Dakota?"

"Gina! I told you, that bitch never liked me."

"Girl, Gina ain't no competition for you." Kima said dismissively.

"I know that, but a bitch is *trying!*" she emphasized and took another swig of wine.

"Like, how?"

"Well, she…" Dakota thought for a moment. "Shit, I don't know, but she's up to something I can feel it. And you know my feeling always be on point. Like for real, for real."

That got Yakima's attention, Dakota's intuition was very strong.

"Yeah, a woman can always tell. So, what you wanna do?" Yakima asked.

"I want her to know, that I know, what she's trying to do, and it ain't gonna work."

Yakima turned back to her recipe. She knew Dakota was tipsy, and a little stressed from Alex showing up out the blue like that, but she had a point. Her feelings were usually right. Besides, Yakima's horoscope this morning said she would have to help a close friend today. She thought it was the situation with the roses, but it was deeper than that. She knew Dakota would help her if the shoe was on the other foot. She thought about it for a minute.

"Aight, here's what we gone do…" and she laid the plan out.

Gina was going to know that she chose the wrong one to fuck with.

Brandon's phone rang; just who he wanted to hear from.

"Hey Ma! How you doing?"

"Hey baby, I'm good. How are you?"

"I'm good. Hey, I've got a question for you?"

"Shoot."

"How long has Gina been coming over to your house?"

"I guess, ever since that Sunday we all had dinner together. Why?"

"I don't know, it just seems like every time I talk to you now, she's over there."

"Yeah, poor thing. All her friends from this area have pretty much moved on, and well, with you getting married and all, she really doesn't have too much to do in her free time."

"Yeah, I guess you're right. Do you know where she lives or works?

"Yes, she works for the District Attorney's office and she lives over there in those expensive condos, they just built."

"The ones they created the new exit for?"

"Yes, those. You should go see her from time to time. Take Dakota, maybe they could get closer. I know they weren't that close in school, but y'all all grown now. Besides she's been asking me the same questions about you."

"Questions like what Ma?"

"Where is your shop, where is your house, Dakota's spa…stuff like that."

"Did you tell her?"

"Only where your businesses were; I figured if you wanted her at your house, you'd invite her yourself."

"Thanks Ma. I love you."

"Whoa, hold up Mr., how's the plans going for the wedding? Y'all got a date yet?"

"It's good Ma, but you know I'm gonna let you and Dakota work all that out. I'm just paying for it." He laughed.

"I can't wait! I've been picking up bridal magazines, decorating books, all kinds of stuff."

"I'm excited too, Ma. I'm glad you're happy."

"I am baby, tell Dakota to call me."

"Ok, I will. I gotta go. Love you!"

"I love you too, bye."

Brandon knew exactly where his mother was talking about. He thought he'd pay Ms. Gina Hefel a visit.

CHAPTER 23

Gina's doorbell rang. She knew who it was before it even rang. She checked herself in the full length mirror and headed to the door. She didn't want to keep her guest waiting. She pulled her blouse open, just a little more and opened the door.

"Well, hello handsome." She greeted her guest.

"Hey. Gina, right?" he asked.

"Yes indeed. Get on in here." She smiled and opened the door wide.

Alexander walked through the doorway, unsure why he was even there. He looked around cautiously and then looked at Gina, waiting for an explanation.

"So, I received your picture and your note saying it was urgent. What's this all about?"

"Well, I knew the picture of you and Dakota together, would get your attention. And since I wanted to see you, I figured I'd use the picture to entice you to come over."

"Ok. I'm here, what can I do for you?" he asked eyeing Gina distrustfully.

"Oh, what's the hurry?" she asked, as if they were old friends. "Sit, relax, have a drink." She said, patting the seat beside her, on the couch.

"No, I'm good. What's up?" he stood his ground.

"Well, I did have a proposal for you concerning your precious Dakota, but if you don't care about what's been happening to her, maybe I had you pegged all wrong." She watched his reaction closely. "Maybe you should just go."

Gina got off the couch, trying her best to look disappointed, and walked past Alexander, without eye contact. She opened the door, and waited for him to make the next move. His back was to her, so she couldn't read his face. She sighed loudly, hoping to cause him to react.

Alex thought to himself, *"Why would this woman, who Dakota clearly doesn't like, care to help Dakota. Why did she send the picture of me and Dakota together? How did she even find me?"*

He turned, walked towards the door, and closed it.

"What do you have to drink?" He asked and took a seat on the couch.

Gina was doing her happy dance, on the inside, but didn't dare show Alexander how happy she was that he was staying.

"You look like you can handle whiskey. Yes, no?" she swung the bottle of whiskey by flicking her wrist back and forth, to entice him.

"Sure. Make it a double, and let's get down to business." He said plainly.

"Ooo, let's get down to business, huh? You have no idea, dark chocolate." She thought as she poured two drinks into the glasses that were already sitting out on the countertop. One contained the drug she'd gotten from Dex. Careful, to leave hers on the counter, she walked over, handed him his drink, and returned to get hers. Sitting on the opposite side of the couch, she folded her leg underneath her.

"So, let's get down to business, as you so aptly put it."

Alexander nodded his agreement and placed his drink on the coffee table, eager to find out why Gina wanted to see him.

She noticed that he didn't even sip his drink, so she took a good swig of hers, hoping to prompt him to drink his, as well.

"Well, I noticed how closed you and Dakota were the day I met you. And I wasn't sure if you were aware of her current situation."

"What situation is that?"

"Her recent engagement."

"Yes. I am aware."

This shocked Gina. She wasn't expecting him to know, since it was so recent.

"Well, she is a sneaky little bitch…I shoulda known she was still in touch with his ass." She tried to keep calm. She had a plan to carry out. She thought about Brandon, and got back on point.

"Good. I figured y'all kept in touch."

"And how does that concern you?" He asked dryly.

She felt like she was losing control of the conversation already. Time to regroup.

"Wait a minute," she said sliding closer to Alexander. "Why not have a drink and hear me out?"

Alexander, leaned back and crossed his arms.

"I promise I don't bite."

"I'm not worried about that," he said loosening up a bit. "I just don't know why I'm here."

"Ok, real talk. I want Brandon, Dakota's fiancé. And, I know you want Dakota, so I figured we could help each other out."

"It seems to me, that they've made their choices. Why should we interfere?"

"Well, it does seem that way, but Brandon and I are still fucking, so he's just being greedy. He's just trying to lock her down and still be free to do what he wants."

Alexander thought about it for a moment. He did want Dakota, and he didn't want to see her get hurt, but all of his senses told him to get up and leave this place. But he ignored his feelings, because he wanted to get as much info from Gina as possible.

"You have my attention…"

"Good. Brandon and I have been together since before we ever met Ms. Dakota. We were always meant to be together, but as you can see, something went wrong."

She paused and took a dramatic swig from her drink. She looked him up and down, as he did the same to her. She could tell he didn't trust her; he really had no reason. But, she needed him to drink from his cup, she had to turn up the heat a little.

"Not much of a drinker are you?" she asked him.

"I only drink when I want to relax" he replied.

Was that a half a smile on his face? Or was Gina imagining what she wanted to see? And was he throwing her a hint? Well, she had caught it.

"Would you like to relax with me?" she leaned back so that he could clearly see what she was offering.

He looked her up and down, surveying what she was offering. She wasn't his type, but she was sexy as hell.

"Sure. Why not, we're here."

Gina jumped up.

"I'll slip into something, a little more comfortable, and we'll finish these drinks. Then we'll talk plans…later." She smiled at him and went upstairs to her room.

Alone in her room, she slipped into a matching bra and panty set. Lace was her signature material, and this racy, red set looked perfect against her beautiful brown skin. She figured she didn't have to do much to get Alexander to relax, and let down his guard with her; that's really all she needed. She wanted a little time, making him anticipate her more. She really loved making men wait; they were easier to manipulate when their 'other' heads took over. She checked herself out in her full length mirror and decided she had this in the bag. Pleased, she turned and headed back down to her prey.

She wondered if he'd had any of his drink; she hoped so. Walking up behind him, she tried to tell by his body language. He looked normal, but then again, she wasn't really sure what to look for as far as the effect the drink should have on him. However, his glass was down to the ice, so she offered him a refresher.

"Can I get you some more?" she asked taking his glass, and watching his reaction closely.

Alexander, just looked at her for a moment; moving only his eyes.

"*It's working!*" Gina thought excitedly.

"Sure, if you're refreshing yours as well." He said at last.

"Of course." Gina replied, and downed her drink in one swallow.

She walked back towards the kitchen area, which was open to the living area, disappointed that he hadn't commented on how good she looked in her lingerie. But then again, he wouldn't be commenting on anything soon, she thought to herself. Pleased with her deception, she quickly poured two more drinks and returned to the couch.

"What do you do Gina?" Alexander asked, taking his drink from her hand.

The question caught her off-guard but she saw no harm in answering it.

"I work for the Assistant DA. Why?"

"So, what is your agenda?" he asked ignoring her question.

"What do you mean?" she asked innocently.

"Why on earth would you think I would help you hurt Dakota?" he said bluntly.

"I don't want to hurt her, I want to help her see how Brandon really is. He wants his eat and cake too." Alexander looked at her oddly. The drugs were kicking in.

"*Wait that didn't come out right.*" She thought to herself.

"I meant, wants his cake and eat it too!" she laughed shaking her head, trying to clear it.

"What makes you think he wants you?"

"I told you, we are…" she thought for a moment but the words wouldn't come, "doing it." She finished.

She wondered what was going on here. Her head felt light and her limbs felt heavy. Her words were eluding her, and with such a diverse vocabulary, she couldn't understand why. And now, it seemed that Alexander was staring at her extra hard.

The drink in her hand felt like it weighed 100lbs. she attempted to put it down on the table next to her, but instead it tumbled from her hand. Now her legs were wet and cold, but she couldn't move to wipe it up. Panic struck her, all of a sudden, as she remembered the drug she put into Alexander's drink, but he seemed fine.

"What's wrong?" Alex asked moving closer to Gina on the couch.

All she could do was watch and wait; she couldn't respond.

"Cat got your tongue? Or is it because you drank my drink, instead of your own? What was in there anyway? What did you plan to do to me afterwards?"

Alex reached out to lift Gina's hand into the air, and let it go. It promptly fell back into her lap. He let out a little laugh. He reached into his pocket and pulled out his cell phone, and clicked a few pictures of her from different angles.

All Gina could do was watch, but she wanted to scream out at him. How dare he switch their drinks? How dare he take control of her like this? She was outraged, but not even the slightest contempt showed on her blank face. She wondered what he was going to do with the pictures he'd just taken.

"Listen, I don't know what kinda games you are up to, or who you're used to playing them with, but I'm not the one." Alex told her. "Whatever you were cooking up here has obviously back fired on your ass. So, let me give you some free advice, miss me with the bullshit. As far as Dakota is concerned, stay out of it. I think I'll contact Brandon myself." He looked down at his phone, "With these pictures, I'm sure he'll at least hear me out."

Alexander, got up to leave, and picked up both glasses, to take with him. The glasses were the only things he'd touched in her apartment, which may have his fingerprints.

"I don't know how long you'll be sitting there, looking like the fucking Tin Man, but I hope it's long enough to rethink your plan. Forget my name, and don't ever contact me again. Is that clear?"

He waited for a moment, then laughed again, realizing she was stuck-on-stupid.

"Blink once for yes, twice for no." He said as if talking to an invalid.

Gina was furious. She wanted to slap the shit out of him, but she could only move her eyes. And since she was ready for him to leave, she blinked once, for yes.

"Good. Enjoy your evening Dum-Dum." He said with contempt. He grabbed the door knob through his jacket and left, leaving her front door wide open.

Gina watched in horror as he left her door open. Not only open, but wide open! He was really asking for it. She felt a slight chill as a breeze entered her condo. She could only pray that none of her neighbors walked by her door while she was spread out on the couch in just her skivvies.

After spending a humiliating two hours frozen in one position, Gina struggled to get off of the couch. It took way more effort than she anticipated to even close her door. But once she closed and locked the door, she was so tired she passed out on the couch for the remainder of the night.

Now, it was morning and reality was sinking in about her dosage. She had put three big drops into the drink because of Alexander's size, but she was a lot smaller than him. She was staring at her face in the mirror, praying there was no permanent damage. She smiled and dropped the smile. She lifted her eyebrows individually and flared her nostrils all in an effort to make sure that everything was working the way it was supposed to work.

She thought back over her ordeal. One thing for sure was that she had time to rethink her plan. She was livid with Alexander, but she realized that she should leave him out of the picture. Besides she really just needed a test dummy for the drug, to see how it actually worked. Well, she got her answer. Now she knew exactly how it worked.

She had no plans of giving up on Brandon though. He was still going to be hers, come hell or high water. As if she'd thought him up, she received a text from Brandon. He wanted to see her tonight. Gina, couldn't believe her luck. She texted back.

Where & when

Same spot, room 112 @7 sharp...key @ desk

K... can't wait

She knew Brandon couldn't stay away from her. She wouldn't miss this date for the world.

CHAPTER 24

Brandon had been trying to figure out a good time to get away and see Gina, he wanted to find out where her head was, with regard to his relationship with Dakota. Then this morning Dakota told him that she and Yakima would be interviewing wedding planners and then going to happy hour tonight. So, he was free and clear to get up close and personal with Gina. She was going to tell him why she was stalking him through his mom.

He figured now was as good a time as any to head out; it was 6:30pm. He jumped on the interstate and let his Audi loose. He loved how he flowed through traffic in his luxury sports car. The cars speakers were bumping to Kendrick Lamar *We Gone Be Alright*. Brandon's mind was filled with thoughts of Dakota. He would do whatever to protect her and make sure their life together was secure. He pressed the gas a little more; anxious to get this over with.

Gina was on her way to see Brandon. Her body ached to feel him inside of her again. She knew he couldn't resist her; why he tried was beyond her. Dakota didn't have shit on her, and they both knew it. She smiled to herself, just thinking about how crushed Dakota was going to be when she found out how Brandon had played her. Tonight she wanted Brandon to tell her that he was leaving Dakota for her. She had some tricks up her sleeve, things that had made married men say whatever she told them to say, even though they knew they were being recorded. She knew tonight was the night and she couldn't wait to get upstairs to her man.

She pulled into a discreet parking space on the side of the hotel. She had to remind herself to slow down as she walked into the lobby. Confidently, she sashayed up to the desk and gave her name.

"Yes, Ms. Hefel, we have a key for you. Do you have your ID?"

"I do. Here you go."

"Thank you. Here is your key. Its room 112."

"Has the other guest arrived yet?"

"Yes ma'am."

"Thanks."

Gina felt like she was floating on a cloud as she headed to her rendezvous. She slid her key into the slot and turned the knob to let herself into the room. Suddenly, the door was snatched out of her hand. A large, strong hand grabbed her arm and dragged her into the room. Just as she thought to scream for help, another hand clamped down on her mouth and nose like a vice grip. She could feel something small and round in her mouth. Whoever was holding her, must have popped it into her mouth right as they clamped down on her.

The arms holding her were big as hell, and strong as shit. She wasn't getting loose.

"Swallow that ecstasy, if you wanna breathe bitch." The voice behind her advised.

Panic tried to take over, but Gina wanted to make it out of here alive. She'd never taken ecstasy, but she figured it wouldn't kill her to swallow it, so she did. But the hand still didn't move to allow her to breathe. Gina lost it. She began clawing and kicking at her captor, until his other hand went to her throat. Her heart was pounding and she felt herself blacking out, so she stopped. And, finally the hand slid down off of her nose, but still covered her mouth.

She breathed in as hard as she could through her nostrils and attempted a muffled scream.

"Shut up bitch, I won't hurt you if you do what I say." The voice advised again.

Gina knew this wasn't Brandon, but couldn't figure out why Brandon had this person in their room. Where was Brandon? She wondered. She nodded her agreement to her captor and his grip loosened a little. He led her over to the bed, and forced her down onto the mattress. She looked at him for the first time. He was huge. His face was covered in a scary clown mask.

"Who are you? What do you want with me?" Gina dared to ask him.

"I don't want shit from you, and neither does Brandon."

She refused to believe that Brandon had anything to do with this.

"Says who? Is Brandon here?"

"Hell naw, he ain't here. I told you, he don't want your raggedy ass, you bout to see what I mean soon as that pill kick in. and if it take more than 10 minutes, you getting another one."

Gina was starting to feel the effects of the pill already and did not want another one. She glanced around the room and noticed a camera set up on a tripod at the end of the bed. She briefly wondered what that was for, and what this man had planned for her. She could feel the pill kicking in and decided to scream for help. This time no hand clamped over her mouth, instead a gag ball was stuffed into her mouth and tied tightly around her head.

Her captor grabbed one of her nipples in his enormous paw and squeezed and twisted it. To her horror, she moaned in pleasure. This brought a gruff laugh from behind the clown mask. Quickly, he began to undress her. He snatched at her clothes carelessly, but he didn't tear anything. When he had her naked he turned on the camera.

He rubbed her all over. His big rough hands scraped her skin, but it felt so good she could only whimper in delight. He rolled her over and spread her legs open. Her juices started flowing. He pulled her ass wide apart, to the point she thought she would split in half. But even that felt good to Gina. He let her ass go and abruptly slapped her across both cheeks. This brought more groans from behind her gag ball.

"Turn over!" he yelled at her all of a sudden.

Gina did as told. He handed her a long vibrating dildo. It was longer and wider than anything she had ever played with before. She looked at it achingly. Then he handed her a shorter toy. She wondered what he want from her, but she didn't have to wonder long.

"Put the short one in your ass and the long one in your cunt. Put all of it in, and I mean every fucking inch. Got it?" he barked at her.

She nodded.

"Open your damn legs bitch."

He squirted her with baby oil and told her to get busy. He grabbed her feet and pushed them up towards her, so that her knees feel out to her sides. This way he could get a better view of what she was doing. Just that little touch got her even wetter.

Gina took the butt plug and pressed it against her ass hole. The end was bulging and seemed not to fit at first. The pressure felt good though, so she kept pressing it until it ultimately slipped into the rim of her ass. The pain was like pleasure she'd never felt before. She pushed it in to the hilt.

"Good job whore" her captor encouraged her. He was stroking his dick watching her behind the camera. "Now get in that pussy."

It took both hands to get the head of the dildo into her hole. She was already stretched from the fat butt plug pulling her skin taut. But, somehow she got the tip inside.

"Turn it on and push that shit up in there." He instructed her.

Gina couldn't figure out where the switch was to turn it on. So, her captor got up and switched it on and began massaging her thighs. She began grinding on the dildo and pushing it deeper inside of herself. She had it about half way in when she stopped pushing.

"I said every inch! Put it all in…or else." He said walking to the head of the bed.

Gina pushed and pulled at the dildo. It felt delicious but she couldn't fit anymore inside. Her captor seized her hair, wrapped it around his fist, and pulled her head to the edge of the bed where he stood with his dick out. This turned her on even more and she pushed harder, grinding as hard as she could on the hard plastic.

He laid his dick across her face, right under her nose. With the gag ball in place and his dick covering her nostrils, her air supply was temporarily cut off.

"Push slut"

She pushed with both hands, feeling like she would rip. He lifted his dick and rubbed it around the rest of her face. He watched in disbelief as she got down to the last inch of the dildo. He slid his dick back under her nose and flicked her nipples as hard as he could. She moaned and he knew that was the last of her air, but he wasn't moving until the whole dildo was in her. He watched as a vein popped up in the middle of her forehead. Her eyes bulged as she lifted her ass off of the bed in an effort to get the last inch inside.

Gina slipped her head to the side and snatched air into her lungs and pushed with all her might. He grabbed her face with both hands and held it in place. She began shaking all over, but amazingly the full length of the dildo was in; suddenly the butt plug shot out of her ass and she passed out.

Brandon knocked on the door to Gina's condo even though he didn't see her car in the parking lot. He waited for a few minutes and decided to wait in his car for her to return. But, after 45 minutes, he gave up and went home.

Alexander scrolled through the pictures he'd taken of Gina. He wondered how much of her story was true. *Was she really involved with Dakota's fiancé? Was this dude really fucking around on Dakota? And if so, how could he do her like that?* Alex knew, if she were his, he would never hurt Dakota that way. But then again, he knew he couldn't trust a chick that was planning on drugging him. He wondered how that night ended for her.

Gina was definitely resourceful; she'd found out enough information about him to send the picture to his house. If she was that determined to break up Dakota's relationship, what else was she capable of doing? He imagined Gina slipping that drug to Dakota and knew he had to make a move. But, Dakota had made it clear, at her spa, that things were different now that she was engaged.

He tried to let go, but he couldn't shake the feeling that he was supposed to help Dakota somehow. Did he still have feelings for her? Did he want her all to himself? Yes, but even if he couldn't have her, he wouldn't stand by and let her get hurt. He cared about her too much for that.

CHAPTER 25

An alarm was going off, somewhere far away. What is that noise, Gina wondered. It seemed to be getting closer and louder. She rolled her head side to side, in a vain attempt to silence the noise.

"*That's not an alarm*" she realized, "*that's a phone ringing.*"

Her eyes felt so heavy, she couldn't open them. But at least the ringing stopped, and she drifted back to sleep. When the ringing started back she forced her eyes open and tried to remember where she was. The phone wasn't hers, but it was laying on the pillow next to her head. *Ring! Ring!* She grabbed it, opened the little flip phone and placed it to her ear.

"The next time you want some of Brandon's dick, you gonna get the same treatment hoe. So forget about him or next time it will be worse, and I'm not playing with you bitch." A female voice told her.

The line went dead before she could reply.

Was that Dakota on the phone? It didn't sound like Miss Priss to Gina. But who else could it be? Was Brandon in on this? Why would he let them do this to her? Gina lifted her head from the pillow and the whole room swung to the side. She lay there feeling her nakedness trying to gather her thoughts. Disjointed memories from the night before flashed through her head.

She felt so defeated she began to cry. Her tears were partly from the humiliation she felt at having done this to herself, she vividly remembered stuffing the dildo into herself with all her might, but also because she remembered the camera at the end of the bed. What were they planning to do with the video? Gina had blackmailed so many people and now it seemed that it was her turn to get the shitty end of the stick. She hated being outwitted. Her body hurt, her head hurt, and most of all her feelings hurt. She cried until housekeeping knocked on the door.

"Pull it together Gina." She reminded herself.

She pulled her body out of the bed and found her purse. Surprisingly, nothing was missing. She found a twenty and cracked the door open.

"Give me about an hour." She said sliding the twenty to the young lady in the hall.

"Forty minutes." She replied dryly snatching the twenty.

Gina closed the door and got in the shower.

"What did she say?" Dakota asked

"She ain't say shit, I didn't give her time." Yakima told her.

"You think it worked?"

"She got the message loud and clear. Every time she even think about Brandon she gone get mad. She gone hate his ass, cause she ain't gonna know if he was in on it or what."

"You sure Big Man didn't fuck her?"

"Naw, if he did, he fucked her off camera. We'll get the disc later today, if you wanna look at it."

"Hell no I don't wanna see that shit."

"I do, I know she gotta feel stupid as hell that she did that shit to her damn self."

They both laughed at that.

"What about the phone?" Dakota probed.

"It was a prepaid and we just called her from the lobby phone. There's no way to trace any of this shit back to you, so just chill. I told you this plan would get her out of your hair, and she gone."

"You're right. Let's get outta here before she leaves and sees us though."

"True, let's be out." Yakima agreed.

Brandon couldn't get Gina out of his mind. He decided to swing by her condo one more time before he had to go taste cakes with Dakota. As he left the Babershop, he jumped on the interstate and arrived in less than 10 minutes at Gina's condo. He saw her car in the parking lot. He wondered how she'd react to him showing up at her place like this, but it had to be done.

He reached for his car door handle and his phone rang. The number wasn't blocked but it wasn't in his contacts. He answered.

"Yeah?"

"Hey man, you don't know me, but we both know Gina."

"So? Who is this?"

"Again, you don't know me, and actually, you don't have to listen, but I have some info on Gina that you need to know. That is, if you're interested."

Brandon wondered what kind of bullshit this was, yet he wanted to know why this man felt the need to give him information about Gina. He decided to listen.

"I'm listening."

"Watch out for this chic, she says that you and her are hooking up, and she wants to let Dakota know."

"Whoa, wait a minute. What you know about Dakota?"

"I don't, that's just the name Gina said when she told me her plan."

"So, you don't know me, you don't know Dakota, but you felt the need to tell me that Gina wants to break me and my girl up. Is that right?"

"Pretty much."

"Why, man?"

"Just because, I'm tired of this bitch winning and ruining everything she touch. I know a couple of guys that have had run-ins with her in the past, and she always plays dirty. And she always gets her way. This chic's been running amuck and it's time to stop this shit."

"Yeah well, I'll take it into consideration. Me and her go way back, I don't think it will go down like that between us."

"Maybe. But if she tries to give you anything to drink, don't drink it. She tried to drug me with something in my drink, but I switched it up on her. Whatever it was made her just sit there like a statue or something. Believe me, don't trust this bitch any further than you can throw her, for real."

"'Preciate it my dude. Good lookin' out."

Brandon hung up. He sat in the car a while longer, wondering what to do. What happened to his Gina throughout the years? Was she really that ruthless? He doubted she would be like that with him. He decided to go talk to her anyway, but he noticed the time. He only had twenty minutes before he had to meet Dakota downtown and taste cakes in order to choose a cake for their upcoming wedding.

"This will have to wait till I have time to get some real answers. I can't be late for our appointment." He thought to himself, cranking up the car and pulling out of the parking lot. In his heart, he wanted to let Gina know that they were still cool, and could still be friends, just not cut buddies. His heart belonged to one woman, and that was Dakota. He didn't really believe what some random dude told him about Gina, she wouldn't treat Brandon that way. As he merged into traffic on the interstate, he promised himself that he would talk with Gina face to face before the week was out, and squash all this bullshit.

Swaddled in jogging pants and an oversized sweatshirt, Gina lay in bed sipping hot chocolate, watching her all-time favorite movie, *Love Jones*. She was still upset by the embarrassing video she inadvertently made last night, and wondered what role it would play in the future. She had cried so much, she just couldn't anymore. Now she was numb, and wanted to stay that way until she had to return to work on Monday morning. She didn't want to go anywhere, or see anyone, except maybe Brandon, all she wanted was to close the world out and try to feel better about herself and her situation.

Normally, she loved the bright sunshine, but today she wanted darkness and seclusion. She pulled herself from her comforter and got up to close the blinds. Was that Brandon's car in front of her house? What was he doing here? He must be here to see her, she thought. But why?

"Because he's sorry for what happened to me. He's come to apologize and to take care of me." She spoke to herself as if speaking to someone else.

Gina realized that she was holding her breath. She took a deep breath and closed the blinds, so that he couldn't see her watching him from the window. Happiness flooded through her, at the thought of Brandon coming to her aid. It was just like in the movie *Love Jones* when Darius pursued Nina. She imagined

Brandon quoting Darius, "You said it was bad timing, so I figured if I asked again, maybe you'd say yes, and if not that time, then the next time, till the next time became the right time."

He did love her after all. She slid the blinds apart, just enough to peek out, and to her surprise, Brandon was gone. Just as quickly as happiness found her, it left her. As a matter of fact, she was pissed. She thought she saw, Brandon on the phone, it was probably Dakota, talking him out of checking on her. Misery washed over her, sending her back into depression. Sliding back under the covers, she vowed to get her revenge on both of them for hurting her this way.

Alexander hung up the phone with Brandon. He knew he had done the right thing, but secretly wished that Brandon would get caught up. Maybe then, Dakota would come running back to him.

CHAPTER 26

"I think we have everything covered. We've chosen the date, the venue, the caterer, the photographer, the florist, the cake, the gown, the tux and the wedding party. The invitations have been ordered, and the save-the-date cards have been sent. Can you think of anything else?" Dakota asked Brandon.

"Nope, I think you've got it all covered. You are brilliant and talented. I never doubted you would pull it off so quickly."

"Thanks, babe. I feel like we've waited long enough, I'm ready to start the next chapter in our lives."

"Just think, in 6 short weeks, you will be Mrs. Brandon West!"

"I can't wait." Dakota leaned in for a kiss.

Everything was working in her favor, Dakota thought to herself. No more worries, or wondering when she would be Mrs. West, now she had a date, December 5. She would have a Winter Wonderland Wedding. Her gown was all white satin trimmed in rhinestones and white fur. She would look absolutely fabulous and so would Brandon in his dashing white tuxedo. Then the happy couple would party with family and close friends before heading out on the long awaited European honeymoon.

Their honeymoon would take them through London, Paris and Rome. Dakota's deepest fantasy was finally becoming a reality. Everything was perfect, just the way she'd always imagined it. And soon after, there would be the pitter-patter of little feet running through their luxurious 3200 square foot home; making the house feel more like a home. All of the trials and tribulations that she and Brandon faced in the past, now seemed worth it. They were stronger than ever as a couple. No one could come between them.

Gina stared at the save the date card, which could have only been sent by Mama J, as if it were a handful of maggots. She felt disgusted at the thought of Brandon marrying Dakota. Although she no longer wanted Brandon for herself, she'd be damned if he would marry Dakota's funky ass. But she was glad for the wakeup call; it was time to take action against this fiasco.

She grabbed her cell phone and texted.

Missing u like crazy. Come c me 2nite. I know u know the address.

Then, picking up the save the date card by the edge, as if it were poisonous, she tossed it into the trash, where it belonged. Setting the alarm, she left for work, knowing she would see Brandon later. She smiled at the thought of how she planned to molest him; she was going to enjoy every moment of it.

It was a slow day at work. Gina was bored and ready to go when Dakota crossed her mind. It dawned on her that it was time for Dakota to get in on the fun. Gina decided to look her up on Facebook and send her a private message. It was easy enough to find her; she had damn near all of her personal info on her profile.

"Such a dumb-ass." Gina thought to herself.

Gina's Facebook account, on the other hand, was as vague as they come. She had a picture of a flower as her profile picture and her favorite quote was her cover photo. Her name was Secret Keeper. None of her personal or identifying information was on her page, and the only photos on her page were reposted from her friends pages. Coincidentally, none of her Facebook friends were real friends, who could be connected to her in anyway, they were all just people that requested her friendship on the social media; she didn't know any of them.

She didn't send Dakota a friend request, instead she clicked 'follow' so that she could see what Dakota allowed the public to see on her page. But by only following, she couldn't post on Dakota's timeline, so she sent her a personal message.

Hey hoe I know that was your ass that set me up last week. Just know that you don't put no fear in my heart, watch your back bitch.

Unfortunately, Dakota wasn't on the book right then, she could tell by the indicator next to her name that she was offline. This didn't faze Gina because she knew sooner or later she would see it. And this was only the beginning; she had so much more in store for the happy couple.

Gina's spirits were lifted by all of the devious plans she had. She didn't have to come up with anything new, most of her tricks were oldies but goodies. She'd used them over and over again, with exceptional results. The best part of it all was that she would still get her way and a front row seat to watch it all fall apart.

Brandon read the text and decided not to respond. He realized that he had put this meeting off for too long. It had to be done tonight. He hoped that Gina would tell him what he wanted to hear; that they could go back to being friends. If she didn't, she would just have to be cut off. It was as simple as that. Dakota was more important to Brandon, and he would do whatever it took to protect their relationship from fuckery and foolishness.

Deleting the text, he thought about what he would say to her. A couple of scenarios played out in his head, but they all seemed so planned out. He'd prefer to just keep it real with Gina, he figured she'd be more receptive to that. And hopefully they would end on a good note, but he knew he needed some time, so he wouldn't feel so rushed to get to the point.

"*I'll let Dakota know that I'll be a little late tonight.*" He thought.

He called her at her office.

"Hey babe! What's up?" She chirped happily.

"Not much, you were on my mind."

"Oh how sweet. You were on my mind too."

"Yeah? Good thoughts?"

"Always…"

He could hear the smile in her voice and he knew she meant it.

"Good, I like that. Listen, I need to work a little later, if that's not interfering with anything we had going on tonight."

"No, we don't have anything planned for tonight. But don't stay too late, I miss you already."

"Don't worry, I won't stay any longer than I have to."

"Cool, I'll see you later then."

"Aight. I love you."

"I love you too, bye."

"Bye."

He hated lying to her even though it was for a good reason in his mind. He finished up a sketch he was working on for a new client, and decided to head out to Gina's, he wanted to get this over with as soon as possible, and get home to Dakota.

Gina washed in her favorite body wash, then applied the matching body butter. Her skin felt like silk as she rubbed the body butter all over her wet skin. She imagined her hands were Brandon's touching all of her intimate places. Massaging and gently caressing her soft skin. Lingering longer on her firm breasts and between her supple thighs. Gina had to catch herself from masturbating; she had to finish getting ready before Brandon arrived. She quickly slid on a short, sexy nighty and headed downstairs.

She hadn't heard back from him, but she knew that she would see him tonight, it was just a matter of time. She was so confident that he was coming, she already had a special glass ready. This time she had two different glasses. She would be sure there was no switching of drinks, if she had to leave the room for any reason.

Her heart fluttered at the sound of the doorbell; she knew it was him.

"Who?" she called out.

"It's me Gina." Brandon called back.

"You alone?"

"Of course…open up."

Gina opened the door just enough for Brandon to enter. He slid in and looked to her to figure out why she was acting so funny. Instead, he was distracted by the revealing lingerie she was wearing.

"Were you expecting company?" he asked

"Yes. You." She smiled and threw her arms around his neck.

This caught Brandon by surprise. In his awkwardness, he allowed her to hold him for a minute or two. Her heart was beating so fast, he wondered what was wrong. Eventually he wrapped his arms around her and hugged her back. As soon as he did, she pulled away from him.

"Well, don't just stand there like a stranger, come on in and make yourself at home."

"Thanks. Where we at, over here?" Brandon pointed at the living area.

"Yeah, have a seat. I'll make us some drinks."

"Cool, nice spot. I like this, how long you been here?"

"Thanks. I've been here about 7 months now; loving it. Oh and congrats on your engagement! How about a shot, to toast to your upcoming nuptials?"

"True, let's do it. What you got?"

"I've got some Hennessey. I've made a delicious drink with it called, *Between the Sheets*, but we'll shoot it straight first. Can you handle that?"

"Who you kiddin' with? You know I can drink you under the table." He chided her.

"Maybe you can, maybe you can't anymore, but we don't want you going home drunk, so I guess we won't find out tonight. Huh?" she teased.

She handed him his shot and sat his drink on the coffee table, returning to the kitchen to retrieve her drinks from the breakfast bar. Her walk was slow and deliberate. She threw in a little extra sauce for his viewing pleasure. Leaning seductively across the countertop her juicy bottom was revealed from underneath her gown, when she reached for her drink.

"Want anything to eat?" she offered, looking over her shoulder at Brandon.

"Uh, naw, I'm good." He said turning away quickly.

Gina sashayed back over to the couch and sat close to Brandon. She lifted her shot glass into the air and smiled her most charming smile.

"Here's to getting everything you and Dakota deserve!" she toasted.

"Here, here!"

She put her drink to her lips, but waited until Brandon had downed his drug laced shot first. She hoped he would drink most of his drink to balance out the fluid needed for the amount of drops she put into his shot. She didn't wish harm on Brandon, but if he wasn't going to be with her, well…

"*It's Dakota's cross to bear if he ends up fucked up permanently.*"

After downing her shot, she grabbed her drink and took a swig, hoping he would follow suit.

"Wow, I forgot how that burned." She joked.

Brandon agreed and took a good swig out of his drink as well. Gina eyed him carefully, looking for any signs that the drug was working. She thought it would work even faster on him than it had on her, since she put it in a shot. She assumed he had come over straight from work and didn't have anything on his stomach; she crossed her fingers. Time to make her move.

CHAPTER 27

Gina picked up a remote control, pressed a couple of buttons and *Moments in Love* by Art of Noise flowed from her Bose surround sound system. She slowly got off the couch and began to dance seductively for Brandon. He reached for her, but she eluded his grasp and continued her dance.

"Gina, we need to talk, real talk."

"Do we? About what?"

"Yes." He paused. "We do."

"Ok. What you wanna talk about?" she asked kneeling in front of him and undoing his belt buckle.

He grabbed her hands and she could feel that he had a slight tremor. This brought a smile to her face. She grabbed at his shirt with her teeth. Releasing her hands he attempted to stop her and grab her face, but he couldn't coordinate his hands enough to be effective.

"What the hell..." he half muttered. Brandon couldn't figure out what was wrong. His body felt like he'd had about 12 shots instead of just 1. He couldn't move or talk the way he wanted to, but his mind was pretty clear. Gina seemed fine; she was all over him. He couldn't stop her. This wasn't why he came over here, he needed to talk to her, but she had her own agenda, it seemed.

Suddenly, Brandon remembered the anonymous call he received about Gina. Didn't that guy tell him not to trust Gina? He said, "*But if she tries to give you anything to drink, anything, don't drink it. She tried to drug me with something in my drink, but I switched it up on her. Whatever it was made her just sit there like a statue or something.*" And Brandon also remembered thinking Gina wouldn't do him like that.

Gina could tell that the drug had kicked in. she dropped the pretense and began to remove Brandon's pants and underwear. It was a struggle; he was like dead weight. It didn't matter though, she was determined to have what she wanted. With his pants down around his ankles, she took her gown off and rubbed her breast across his naked legs. She massaged his manhood, kissing and suckling it until it began to grow in her hand.

Brandon received some of the best head he'd ever received in his young life. He rationalized in his head that if Gina was ok, after being drugged, he would be too. He also knew he would never trust her again. But for now, nature had taken over, and all he could do was watch and unwillingly receive.

"Why are you making me do this to you, Brandon? We could be so good together, but you just didn't recognize the good thing you had, when you had it. So, now you have to learn the hard way." She shook her head. "You gonna miss me though."

Keeping eye contact, she straddled his lap, and took him inside of herself. She was so wet that she slid down further than she intended. She gasped and grabbed the back of his head, pushing his face into her breasts. Her hips rocked back and forth rhythmically and her legs moved her up and down his shaft effortlessly.

"You like this, baby? Huh? Do you?"

She looked at him as if he were going to answer her. Of course he couldn't. This didn't bother her at all.

"Here," she grabbed his hands and put them on her ass, "feel that? It's soft and juicy, just like you like it, right baby? You feel so good inside of me. Remember the first time you fucked me like this?"

She laughed and grinded harder on his lap.

"You probably don't, but I do. I fed you some brownies laced with marijuana and rode your ass like my little pony!"

She let out a high pitch laughed that bothered Brandon, as if this whole situation wasn't disturbing enough. He was starting to wonder about her sanity; she seemed off her rocker. But there was nothing he could do about it now.

"*She might be crazy, but damn this pussy good as hell.*" He couldn't help thinking about how good she felt.

"I could have given you this all the time, but you didn't want it. Did you?"

She twisted his nipples as hard as she could, watching his lack of reaction.

"Why didn't you want me Brandon?"

She grabbed his face in both hands, kissed him deeply, and pulled back and slapped him hard across his face.

"Answer me! Whyyyy?"

This was turning her on more than she ever imagined it would. She was in complete and utter control, and loving every second of it all. He didn't know it, but he was going to give her everything she ever wanted from him.

"I'm cuming baby! Ooo you feel so good...cum with me. Cum inside me, Brandon."

Her orgasm hit her like a ton of bricks. She held on to Brandon as her body was racked with waves of spasms. She was far from finish though.

"Did you cum? No? Well, we just have to fix that, don't we?"

She got off him and turned around, positioned herself over his dick and inserted him back inside of her wetness. Once she had him all the way inside of her snatch, Gina leaned back and slowly rocked her pelvis. She took every inch he had to offer. She pulled his hands up to her tits and squeezed them with her hands and began sucking his fingers. Her juices were sopping Brandon's stomach and thighs, he felt his nut coming, but he didn't want to bust inside of her.

"This ass feels good rubbing on your wash board abs, don't it baby? This pussy wet enough for you? Don't try to hold back on me now..." she purred into his ear.

Impulsively, she leaned forward putting her hands on the floor and bounced her ass in his lap. Brandon couldn't take anymore, watching his dick disappear in her like that. He let go and came hard inside of Gina.

"Yesss baby! Give me all you've got! Give it to me, give it to me, give it...I'm cuming with youuuu!" she shouted and rode him like a wild stallion until her orgasm receded.

Without warning, Gina got up and walked into the kitchen. Brandon could hear her opening and closing drawers as if she were looking for something. Fear kicked in. What if she intended to harm him? What could he do? He heard her coming back towards him.

"Want some more to drink?" she teased him.

Relief flooded his mind as she plopped down on the couch and downed another drink. But she did have something in her hand, he just couldn't make out what it was.

Gina looked at him for a long while, not saying anything. Then she leaned across his lap and patted his pants pockets. To his disbelief, the feel of her breasts rubbing his thighs, had his dick getting hard again. When she sat back up, she had his cell phone in her hand.

"Hey let's play truth or dare! You down? I'll go first. I choose truth. Ask me anything."

She sat quietly for a moment as if waiting for his question.

"This bitch is really crazy..." Brandon thought and tried to move his fingers or toes or anything. He needed to get the hell out of here fast. But nothing moved.

"Yes." Gina replied as if he had asked her a question. "I do love you Brandon. I've never told you that outright, but I know you always knew. Didn't you? Ok, let's kick it up a notch. Time for a dare."

She picked up his phone and stood up. Brandon's heart dropped from the devious smile on her face.

"I dare you to send Dakota a picture of the fun we're having right now."

Without pretending to wait, she stood on the couch and threw one leg across his shoulder, placing her Brazilian bikini wax on his mouth, and positioned the camera to snap a picture.

"Oh, wait, let me slide down a bit, we don't wanna cover your face."

She tilted his head back against the pillows on the couch and put her clit on his chin.

"Smile!"

Brandon stared at her in disbelief. He really expected her to put the phone down, so when the blinding flash brought tears to his eyes, he felt like crying for real.

Gina burst into laughter, looking at the photo. She turned the phone so that he could look at himself. He didn't find it funny at all, in fact he wanted to punch her in her ass, but he couldn't even ball his hand into a fist.

"You look like a deer in head lights." She mused. "Now, how do you send this to someone? Oh, never mind, I can figure it out." She said nonchalantly.

She was sitting on his lap as casually as pie sitting on a window sill cooling. Brandon was past angry. He went from zero to a hundred real quick.

"Mmmunnn…"

Gina froze. She watched Brandon closely. She could see the hate in his eyes. Then suddenly, his nostrils flared ever so slightly.

"Oh, ok, you're tired of this game? I get it. Maybe, uh, it's time for you to leave."

She pressed a few more buttons on his phone, jumped up and ran upstairs.

Brandon tried to move his fingers again, and to his surprise his first finger, on his right hand curled. It took all of his concentration though, so he knew he wasn't about to get up and leave just yet. Gina on the other hand, had changed her tune.

"Where is she? What is she getting?" he began to worry again.

When Gina returned, she was fully dressed in a jogging suit and sneakers. She headed directly towards the couch, grabbed whatever it was that she'd brought out of the kitchen, and swung around towards him. They were both shocked when Brandon's arm moved up to block her from harming him. Gina quickly pinned his arm down under her leg and pulled the top off of the permanent marker she held in her hand.

"Sorry about this, but you brought it on yourself."

She roughly grabbed his dick, which was no longer hard, stretched it out and wrote her name along the shaft.

"I'm gonna kill this bitch!" he thought as he watched in astonishment.

Then she leaned back on the couch, placing her cheek next to Brandon's and took several selfies with her cell phone. Finally, she got up and pulled his legs out from under him and began pulling up his pants, but they got caught on the edge of the chair. Not deterred, she pulled him lower on the couch until his ass was hanging off and only his upper body remained on the chair.

She quickly pulled his pants up and fastened them, but she took his belt off.

"Just a little keep sake." She winked at him. "Now it's time for us to part ways. I wish we had more time together, but your drug is wearing off.I wish things could have been different between us, but you want a simple bitch, so I hope you enjoy your simple life."

Gina patted his pockets one more time and felt his keys in his right pocket. She slid his cell into his left pocket. And grabbed his ankles and pulled with all her might. Brandon was grateful that her floor was carpeted as his head bounced from the impact. He couldn't believe that she was pulling him towards her door. Did she really expect to be able to lift him into his car? He thought she might be crazy enough to try, and he wasn't looking forward to being dragged across the concrete parking lot.

Gina dropped his legs, opened the front door and peeped out. She waited for a moment to see if she saw any of her neighbors coming or leaving. It was all clear. She went back inside and quickly dragged Brandon across her threshold, and propped him up against the wall of her walkway. Closing the door behind her, she locked it and knelt down next to Brandon.

"The effects should wear off in a few minutes." She looked at her watch for confirmation. "You won't feel one hundred percent right away, but you're a big strong man, you should recover enough to drive yourself home." She patted his face.

"Www...why?" Brandon struggled to say.

"I know you don't understand, but I've loved you for so long Brandon, and you never appreciated it. You turned me against you. I know we'll never be what I want us to be, so if I can't have all of you, I'll take what I deserve. I think I've got that now, so take care."

She walked over to her car and started to say something else, changed her mind and drove off.

Approximately five minutes later someone pulled up and helped him to his car. He told them that he had narcolepsy and they offered to call an ambulance. But he assured them that he was fine. It was a struggle, but he made it home safely. He was never happier to pull into his own garage in his life. But what would he say to Dakota? He knew he smelled like sex and Gina, not to mention her name in permanent ink on his member. There was no explaining that shit. Plus the picture Gina sent from his phone should have had Dakota waiting for him in the driveway.

He said a short prayer and went inside.

CHAPTER 28

Brandon set the alarm after doing a quick walk through of the downstairs. He crept up the stairs like a thief in the night. Pausing to listen at their bedroom door, he was grateful to hear Dakota lightly snoring peacefully. He eased the door open and looked at his wife to be. She looked so innocent and tranquil. He snuck into the master bath and turned on the shower and began to undress. He was thanking his lucky stars, when the door opened and Dakota walked into the bathroom.

"Hey babe, I thought I heard you come in."

"You couldn't have heard me over all that snoring. You were calling the hog's just now." he teased her.

She laughed and swung at him.

"Well, actually I had to pee." She confessed and went into the water closet.

Brandon grabbed his rag, stripped and jumped into the hot water. He quickly lathered his face and rinsed it just as Dakota emerged from the toilet room. She turned to walk back into the bedroom.

"Damn, I can't even get a kiss after a long day?" he tried to sound hurt.

"Of course babe. You want me to get in with you?"

Brandon immediately thought of Gina's name written on him.

"No, I know you're tired, you were sleeping so peacefully. Just give me a kiss, I'll be in there shortly. I'm tired too." he admitted.

She leaned into the shower and kissed him and went back to bed.

Brandon scrubbed his body like he was just released from jail. Afterwards, he put on cologne, some drawers and pajama pants. Feeling partially safe, he eased into the bed and snuggled up behind Dakota. Soon, they were both snoring.

The next morning, Brandon woke up at his usual time, but he couldn't pull himself from the bed. Eventually he drifted back off into a fitful sleep. He dreamt that Gina had him again, and this time she wrote her name all over him. He struggled in his sleep to get free from her web. She had transformed into a giant poisonous spider and was wrapping him in a cocoon when he began moaning uncontrollably.

Dakota woke up and tried to wake Brandon up from his nightmare. He was kicking his legs furiously, and was all tangled up in the covers. He was sweating profusely, and when Dakota tried to wipe his forehead, he began screaming. This scared Dakota.

"Brandon wake up! Wake up!!" she yelled into his ear.

Suddenly he opened his eyes and sat straight up in the bed. It took a moment to realize that it was all a dream. It was so vivid, he didn't know what to believe.

"Are you alright? What were you dreaming about?" Dakota asked worriedly.

"I, I was being attacked by a giant spider."

"What did you eat last night?"

"Huh?"

"You must have eaten something that didn't agree with you last night. What did you eat?"

"I can't remember." He dodged her question and wiped his forehead. He was washed down in sweat. He stared at his hand in disbelief.

"It's probably those hot ass pajama pants you slept in." Dakota said. "Come on, let's take a shower together."

"You just wanna get me naked."

"It's quite possible…"

Dakota pulled at his pajamas, but Brandon had a grip on them.

"I know your nasty side, but I gotta work out. I can't believe I overslept."

"I can't either. But you deserve to sleep in every now and then, you know."

"I'll keep that in mind. But don't wait on me babe, I'm just gonna do a quick couple of circuits."

"Ok"

He waited for Dakota to get in the shower, and he picked up her phone. He searched through her texts and emails, but he couldn't find any pictures or anything sent from his phone at all.

Did she delete it? Or did it not download? Brandon, thought that he'd better check his own phone; maybe Gina didn't press send.

He grabbed his phone and headed down stairs. Halfway down, he had to sit down. She did press send, she sent it to herself with the caption "damn you taste good". There were so many ways she could use this against him. Brandon felt like someone had sucker punched him. He had to tell Dakota before Gina did, but how?

Dakota stood under the running shower wondering what was up with Brandon. It was nothing she could put her finger on, but something was off with him. Maybe it was just the stress of the upcoming wedding preparations. They had been running the streets a lot lately, and Brandon had been a homebody for so long, it was probably starting to weigh on him. She decided to plan a relaxing weekend for the two of them this weekend.

She made plans in her head as she dressed and prepared for her day. She was off today, so her plans would begin once Brandon left work this evening. She wanted him to know that she was paying attention, and that his well-being was a priority to her. But for now, she had an appointment to keep.

Dakota reclined her seat a little more, so that she was almost laying down while getting her pedicure. She was at Yakima's shop. It was busy as usual. Yakima was working on a client, so Dakota decided to pull up Facebook on her phone. She was scrolling when she noticed that she had a personal message. She clicked on it and read the message.

"*Who the hell is this?*" she thought.

Pissed, she clicked on the person's name to go to their page. After a few clicks she realized this person purposefully didn't identify themselves. So, she re-read the message.

Hey hoe I know that was your ass that set me up last week. Just know that you don't put no fear in my heart, watch your back bitch.

She wracked her brain for a few minutes trying to think of anyone that would send her a message like this.

"It's Gina. This bitch didn't learn her lesson and now she's got the nerve to threaten me?" Dakota could actually feel her blood pressure go up.

Fuck you trick. Watch YOUR back you thirsty bitch. You can't have Brandon he's mine

Dakota messaged back. She could see that Gina was available on her mobile device. A message popped up.

Oh really? That's not what he says…

Dakota could feel the hairs standing up on the back of her neck.

And then a screen shot picture popped up; it was a texted picture of Brandon eating pussy and the caption said, "damn you taste good"

Dakota saw red.

Another message popped up

Maybe I can have him when I send him this…

The second picture was of Dakota and Alexander kissing on the deck of a restaurant. It took all the wind out of Dakota's lungs, but she managed a small scream.

Yakima looked over at her best friend and immediately knew something was tremendously wrong. She was at Dakota's side as the first tear fell.

"What's wrong? What happened? She questioned Dakota thinking something happened to somebody in her family. Dakota looked so distraught. She had her hands over her face shaking her head back and forth frantically.

Yakima couldn't get an intelligent word out of her. She snatched the phone from Dakota's grip and read what was on the screen. She quickly turned and barked an order to one of her technicians in Korean. The woman came from the back and began working on Yakima's client. Yakima told the technician that was working on Dakota's feet, to dry her feet and put her shoes on.

She pulled her friend to a sitting position, uncovered her face and said, "Come with me."

Yakima grabbed their purses and walked Dakota out to her car. Once she got her in the car, she pulled off, not knowing where they were going. All she knew was that she had to get away. A little while later, they ended up at a park. Yakima cut the engine and turned to her friend.

"Listen to me. You are gonna have to fix this before it gets out of hand."

"How?"

Tears were streaming down Dakota's face, but she didn't make a sound.

"You've gotta tell Brandon before she does. This bitch is out for blood."

"I can't tell him, he won't believe me, and obviously he wants her."

She sounded so helpless and pitiful, Yakima wanted to slap her face.

"What the fuck? What are you saying? You just gonna roll over and let this hoe have your man?"

"You see the picture of him eating her pussy don't you?" Dakota shot back.

"So, that shit could be photo shopped." Yakima didn't sound too convincing, but she pressed on. "Besides, even if he did eat it, it's just pussy. Stand up for yourself! You've done shit too, but that doesn't mean you don't deserve happiness."

"She probably already sent the other picture to him..."

"Good. You can easily explain why you were kissing Alexander, y'all were seeing other people at the time. And didn't Brandon suggest you see other people?"

A glimmer of hope crossed Dakota's face.

"Yeah he suggested it."

"Well go explain this shit away. But you gotta tell him right now. Don't let him simmer in this shit."

Yakima cranked the car and backed out.

"Here call him and tell him to meet you at the house right now." she handed Dakota her phone.

Another message popped up

You stupid bitch that dick has my name all over it...bet you didn't get none last night, and you won't get none tonight either... lol

Enough was enough! Dakota decided she would fight for her man. She wasn't going to let anyone come between her and the life she deserved. It was time to stop letting things happen, and time to start making things happen. From now on, she would stand up for herself. She knew she could trust Brandon and she knew Gina was trying to get into her head. But she was better at this game than Gina could ever imagine.

She messaged Gina back.

Send whatever you want to send...we both know who ain't getting his dick no more... thot #hesmine #mrswest

A calm fell over Dakota like she'd never felt before.

CHAPTER 29

"Brandon, I need you to come home, we need to talk."

"What happened? Are you ok?"

Brandon sounded nervous, obviously he hadn't seen the picture yet, and he didn't know she'd seen his photo yet either.

"I don't know if I'm ok or not, but we need to talk face to face. Now."

"Ok, I'm leaving now. What's this all about, D?"

"Just come home, baby."

Dakota hung up and looked at Yakima.

"I hope you're right, girl."

"Have I ever steered you wrong?"

"Hell yeah! I can think of a couple of times…"

"I mean, when it really mattered, bish! No, right?"

"No, not when it really mattered." Dakota conceded, laughing.

"Alright, then. Now remember the law of attraction, focus only on what you want, not on what you don't want. Talk plainly and calmly, and stick to the subject. Don't get pulled into a power play, if you do, neither of you will win. The goal is reconciliation and getting all skeletons out of the damn closet. Clear?"

Dakota stared at her bestie in disbelief.

"Since when did you become Dr. Kima?"

"I'm not, I just know how to focus on the goal. And I know you gotta give a little to get a lot. I've seen that shit modeled by my parents my whole life and it works. I just want you and Brandon to make it. I look up to you guys; y'all represent my relationship goals, for real, for real."

"Now there's the Yakima I know…thanks love. I will stay focused, promise."

Yakima whipped into Dakota's driveway just as Brandon was getting out of his car.

"Go get 'em tiger!" she encouraged Dakota.

Dakota got out of the car feeling afraid and unsure of herself. None of the bravado she had in the car got out with her. She had overcome so many things recently to make this relationship work between her and Brandon. However, this was the biggest hurdle yet. This was not the time to fumble the ball, so to speak. She would have to be honest and completely transparent, if she wanted to clear the air, and start her marriage off with a clean slate.

"*Focus on what you want...*" she heard Yakima in her head as she walked towards a nervous looking Brandon.

"*She looks too calm to have seen the picture, so what's so urgent? Please don't let it be anything to do with Gina,* he prayed silently. *How am I gonna play this shit? Just let her do the talking...*

Dakota stood in front of him.

"Everything alright, Coca?" Brandon couldn't help himself, he didn't want to lose his future.

She hugged his neck tight, "I hope so, babe." She whispered in his ear. She kissed his cheek and walked into the house.

Brandon's feet felt like they weighed a thousand pounds each following her into their kitchen. Dakota sat at the breakfast bar, but Brandon was too nervous to sit, so he stood on the other side of the marble island.

"Brandon, I love you and I want to tell you some things as well as ask you some things. I hope we can be honest with each other, for the sake of our upcoming marriage."

Brandon's throat had suddenly dried up, so he just nodded his agreement.

"I am not proud of everything I've done, but I hope that you can forgive me…"

Her voice cracked, and she felt an overwhelming urge to cry, but that was the old Dakota's style. She knew she had to do something different if she wanted something different. She took a deep breath and found her inner strength.

"*Please don't tell me some bullshit that I'll never be able to let go of.*" Brandon thought.

"When we decided to 'see' other people," she made quotation marks in the air with her fingers, "I went out a couple of times with one guy. We had fun and he kinda took my mind off of what you might be doing."

"So, he made you forget about me? Huh? What kinda fun?" Brandon's voice was rising with each question.

"Brandon, wait, that's not important."

"Oh its not?"

"No."

"Well, please, get to the fucking important part, D."

"*If looks could kill…*" she glared at him, remembering the picture of his face in between Gina's legs. He had the audacity to be angry about a picture he ain't even seen? How dare he judge her, after the shit he had done? She did her best to re-focus herself on the outcome she wanted.

"What's important," she said after another deep breath, "is that Gina saw us out one time and apparently she took a picture of us. She's been holding it over my head ever since and I'm tired of the shit. So I needed to come clean before she showed it to you."

She looked at Brandon trying to gauge his reaction; he looked really angry, like he was trying to get himself under control before speaking.

"So, is that it? Or is there more you wanna tell me?" he said as calmly as he could.

"No that's it."

"You sure?" he pressed

This pissed her off.

"Unless you want some details, that's pretty much it. You don't want to hear some shit that you won't be able to let go of in the future, do you?"

"Maybe. Maybe not. Do you have the picture? Let me see it because I don't keep in touch with Gina for her to be giving me pictures and shit."

"Oh you don't? She asked.

She looked through her phone, found the picture she wanted and gave the phone to Brandon.

He snatched the phone out of her hand and stared at the picture in shock and disbelief.

"What the fuck?" he barely whispered.

"Hmm? What's that you said, I couldn't hear you?" Dakota put her hand up to her ear.

Brandon was looking at his own face and Gina's crotch.

"How long has this been going on Brandon?"

"Ain't nothing going on."

"I would call that, something." She shouted, pointing at the phone. "So, please don't lie to me anymore, how long has it been going on?"

"Once. Well, twice by mistake…"

"Oh? By fuckling mistake?" now Dakota's voice was high-pitched.

"Listen,"

He put the phone down and reached for her hand, but she pulled away. The look on her face made him feel 2 inches big. How was he going to explain this? He had no choice but to tell the truth, as crazy as it sounded. He came around the island, and sat on the bar stool next to Dakota.

"It happened when we were 'out there'. I mean, I didn't plan it, it just happened the first time. And I wish it didn't… honestly, Coca."

He tried to read her face, but she was really holding it together, she had her poker face on. He decided to continue.

"But it did happen. And then she started texting me, calling me, showing up at my mom's house and shit. She was acting all jealous and shit like she thought we was together or something. I just wanted the bullshit to stop. I thought if I talked to her, on some real shit, she would get the big picture, but she didn't. She flipped out like a fatal attraction, and drugged me."

Dakota folded her arms and looked at him like he was completely crazy.

"I know it sounds crazy, but I'm telling you the truth. Whatever she gave me had me stuck; I couldn't move at all. That's when she took that picture…I swear! It was nothing I could do to prevent it."

"Where were you when she took the picture, Brandon?"

He paused for a second, knowing how stupid his answer was going to sound.

"At her house. I see now, that was a bad move on my part."

"So, you went to her house, just to talk? Why the fuck didn't you just call her on the phone? Do you really expect me to believe you didn't wanna fuck her again?"

"Yes. Please believe me, I only want you." He took her hand.

So many thoughts were running through Dakota's head, it actually hurt. She had questions that she wanted to ask, but wasn't sure if she really wanted the answers. Was he being completely honest with her now? Was it really over between them? Was it just a fling, something that she and Brandon could leave in the past? She hoped so.

She took a deep breath and held it for a minute, trying to calm her heartbeat. She really wanted to trust Brandon and get on with their happily ever after, but it was easier said than done.

"Is it really over?"

"It is. There's nothing, absolutely nothing going on with her or anyone else. All I want is you."

Dakota thought about Alexander, and how hard it had been to stop thinking about him, and wanting him. She was able to stop because she wanted Brandon more. She had never been insecure, and she decided she wasn't going to start now. She trusted Brandon and he trusted her, they could definitely start a marriage built on trust.

"Alright, I trust you and I'll always trust you, so don't make me regret it."

"Thank you baby, I won't. And I trust you too, and always will."

They held each other for a long while, neither wanting to ever let go.

"But, just so you know everything, she has more pictures and I don't know what she plans to do with them."

Dakota broke free from his embrace and stared at him. Then she snickered and then giggled, finally it turned into a deep belly laugh. Brandon stood there trying to figure out if she was losing it, or if he had missed the joke. Eventually her laughter trailed off.

"Well that's what you get for messing with a messy, attention needing, miserable ass hoe. Of course she has more pictures, anytime she thinks we're happy, she'll wanna throw a monkey wrench our way. But you know what? I can beat her at her own game. And in all fairness, I should tell you that I have a video of her that I'm sure she doesn't want anyone to see. Just don't ask me how I got it…it's a long story. Just know that I can get grimy with the worst of them and still come out smelling like roses."

She smiled at her husband to be and he pulled her into his arms shaking his head. Both were grateful to have the air cleared, and to have dodged the bullet. Everything could have really gone left, and they both knew it.

"And one last thing…"

"What the fuck now?" Dakota thought.

He paused so long, Dakota thought he forgot what he was about to say.

"Yes?"

"She wrote her name, in permanent marker... on my member."

"See!" Dakota threw her hands up in the air, "Now this bitch gone make me fight her ass! What kinda trifling, trick ass, shit is that to do to somebody? She wants me to act an ass. She wants me to show my natural ass out in these streets when I see her ratchet ass!" Dakota banged her fist on the island as she ranted.

And just as suddenly as she started she stopped and burst into laughter again. She felt like she was losing her mind, and she could tell by the look on Brandon's face, he thought she was too. But her head was clear, and a plan was hatched. She would get rid of Ms. Gina once and for all. She put that on everything she loved.

CHAPTER 30

It took a lot of prayer and meditation to let go of the information she recently learned, but Dakota didn't want to carry around negative energy. She decided they needed a couple days away from the outside world, she planned to create an oasis at home for her and Brandon. The whole weekend was spent in pajamas, house clothes, or no clothes at all. They completely immersed themselves into each other. They ate delivered food, watched movies, played pool, and talked about their future plans.

They reconnected on a higher level. They got into each other's minds and built on a mental level. This connection intensified their love making. It was pure and real.

Dakota loved when they made love this way. It was orgasm after orgasm, and then he would just lay inside of her, caressing her body. Kissing her deeply and intimately, like he never wanted to stop. Slowly, he stroked in and out of her, softly touching her tender spots. Real, true love making. Her multiple orgasms piled on top of each other feeling like she were having an out of body experience; she never wanted to be apart from him.

By the time the weekend ended, they were ready to face the real world as a unified front. Dakota was grateful to be back at work, she had some plans that would allow her to expand and see more clients. She was putting the finishing touches on a meeting agenda, when her assistant tapped on her door with a delivery.

"Come in Kim."

"This just arrived. It says important on the envelope, so I thought I'd better get it to you."

"Thanks."

Dakota looked at the manila envelope for any clues to who sent it, but there were none. It was addressed to her spa with attention to Dakota Morgan. Dakota picked up her letter opener and tore open the envelope. She tilted the envelope and poured its contents out onto her desk. There were six, black and white, 5x7 pictures and a note. She flipped the pictures over, one by one, each turned her stomach more than the last. Finally she read the note:

Enjoy bitch, I know I did!

Seeing Gina and Brandon together in such intimate poses made Dakota want to throw up. She gathered the pictures together and put them back into the envelope, and leaned back in her plush chair. She knew the response Gina hoped to elicit from her, and she refused to give her what she wanted. Instead, she quieted her mind and thought for a moment.

Suddenly and idea came to her. She picked up the phone and pressed Kim's extension.

"Kim, don't we have a profile on the majority of our clients?"

"Yes, they fill it out during their first visit to receive 15% off of a future service, but not everyone participates."

"That's fine. Do me a favor. Go through the database and see if we have anyone that works for the Assistant D.A.'s office, and get those names to me ASAP. Thanks."

"Ok, I'm on it."

Dakota thought some more, and figured Gina was probably stalking her social media too. *"Let me give your looking ass something to look at trick."*

She pulled a USB cord from her desk drawer, connected her phone, and uploaded all her photos to a folder. Then she picked a few of her favorites, of her and Brandon together, and posted them to Instagram and linked them to her Facebook and Twitter accounts. She was sure to include cute captions like *he loves me, meant for each other,* and *wedding of the century coming soon,* and to hashtag each with #Mr&Mrs #TrueLoveAlwaysWins #NotEasilyBroken

Her phone rang.

"Dakota, I have the names you wanted. There's only two." Kim informed her.

"No worries. Who are they?"

"Carla Wright and Lisa McCelvey."

"Great get me their numbers & email."

"Coming right up, I'll text it to you."

"Perfect."

She hung up, very pleased with herself. This plan could really work, if she played it just right.

First, Dakota called both women and left voicemails informing them that they had been randomly selected from a list of preferred customers to receive one free spa service up to a $50 value. She let them know that they only had to arrange a time for the gift certificate to be delivered at their workplace as part of an advertising promotion. Then she emailed them both the same information. Now all she had to do was sit back and wait.

Dakota knew both Carla and Lisa were regular clients, and she didn't mind giving away $100 in services to them, especially if it would give her a reason to show up to Gina's workplace. She relished the thought of Gina stressing over why she was there.

"So, you wanna send packages to my place of business? When I deliver some to your workplace we'll see how you like it."

"Yakima on line one." Kim notified her.

"Thanks, put her through."

"Hey girl, I was just thinking about you. What's good?"

"It's all good, and I was thinking about you too, but you see how I picked up the phone and called you? That's what friends do when they thinking 'bout each other." She said in typical Yakima style.

"And that's neither here nor there, especially after I catch you up on the latest drama."

"Spill it bish, I've been waiting all weekend."

"Ok, so he took the news about the picture with Alex pretty well, as well as could be expected anyway. And she had never actually sent the picture so go figure. But she did send me a picture of her and Brandon. Girl, when I tell you that this nasty trick had a picture of her stank ass cootchie on his chin, I am telling you the truth!"

"Whaaaaat? No way in the hell!"

"Yes, girl. But wait, that ain't all. He goes on to tell me that she drugged him and took the picture while he couldn't move. I still don't know if I believe that shit or not."

"Wait a minute, he probably telling the truth. You know Ariel, who works at that biochemistry lab, making all those new drugs and shit? She told me that they had developed some shit like that, but it was supposed to be for military use only."

"Gina's sneaky ass probably blackmailed someone to get it. Anyway, he said she took more pictures and he didn't know why she didn't send them. Well, they showed up this morning via messenger, at my damn office! Can you believe the nerve of this trick?"

"Ooo, she out for blood, huh?"

"And you know I had to keep my cool throughout the whole confession, but when he told me that she actually wrote her name, with a sharpie, on his dick, I fucking lost it!"

"Oh hell to the naw! I know you lying Dakota. Please tell me this bitch did not stoop that low! Theses some new-age thots we dealing with in this day and time."

"Just ratchet for no damn reason…"

Yakima started laughing.

"Sorry, I don't mean to laugh but, how did y'all get the name off?"

"Chile, I had to laugh too. Shit it was either laugh or cry, at the time I thought I was losing my damn mind."

"I bet you did."

"But we just used some hand sanitizer and it faded it pretty good. The rest washed off over the weekend. But that was some shit to get over, girl."

"Well you made it through. And you did it without catching a case. I'm proud of you."

"You're about to be even prouder of me. I came up with a plan to get rid of this nuisance all by myself. Let me run it by you."

"Run it."

Dakota explained that she would send Gina a snippet of the video made in the hotel room, telling her that she was going to expose her as the tramp she is, at her job. And how she planned to show up at Gina's job with two manila envelopes, just like the one Gina sent to Dakota's office. She would be delivering the gift certificates to her clients, but Gina wouldn't know why she was there or what she was giving to her co-workers. This should arouse her suspicions, and may even cause Gina to confront Dakota.

"What do you think?"

"It sounds ok… for a first attempt at being evil, but you've got so much to learn little one. Has nothing rubbed off from me over the years?" she asked sarcastically.

"What would you change?" Dakota wanted to know.

"For starters, you shouldn't upload anything that could be traced back to you. Second, what do you expect to accomplish if she does confront you? And third, why not get the video to her boss, and get her ass fired?"

"I don't know how to upload it without it being traced back to me."

"Let me handle that part. Remember Tim, the one I had a threesome with? He's like a technology nerd, he knows all kinds of ways to get shit done electronically. So that takes care of part one and three, but I still don't know why you want her to confront you."

"If I can get her to act an ass at her job it will put the spot light on her and they will be more susceptible when they do see the video. And they won't have a problem letting her go before she ruins their image.

"Well played. So all my teachings have not been in vain?"

"No, not all of them." Dakota laughed. "So how soon can you get in touch with Tim?"

"I emailed him while we were talking; we're meeting up for happy hour this afternoon. Wanna join us?"

"Can't wait. See you there."

"See ya."

Dakota loved her 'evil scheme'. She was always the one who took the higher road, but now was not the time to be diplomatic, now was the time to fight dirty for what she wanted.

CHAPTER 31

Gina looked at Dakota's pictures on her Facebook page and wondered if she had seen the pictures she had delivered earlier. She knew they were delivered, but guessed that the package wasn't opened yet. If Dakota had seen the pictures that Gina sent, she wouldn't be posting all of this lovey-dovey shit, in fact she wouldn't even be with Brandon anymore.

"But it's just a matter of time before you see just how close Brandon and I are." Gina thought to herself.

Gina knew there was a chance that she and Brandon could get back together if Dakota were out of the picture. She really wished that Dakota would just die and save them all the trouble, but that didn't seem likely so Gina had to drive her away. She had waited this long, she could wait a little longer. Soon, social media would be filled with happy pictures of Brandon and his true love, Gina. If her dreams were any indication of the change coming, she shouldn't have long to wait.

The recurring dream always starts out the same, but every now and then it has an alternate ending. This time the dream began, as it always did, with a photographer taking their family portrait.

They are in their home, on a sprawling estate in the mountains of North Carolina. It's Christmas time and the family is positioned in front of their enormous fireplace. There's a roaring fire crackling, and they are gathered on a huge bear skin rug. Everyone is laughing and smiling. The photographer is snapping away, getting great photos of the happy family.

Brandon is lying on his side and Gina, their two boys Bradford and Bentley, and a daughter Challis, are all kneeling behind him. The children are 6, 4, and 2 years old. Eventually the children become too boisterous and the photo session is ended. They head into the kitchen to snack on some holiday deserts that Gina made. Brandon is lifting the children into the air, one by one, and giving them an airplane ride when the doorbell rings. Gina knows how much the children adore their father, and doesn't want to interrupt their fun, so she goes to answer the door.

However, when she opens the door, there's no one there, and when she returns to the kitchen, there's no one there either. She is all alone. She spends the rest of the dream searching in vain for her lost family, and usually wakes up in tears. The dream is so real, she is sometimes thrown into a deep depression afterwards. It feels like she's suffered an actual loss.

But not this time, in this version of the dream, when she answers the door, there are two men and a woman. The men are dressed in all white uniforms and the woman is in a nurse's uniform and has a clipboard in her hand. They greet Gina as if they've known her for years. Gina is cordial, but doesn't know any of them, but she is soon in a struggle for her life. The woman tells the men to take Gina and put her into the vehicle. Gina fights them but they overtake her. Her family comes to the door to see what is going on. Brandon attempts to come to her, but the nurse stops him and has him read what is on the clipboard she's holding. The children are crying and calling for their mother. Gina fights even harder to break free, but the men get her into the vehicle.

She looks out of the window and sees the sadness on Brandon's face as he ushers the children back inside. She can't believe her eyes. Why isn't he coming to her rescue? In frustration she throws herself to the floor, except the floor is soft, a little too soft. Gina realizes that she's in a padded room. The window no longer looks out at her beautiful home, now it reveals a long lonely corridor. The nurse is walking towards her room. As she gets closer, Gina gets a better look at her and realizes she knows her after all; it's Dakota. Gina beats on the door with all her might, but it is no use, she only wakes up tired. Gina wondered if the alternate ending to her dream was a sign that the dream could actually come true. Not the part about losing her family, but having the family in the first place. She wanted that more than anything in her life.

Gina wanted to turn up the heat a little. She decided to post some of her own pictures. Scrolling through Dakota's recent uploads, she choose the one with the most likes, clicked comment, and uploaded one of the selfies she'd taken of her and Brandon.

"This should get your attention…" she laughed to herself.

She wished she could see the look on Dakota's face when she scrolls through the comment section. There would be no way to ignore it when all of her friends see the picture. Little miss thing will be so distraught, but it wouldn't even come close to the pain

Gina suffered over the years. Now it was payback time and Gina had plenty to go around.

Dakota pulled into a parking space right next to Yakima's car. Chill 'n Grill had been their happy hour spot since they were old enough to drink. Dakota remembered one time, she and Yakima were so drunk that they tried to jump a guy in the bar. He was easily holding them both at bay, neither of them weighed 110 pounds, at the time, but they were put out of the bar; it only took one bouncer to carry them both out. They even had the nerve to ask for their money back, so the bouncer gave them money out of his own pocket. And they came back the next week.

Shaking her head at the memory, Dakota saw Yakima and Tim sitting in their usual booth. There were hugs all around. Dakota ordered her usual dry, vodka martini and chatted with Tim until it arrived.

"Now, let's get down to business." Yakima told them.

"Yeah, Tim what can you do to help us with this video we have of Gina?" Dakota asked.

"Well, Kima was filling me in a little about what's been going on, and catching me up on all the dirt. I wanna help you get this dirty bitch back. I know she's a dirt dauber 'cause she tried to blackmail me before. And honey when she's got you by the short 'n curlies she won't hesitate to pluck you bald, if you let her. So I'm down for whatever y'all need me to do to strike back against her."

"Good." Dakota agreed.

"So, here's the plan. We get her to think Dakota is going to deliver the video to her job, but instead we upload it to the company website or to the D.A.'s email. But of course we don't want it to be traceable to us, so that's where you come in. Is that something you can handle?"

"Handle? Ha! I created that ish bish!" Tim snapped his fingers and continued. "I'll even do you one better…we can send a series of videos all starring Ms. Thang. How you like that?"

"No, we only have one video." Dakota said.

"Yes. You have only one, but I have more than you can imagine."

"What the hell you talking about?" Yakima chimed in.

"Well, my dear, a little while back, the wicked witch summoned me to install video surveillance in her home for the explicit purpose of capturing unsuspecting suckers in action. See, I know how she gets down. I told you she blackmailed my ass before, so I figured I would link her surveillance to my computer and I'd be able to return the favor one day...."

He looked at them both in a dramatic pause...and smiles crossed all of their lips.

"And that day is today baby!" Yakima high-fived Tim.

"It is indeed. So, I suggest we not only send the videos to the D.A. but to the entire staff's computers. And on the last video we loop it so that it plays over and over until all work is at a standstill. They will be running that witch out the door, to burn her at the stake!"

"Good for her ass! That's what she gets for fucking with a boss! She gon learn today."

"How soon can we get this ball rolling?" Yakima wanted to know.

"I can get the videos together by tomorrow. I will need a little longer to get into the D.A.'s computer system, but I know a guy that can help with that...all together I'd say we could ruin her career in about a week. Is that good for you D?"

"Perfect. Thanks for helping ya girl out, Tim. I owe you for real, for real."

"Well I do it 'cause I love you, but a spa package ain't never hurt nobody. I'm just saying." He said hugging Dakota."

"Consider it done!"

"Aww, get a damn room with all that hugging and shit!" Yakima chided them. "We need more drinks, this round's on me."

They ordered another round and laughed and talked for another hour. After all was said and done, Dakota could actually relax. She felt like she had a lock on the situation, and a weight had been lifted off her shoulders. She felt ten pounds lighter.

After happy hour, they parted ways. Yakima was meeting up with more friends to continue the turn up, and Tim had a date with his fiancé. Dakota was headed home to spend some quality time with her bae, Brandon. She couldn't wait to give him all of the details of how they were going to get rid of Gina. She had a 15 minute drive, so she called in an order of Chinese food to pick up on the way home.

She pulled into the drive through line and the phone rang. On-star announced that it was an unidentified caller. Dakota had a bad feeling in her stomach. Her number was never given out randomly, she had a business cell for her clients, for anytime she signed up for a service that required a phone number, and all other shenanigans. So, who was the unidentified caller, calling her cell? Dakota thought she knew.

"Hello?"

"Dakota?"

"Yes. Who's calling?"

"You know who this is. I'm calling to decline the invitation to your wedding. I just received it in the mail today, but I just can't participate in the foolishness. I won't be an enabler to your delusions."

"Delusions? Bitch you are the one that's delusional."

"Whatever. I won't be in attendance to watch Brandon throw his life away with a tramp like you."

"You won't be there because you are not invited you fucking psychotic bitch. You probably saw your mother's invitation, but let me give you a clue, since it's obvious you don't have one, if you come anywhere near my wedding, I will have you fucked up."

"Don't feed me that bullshit and think you put fear in my heart, because you don't; you never did. I do what I want, and I get what I want. Enjoy your little 5 minutes in the lime light, because the memories are all you'll have soon…"

Dakota hung up. She couldn't believe how crazy Gina really was; like she should be committed somewhere. In what universe did she believe her and Brandon were a couple? This bitch needed a shrink, like real quick! She was glad Gina didn't know where they lived, because she would have to kill her ass. But, soon she would be a bad memory and that's all.

CHAPTER 32

Gina's phone chimed. She got excited because it was a text from Brandon. Brandon had his own personal ringtone and notification tone in her phone. Snatching the phone off the bed next to her, she read his text.

I've got a surprise for you...will send to your job tomorrow

What kind of surprise could Brandon have for her, she wondered. It really didn't matter, because whatever he had, she wanted. Before she could think about it too long, her phone chimed again.

Do you like surprises?
You know what I like daddy
No actually I don't...this is Dakota
U sneaking on his phone to get at me. Getting desperate?
No just chilling with bae

The phone chimed before she could reply. She stared at the selfie of Dakota and Brandon snuggled up together on a plush looking bed covered in pillows. Their smiles looked so genuine; they looked so happy. But she refused to believe they were together, she clung to the idea that Dakota was sending these things without Brandon's knowledge. There was no way that Brandon would participate in hurting her. She wanted Dakota to know that she wasn't fooled.

Cute throwback
Current situation
Yeah? Send another one

When the picture came Gina opened it immediately. It was Brandon and Dakota in the same position, only this time they were holding an index card that said 'Bye Gina'. She was crushed. How could he? She stared at the picture, as if trying to memorize every detail.

"*Oh well, he's probably just trying to appease Dakota by going along with her little tactics.*" She rationalized in her mind.

She knew it was all a ploy to fool her. Obviously, Dakota was afraid of how close Brandon and Gina were, and was trying to run Gina away, but it wasn't going to work. Gina could stay the course, and that's exactly what she planned to do. She had put in too much time, energy and heart, to lose now. She would hold on and soon she would get her way. She always did.

When her phone chimed again, she ignored it.

"You think she got the picture?" Dakota asked Brandon.

"Yep. I think she *literally* got the picture." He laughed.

"Bet she won't post those pictures."

"Nope."

"I still can't believe she posted on my timeline, but I've blocked her ass now."

"Good. Now you won't have to worry about her commenting on anything you post. But I still can't figure out how she got your phone number."

"Ain't no telling. One thing's for sure, she's a resourceful bitch."

Brandon thought back to how Gina had drugged him. As soon as the drug kicked in, she switched up on him like Dr. Jekyll and Mr. Hyde. She got everything she wanted from him including sex, and dragged him out of her house, and left him sitting outside waiting for the drug to wear off. She had all the evidence she needed to blackmail him. Although he was an unwilling participant, the sex was good and he came in her. The thought made him shudder.

Dakota noticed. "What's up babe? You got a chill?"

"Yeah, 'cause you stopped snuggling with me. Get over here."

He pulled Dakota into a massive bear-hug and kissed her all over her face, making her giggle; just the way she liked. He caressed her soft skin and kissed her deeply this time. She returned his kiss with increasing lust. His hands were all over her body. He slid her panties down and she kicked them off. She could feel his need for her; he was hard as steel.

Brandon rolled over onto his back, pulling Dakota on top of him. She wasted no time grabbing his rod and guiding it to her wetness. Brandon was rock hard and she wanted every inch of him inside of her. She slid up and down, lubricating his dick with her juices. This was one of her favorite positions, since they got back together. It made her feel in control and the feeling turned her on even more. In this dominate position, Brandon usually laid back and let her run the show.

Dakota knew exactly what she was doing; she had mad skills in the bedroom. She rode him like a stallion, watching the ecstasy written all over his face. Brandon was on the verge of a nut when she slowed her pace. She rode him slow and sexy, popping her ass each time she slid down his shaft. Her wetness made her pussy sound like someone was stirring mac 'n cheese. Brandon couldn't take it anymore, he tapped her on her hip, to let her know he was about to come. She knew he was on the verge as she popped her pussy back and forth on his long dick. When his body began to stiffen, she jumped off of him and sucked every drop he squirted out, and let it all drain down his pole. She loved that nasty shit.

Rinsing her mouth out in the sink, she heard Brandon come into the bathroom and start the shower. He smacked her across the ass.

"You should have just swallowed it." He joked.

"In your dreams." She said.

But secretly she wanted to swallow it. She had tried before, but it gaged her and made her feel like she would throw up. So, she never tried again. She liked the idea of being dirty and nasty, because it was so outside of her everyday self; just the thought turned her on completely. Her alter-ego was a hot ass little slut that would drop her drawers at the drop of a hat; anywhere, anytime. Dakota figured, everyone has a dark side they wouldn't want anyone to find out about, this just happened to be hers.

"Get in here, I'm not finished with you yet." Brandon called out.

Dakota laughed and got into the shower with him. The hot water flowed over her face and down her body. She loved the three shower heads they had installed, and the way the water hit her from every angle. Brandon had the hand held shower head in his hand and a grin on his face. Dakota knew where this was going.

He knelt down in front of her and put her leg up on his shoulder. Adjusting the nozzle spray he aimed it at her clit. Dakota was instantly engulfed in the sensation. He slid his forefinger into her and she moaned in pleasure. Then he moved the shower head away and sucked and licked her moistness. She gyrated against his face and leaned back against the tiled shower wall. His mouth game was on point, he was talented with his tongue.

"I want you in me." She told him.

Brandon stood and turned her towards the wall. He entered her from behind, pressing her into the cool shower tiles. The water rushed down their bodies as they pumped and grinded on each other. Dakota felt her orgasm coming quickly and she had no desire to hold it back. Her body rocked as she came multiple times, and Brandon never missed a stroke.

He pulled back too far, and slid up into her ass. Her gut reaction was to pull away, but he aimed the hand held shower head at her clit again. The sensitivity of her nerves were on the edge, her legs were getting weak. Brandon sensed it and held her up and steadily stroked her ass, deeper and deeper until he had her pressed flat up against the shower wall. Between the pressure of Brandon's constant pounding in her ass and the jet stream of water on her pussy, Dakota couldn't take anymore. And neither could Brandon, he came with an intensity that threatened to split Dakota in half. His body jerked and tremored as all of his load was spent.

Dakota turned to face him. he was breathing hard, his body was still tense, and the water was dripping down his handsome face and cascading down his ripped abs. she was so grateful that he was her man, and soon to be her husband. She caressed his face and kissed his soft lips. They held each other and swayed in the water as if they were slow-dancing to their favorite song.

Afterwards, the lovers washed each other's bodies; not missing a spot. When they were dried off, Brandon picked Dakota up in his arms like a baby and carried her to their bed.

"I love you." He told her and kissed her deeply.

"I know baby, I love you too."

They snuggled into the spoon position and watched movies until they both drifted off to sleep.

CHAPTER 33

"So, everything is ready to go?" Dakota asked excitedly.

"Yep, I think I'm more excited than you are!" Yakima told her.

"Ok, so I will deliver the packages today and then tomorrow we drop the bomb."

"I only wish I could be there to see her face."

"You and me both!"

They hung up and Dakota informed Kim that she would be out of the office for a few hours and to forward any important calls to her cell. She put the gift certificates into her Louis Vuitton bag and headed out to her truck. She felt like she was floating on air, she was so happy. She texted both her clients to make sure today was a good day to drop off the gift certificates. Both replied yes. Dakota put the truck in reverse and headed out.

When she pulled into the parking lot, her senses were tingling all over. It felt like static electricity, and Dakota recognized this feeling. She sat in the car for a few moments trying to figure out what was causing her to be on alert. She couldn't pin point anything specific, so she chalked it up to excited nervousness. She shook off the feeling of being watched, gathered herself and got out of the truck and walked into the building.

Gina was in a particularly bad mood this morning and just couldn't shake it. She thought about not going in to work, but she was working on a really big case with some of the higher ups that could help her career if she played her cards right. So, she didn't want to miss work. Yet, the crying spell she had last night, had her eyes puffy and she had a headache that just wouldn't quit. It took everything in her just to get dressed and comb her hair. Her makeup was minimal to nonexistent, but she didn't care.

She pulled into her usual spot near the back of the parking lot, but couldn't bring herself to get out of the car. She closed her eyes and took a couple of deep breaths in an attempt to calm the thumping in her head. Nothing seemed to be working, she was just going to have to suck it up. Reaching for the door handle she recognized a familiar looking truck, but it couldn't be who she thought it was. She waited, and sure enough, Dakota Morgan hopped out of the truck and headed into her job.

"What the fuck…"

Her headache was instantly forgotten. Gina grabbed her purse and briefcase and was across the parking lot in no time flat. By the time she entered the lobby, Dakota was gone.

"The young lady, in the white suit, where did she go?" she asked the lobby receptionist.

"She signed in to go to the D.A.'s office."

"Thanks."

Gina stood there for a moment thinking through a couple of different scenarios in her head. In one, Dakota was headed to her boss, Robert Glynn, III, with that damn video from the hotel. If that was the case, maybe Gina should leave and save herself the embarrassment, or she could try to get up there quickly to persuade Robert that she was set up and being blackmailed. In another scenario, Dakota was on her way up to threaten Gina, and instead, Gina could surprise her ass. She knew time was running out to make her move, whatever it was. She reasoned that Dakota didn't have the balls for blackmail, and she would take her chances and go on up.

Gina stepped out of the elevator and glanced in both directions. She didn't see anything out of the ordinary. She checked her watch and was grateful that she didn't have any morning meetings. She headed towards her small office, not speaking to anyone that wasn't above her pay grade. When someone called her name, she turned and her eyes caught sight of Dakota. Gina stopped dead in her tracks.

"Hey, glad I caught you before the meeting this afternoon."

It was Sheldon, a coworker on the same level as Gina, not important in any way that concerned her. She had used him to help her with research a couple of times, but like with anything else, if they couldn't do something for her, Gina wanted nothing to do with people in general.

"I was hoping you were finished with that file I lent you last week, I need it back." He continued.

Gina looked past him at Dakota. She was laughing and talking with a paralegal at her desk. *What on earth could they be talking about? And what was so damn funny? Were they laughing at her?* Too many thoughts were running through Gina's head at one time, she couldn't focus.

"Do you have it?" Sheldon asked again.

"Have what?" Gina snapped at him.

"Uh, the um file that I lent you last week. I need it before the meeting this afternoon. Sorry."

He fidgeted with his tie waiting for her response. Gina softened a little.

"Oh, yeah, it's in my office. Come on."

Sheldon followed her like a little puppy to her office. She glanced one last time at Dakota and rationalized that she must know the paralegal and it was a coincidence that she worked with Gina. She reached her office, found the file, gave it to Sheldon and ushered him out her door. Once her door was closed, she gathered her thoughts and realized that she was being paranoid. There was no way that Dakota was here to see her; or was there?

Gina didn't want to leave anything to chance. She grabbed her coffee mug and headed to the break room, where there was always coffee brewing. She would have to pass right by Dakota to get there, and she had every intention of asking her what she was doing there. But neither Dakota nor the young lady were there anymore.

"Now where could they be?" she wondered.

She continued to the break room and fixed herself a cup of coffee anyway. Just then, she saw the young lady and Dakota walking down the hall. She was pointing as if giving Dakota directions. But to where? That wasn't the way out. Suddenly, Gina realized her boss's office was in that direction. She took off down the hall to catch and confront Dakota.

Gina was speed walking, but she was running out of time, Dakota was dangerously close to Robert's office. They turned the corner and Gina lost sight of them. Panic kicked in and she broke into a run. She never once thought about slowing down or about anyone else other than Dakota. The door to Robert's office closed as she rounded the corner; her heart dropped. She stood there frozen in her tracks trying to think of what to do next.

◇   ◇   ◇

Dakota talked with Lisa as long as she could hoping to see Gina or at least for Gina to see her. But it seemed that wasn't going to happen. Dakota wasn't giving up though, if she had to walk through that whole office, she wasn't leaving until she knew Gina saw her there. She asked Lisa to show her where Carla's desk was, and if she would show her the way.

"Of course, I'll take you over there. She is the D.A.'s legal secretary. Come on."

"Thanks, I can't wait to see the look on her face when she realizes I doubled her gift certificate. The look on your face was priceless."

"And I can't thank you enough Dakota."

"No worries, you deserve it. Don't forget to send referrals our way, we are expanding soon."

"I will send lots, promise. So, here we are, she's right around this corner." Lisa pointed the way to Dakota.

"Hey, do you know a woman here named Gina?" Dakota hoped she sounded casual.

"Gina Hefel?" Lisa asked.

"Yes."

"I know of her, but we're not friends or anything. Why?"

"I was just wondering if she still worked here. She's an old acquaintance, I may stop by and see her before I leave." Dakota lied.

"Well, I think that was her in the break room we just passed, but her back was turned. Do you wanna go back?"

"Oh, no. that's fine. I know that Carla is expecting me, I'll see Gina afterwards. But thanks."

"Not a problem. Here's Carla."

Dakota and Carla hugged and over Carla's shoulder she caught sight of Gina running full speed down the hallway. She had a half crazed look on her face, at first Dakota thought she was running towards her. But when Gina turned the corner she stopped and stared at the door across the hall. Dakota returned her attention to Carla, but kept Gina in her peripheral vision. She didn't trust that bitch, but she wanted her to know she was there.

"Surprise!" Dakota yelled loudly when she told Carla about the increase in the gift certificate.

She was sure she had Gina's full attention, but she never made eye contact with her, even though she could feel Gina's gaze on her. Dakota wanted to draw Gina over to her for the confrontation she was anticipating. Knowing that Carla worked directly for the D.A., she asked her questions about him, and offered a gift certificate for him, hoping that Carla would gesture towards his office. And it worked. Gina was headed directly over to where she and Carla were talking. Dakota braced herself for whatever was about to pop off; she hoped there would be fireworks.

"Well, well, well look who's here in my workplace." Gina sneered.

"Oh, hello Gina. I didn't expect to see you. Is everything ok? You look like you've been crying." Dakota dripped syrupy concern.

"I'm fine, never better." Gina laughed. "What are you doing here, if not to see me?"

"What would ever make you think I'd come to see you? But, if you must know, I'm here to see Carla."

Gina looked Carla up and down like she had magically appeared there.

"Umm hmm. Ok, but watch yourself on the way out, this is not the place for any foolishness."

Dakota stared at her, eye to eye, and turned her back to Gina.

"I apologize for having to leave, Carla, but I don't deal well with simpletons, I will see you soon, and don't forget to give that to Mr. Glynn for me. Thanks."

She handed the envelope to Carla, but Gina snatched it out of her hand. Carla just stared at her like she was crazy. Dakota pushed the issues.

"What is wrong with you Gina? That is for Mr. Glynn!" Dakota shouted loud enough for everyone in the vicinity to hear her.

Gina got right up in her face; nose to nose. Dakota didn't flinch.

"You thought you was slick, didn't you bitch?" she whispered.

Dakota smiled sweetly at her, but didn't answer.

"What's this, huh?" she held the envelope up to Dakota's face.

"It's for Mr. Glynn…" Carla interrupted as Mr. Glynn walked out of his office. But Gina's back was to him, and she didn't see him coming her way.

"Shut up! I wasn't talking to you was I?"

She tore the envelope open and snatched the contents out, but stared at them as if in a daze. Her brain couldn't compute what she was looking at and how it pertained to her.

"Well, what is it, Ms. Hefel?" Mr. Glynn asked directly behind her.

She spun around and looked at her boss, but no words would come.

"Why are you opening my packages and causing a scene outside of my office. Did you know I have a client in there that can hear your entire conversation?"

"I, I apologize…" Gina began, handing the envelope over to him.

"Save it. Take the rest of the day off to think about it."

Gina looked at Dakota, who was shaking her head at her.

"Get some help, Gina." Dakota told her and walked out.

"You are in dangerous territory, Ms. Hefel. Get it together before you return tomorrow."

"I will."

Gina walked back to her office seething with hate for Dakota. She couldn't believe she'd let Dakota get her out of her element at work. She had fallen for her little trick. Everything in her wanted to get Dakota back today, but she was too tired, and a little nauseous. All she could do was go home and lay down for now.

Dakota breezed out of the lobby still laughing at how well her plan worked. She couldn't wait to meet up with Brandon for lunch and tell him all about her day so far. She backed out but had trouble turning her steering wheel. She put the truck in park and got out to see what was wrong. Dakota couldn't believe it; both of her front tires were flat. She looked up and saw Gina exiting the building and knew she'd done it, but she couldn't figure out how or when.

"Car trouble?" Gina called out, and flipped Dakota the bird.

"You can take the girl out the ghetto, but you can't take the ghetto out the girl huh?"

"Fuck you bitch, you better be glad I didn't cut you instead of them fucking tires."

"Do it hoe, if you so bad. If you think I ain't strapped…" Dakota popped her glove box open and reached inside. "I'm right here!"

Gina wanted to hurt her so bad, but her stomach was churning and she felt like she was going to blow chunks right in front of Dakota, but she wouldn't give her the satisfaction. She started running towards her car.

"You better run trick!" she yelled. She was really fed up with this whole situation. She couldn't believe Gina had her out here ready to fight and shit.

Dakota pulled herself back together and had On-Star send roadside assistance to change her tires and had Brandon to pick her up for lunch. She refused to allow Gina to ruin her victory.

CHAPTER 34

Gina only made it two blocks down the road before she had to pull over. She ran into the bushes on the side of the road and let her stomach empty out. She wished she had just stayed home that day like she started to do. All she wanted to do was crawl into bed and sleep the day away. She got home in record time and did just that. She stripped on the way up the stairs and fell asleep five minutes after her head hit the pillow.

She slept hard. And when she awoke it was dark, but she didn't know what time it was. Her digital clock was flashing 12 o'clock so she assumed the power had gone out at one point while she was sleeping. She lay awake in the dark listening to the rain falling outside. Lightening flashed and lit up her room temporarily, followed by loud, crashing thunder. Storms didn't bother Gina, she loved the sound of rain. It was very relaxing to her. Soon her stomach was rumbling as loud as the thunder, so she got up to fix something to eat. Not sure if she had caught a 24 hour bug or not, she opted to warm up some chicken noodle soup and got back in the bed to watch TV.

Sleep overtook her once again, but this time her dreams kept her tossing and turning. In her dream the events of the day turned out completely different. Somehow she got the best of Dakota and was sitting on her chest punching her in the face with all her might. It felt so good to finally let all of her aggression out on the one person she hated the most in the world. The only one standing between Gina and her happily ever after with Brandon. She pounded her face until it was unrecognizable; struggling so much, that she woke herself up.

Gina sat up. She was washed down in sweat and breathing heavily. The dream felt so real and it still had her in its grip. She wanted to finish what she started in the dream. Instead, she got in the shower to wash away the sweat and tried to relax enough to fall back asleep.

Gina slept a little more but never fell back into real sleep, so she was up and ready for work early the next day. She was grateful to feel much better, she wanted to show Mr. Glynn that she could bounce back quickly. She stopped at her favorite coffee shop and got a latte and a cheese Danish. When she arrived at work she felt optimistic about the day ahead.

Once she was settled into her office, she began reading her email to catch up on whatever she'd missed the day before. She wasn't really friends with any of her coworkers and she was pretty sure everyone was discussing what happened yesterday, so she wasn't going to ask anyone what she'd missed. She had several unopened emails to read. After forty-five minutes of reading email after email, she decided to take a break. The first thing she did was try to go onto Dakota's page. She realized that she had been blocked, but that didn't bother her because she had more than one account. She started logging into her other account. Her phone chimed with a text message.

Bye Gina

She wasn't in the mood for Dakota's bullshit this morning. As soon as she logged in, she was going to plaster Dakota's page with pictures of herself and Brandon. Turning back to her computer she thought her screen had timed out because it was a blacked out. Then suddenly a countdown appeared on her screen counting from ten to zero. She figured the computers were being updated or something and paid it no mind.

"I'll go get some coffee, maybe the update will be complete when I get back." She thought.

Gina walked down the hall, avoiding eye contact with any higher-ups and staring down anybody else that dared look at her. She liked intimidating people, she found that it kept them at bay and she didn't have to pretend to be friends with anyone in the office. Especially those who couldn't help her to get ahead. She got her coffee and was deep in thought about which pictures she was going to post to Dakota's timeline, as soon as her computer came back up.

Someone ran past her in the hallway and snapped her out of her daze. She looked up and noticed people gathered around computers in clusters. A couple of them were looking up at her and pointing. She wondered what was going on, and walked faster to get back to her office. On her computer screen there was a movie clip playing, but she couldn't tell what it was at first. She watched a little longer and slowly it dawned on her why the scene seemed familiar. It was the hotel room, she went to thinking that she was going to meet Brandon.

She frantically began pressing keys trying to make the video stop. It just kept playing no matter what she did. Her heart beat sped up and she felt light headed. She fell back into her chair and watched in horror as she stuffed the butt plug up her ass. The memories came flooding back over her and tears welled up in her eyes just thinking about all of her coworkers seeing what was coming next. She was mortified and wanted to get away quick.

She threw her purse over her shoulder and grabbed her brief case and cell phone. Her mind was on overload and she was in a flight response mode. She felt all eyes on her as she tried to escape the spotlight. She desperately pressed the call button for the elevator.

"Going somewhere Ms. Hefel?" Mr. Glynn asked.

"Not, now Mr. Glynn, I don't know who is doing this to me, but I am not responsible for any of this."

"I know that you aren't responsible for sending this video."

She stopped pressing the button and looked at her boss with a glimmer of hope in her eyes.

"But, you are responsible for making such a video in the first place and I'm sorry but we don't need anyone with such poor judgment working in this office. Please don't come back, we'll have your things sent to you."

The elevator doors opened and Mr. Glynn turned and walked away. The people in the elevator shuffled away from Gina as if she were a leper. Gina was so distraught she slid down to the elevator floor and cried like a baby. When the elevator opened on the ground level everyone exited and left her there alone. Just as the doors were closing, Tom blocked the doors. He looked at her on the floor; a broken shell of the woman she was. He helped her up and took her out to his car and drove her home.

Tom pulled into the parking lot of Gina's condo and turned the ignition off. They hadn't exchanged a word during the ride to her place, but Tom needed to know something.

"Here we are." Tom said.

Gina didn't reply, only stared out the car window.

"Do you want me to come inside with you for a while?" he offered.

More silence and staring. It seemed Gina was gone and only this scrap remained. Tom didn't know what to say or to do to comfort or console her, but he had to say something.

"Gina, who did this to you and why?"

He prayed she would answer him, but she did not.

"I hate to bring it up, but I noticed there were other men on some of the videos, and the videos were made in your condo…"

She turned her head and gave him a look as cold as ice.

"You wanna know if you were on any videos, huh?

"Yes. I mean, I don't see any reason why I should have been recorded, but…"

"You weren't."

Relief washed over him, and he offered again to stay with her for a while. Gina shook her head no, and got out of the car. Slowly she made her way to her door, entered and never looked back. That was the last Tom ever saw of her.

Once she was alone inside her home, Gina thought about what Tom said in the car. She hadn't been aware that there was more than the one video of her, which she made at the hotel. He said something about other men, and the footage was shot in her house. The only footage she could think of was from her surveillance equipment. But how did Dakota get her hands on it? This question ate away at her mind for over an hour, until it suddenly hit her. The only person that even knew about the footage or the surveillance was the installer. Tim.

"That low down, ass-waggling, little bitch! He is responsible for this."

But how and when did these two dummies get together and hatch a plan against her? She wondered. It didn't matter now, all that mattered now was revenge. But even revenge would have to wait right now; Gina was exhausted and just wanted to sleep. Usually the thought of revenge, or blackmailing someone had her buzzing with excitement, but she just couldn't shake this feeling right now. She left her half eaten sandwich on the countertop and staggered to her bed and was soon fast asleep.

But she did not get any rest. She tossed and turned; tormented with dreams of Brandon and Dakota. In one, they were hunting her down like prey through a maze. She ran and ran, and the maze got longer and more puzzling with every twist and turn. She tried with all her might, but she couldn't out run them. They found her in each hiding place.

In another dream, she was in an arena fighting for her life as a gladiator, while Brandon and Dakota sat in the place of Caesar. They watched her along with all of the screaming fans, cheering for her demise. Overgrown men swung axes, chains, and swords at her with no regard for her pleas to stop. She begged for mercy, but all of her cries fell on deaf ears. At the very end, a challenger had her pinned on the ground. He looked up to Brandon for instruction, as the crowd chanted kill, kill, kill. Brandon, who was feeding grapes to Dakota, looked at her with contempt and gave the thumbs down signal, which meant kill.

Gina awoke screaming. With no one there to console her, she had to calm herself. It was one of the drawbacks to living alone. Normally she loved being alone, but today she could really use a shoulder to cry on. Just before the dream faded she saw Brandon's face in her mind, and the contempt he had for her, in his eyes; it broke her heart. For the first time in her life, she wished she had never met Brandon West.

CHAPTER 35

It was finally here! The big day Dakota had waited for was here at last. She was up with the chickens, even though her wedding was an after five affair. She had lots of things to do and to have done to her. She stood under the shower and thought to herself, that the next time she got in this shower, she would be Mrs. Brandon West. Just the thought of it made her happy.

"Mrs. Brandon West." She whispered.

She laughed out loud at herself. Why was she whispering? Brandon was not there; they would not see each other until she walked down the aisle. She missed him, but cherished the time old tradition. She couldn't wait to see him in his tux or for him to see her in her gown, they were gonna have some fabulous pictures.

"Aye! Chop, chop in there!" Yakima shouted into the bathroom. "The countdown has begun. Let's go!"

"I'm coming, let me at least rinse off."

"You better run through it like a carwash, ain't nobody trying to be late."

"Umm, we are going to my spa, I think they'll hold my spot." Dakota laughed.

"Bish! It ain't your spot I'm worried about, it's mine. I gotta look good too hun-ty!"

"Alright, alright I'm out! Are you happy now?"

"Yep. Now get dressed. And don't put on nothing that you gotta pull over your head. You getting' hair and makeup done, so if you don't want me to cut your shirt off of you, I suggest you put on a button up."

Yakima was taking her Maid of Honor position very seriously. She was almost as excited as Dakota was about the wedding. Knowing how much this meant to her best friend, she couldn't help but be happy. She wanted today to be perfect for Dakota and Brandon. She had her checklist from Dakota's mom, Ms. Karen, and every single thing on there was getting checked off.

Dakota got dressed in a comfy 2 piece jogger set and her favorite kicks. Barely out of the bedroom, and Yakima was barking more orders at her. All she could do was shake her head and follow instructions as best she could. She bounded down the stairs like a kid on Christmas morning.

"I'm ready for duty!"

Standing at attention, she saluted Yakima. Yakima rolled her eyes, but couldn't resist a smile.

"Aight, I'm driving. Get in the car, I already got everything you need in a bag in the trunk. We'll meet up with your mom at the spa."

They got in Yakima's car and before she pushed the ignition button, she turned and looked at Dakota. She was the closest thing Yakima would ever have to a sister. For a moment, they looked at each other; started giggling and started screaming and slapping fives.

"You getting' married girl! It's about to go down." Yakima said in her Kevin Heart voice.

"I know right?" Dakota screamed.

"We gotta get you to the church on time!"

"So, why we still here, let's be out!"

Yakima threw the car in reverse and headed to the spa with the music bumping.

At the spa they were sipping mimosas and eating a light snack as they got their pedicures first.

"Are you nervous?" Dakota's mom, Karen, asked her.

"No, just really, really excited. I've waited for this day for so long."

"I know. We were beginning to wonder if it would ever come." She joked.

"I started to wonder myself." Dakota confessed.

"Yeah me too." Yakima chimed in, "But I knew it would eventually come to pass. Love always wins in the end."

"Aww how sweet of you to say that Yakima." Karen said.

"Well, it's true. I look at all my parents went through to be together and I know that love wins. They couldn't afford to travel to America together, so my dad came first to earn money to bring my mom. And after years of being apart, he finally had enough saved to bring her here and enough to start his first business. Then they wasted no time making me and the rest, as they say, is history."

"What a lovely story. Dakota's dad and I struggled to get our businesses up and going as well. In the beginning it was rough, and it took a lot of love to keep it all together. It took communication, dedication and being there for each other when it all seemed too hard. But thank God, we made it through. I'm so grateful that Dakota and Brandon don't have that hurdle to cross."

"It's because of watching and learning from our parents that we are in the position we are in. Even Kima, we all learned from y'all's example." Dakota told her.

"Well then, it was all worth it.' Karen smiled. "Just know that whatever hurdles you do come up against, you can make it over if you do it together. Listen to him, let him be a man, and treat him with respect and he will return the same to you. Love him like there is no tomorrow, don't ever be afraid to show your love for him or your children, when you have them."

"I learned from the best, mom."

They moved on to the salon to start on their hair and continued their conversation there. And soon it was time to head over to the church for the ceremony Dakota had waited for all her life. All systems were go. It was time.

The ceremony was picture-perfect. Dakota's father, Nicholas, walked her down the aisle and proudly gave her away to Brandon. Brandon could not believe that Dakota could look even more stunning than usual, but she did. His eyes welled up with tears as she strolled towards him to take their vows to honor, love and cherish each other. He unveiled his beautiful bride and sealed the deal with a passionate kiss. The guests burst into applause and welcomed the newlyweds into their new lives.

The photographer had them set up on a grassy hill behind the church for their photos. The sun was positioned perfectly and the bride and groom were gorgeous together in photo after photo. The wedding party was dressed in burgundy and black, and Dakota was splendid in all white. She looked and felt like a princess. Her handsome groom was the perfect prince in his black and white tuxedo. It was just as she had dreamt it would be.

The reception hall was adorned in luxury. It was as if they had been whisked away to a far-away land. The candlelight set the ambiance and white linen, crystal and fine china topped it all off. There was a band, two bars and servers to carter to them.

Brandon and Dakota sat at the head table along with their parents and best man and maid of honor to welcome their guests and to receive their wedding gifts. The gift table was loaded with gifts of love for the couple. And soon the guests were taking turns standing to toast them. One in particular caught everyone off guard. It was Gina; she stood and put the mic to her mouth.

"Well, well, well, look at the happy couple all decked out with everyone cheering and applauding them." She sneered. "Oh, you thought I wasn't coming? Or did you think you could keep me out? I'm family, I'm the one who's supposed to be all dressed in white today, not you!" Gina slurred and sloshed champagne from her glass as she gestured towards Dakota.

Everyone was in shock. No one knew what to say. Phyllis, Gina's mom grabbed Gina's hand and tried to pull her back into her seat, but Gina wasn't having it. She pulled free and continued her barrage.

"Why is everyone looking at me like I'm crazy? Most of y'all grew up with us, you all expected it to be me up there too. Didn't you? Of course you did, because Brandon and I belong together…" she began sobbing.

Karen got up and motioned to two of her nephews, Micah and Trust, to follow her. She walked over to Gina and took the mic from her hand, and told her it was time to go. She looked at Phyllis as if to say, you can stay or you can go with her, but she is leaving here right now. Gina tried to take the mic back, and Karen's nephews interceded.

"Listen to me and listen good, it's time to go. You were not invited and you will not ruin this day for my baby. You are leaving now." she nodded to her nephews.

They grabbed Gina as she swung on them, but they managed to get her moving towards the door. Phyllis got up to leave, but she turned to apologize to everyone for Gina's outburst.

"I am so sorry to have interrupted such a beautiful ceremony, please forgive her. I don't know how many of you know about her sickness, but it seems to be getting worse and for some reason, she won't take her medication. Again, I apologize."

She walked out with her head down, ashamed. Joan got up and ran to her, gave her a hug, and spoke with her briefly before she left. Brandon turned to the band and motioned for them to carry on with the music. The wedding coordinator took charge from there and had everyone get up on the dance floor to get the festive feeling going again. Everyone was relieved that the altercation was over.

"I can't believe she still thinks you want her." Dakota whispered to Brandon

"I can't either."

"How come you never told me that she was sick? Is she sick like crazy or is she ill?"

"Actually, I forgot about it. I remember she always took medicine when we were younger. It started when her dad passed. But I've only seen her have one episode that even came close to this. So, as long as she took her meds daily, she was normal. I don't know why she stopped taking it."

"Well, she needs to get some help, cause I will still beat her ass, crazy or not."

"You ain't gonna have to fight nobody, especially in this gown. You are flawless right now."

"Right now? I'm always flawless. Shit, I woke up like this."

"Um, yeah, ok. I've seen you when you wake up..." she jabbed him in the ribs, "I'm just saying." He laughed.

"And now we will have the couple's first dance." The wedding coordinator announced.

Lay Me Down by Sam Smith began to play as Brandon escorted his beautiful bride to the dance floor. Dakota was a vision in her designer gown. Brandon held her close and sang softly along with the song into her ear. Everyone was up taking pictures and video of the happy newlyweds. Dakota felt like she was dancing on a cloud. Neither of them could have been any happier.

Afterwards everyone joined them on the dance floor and they partied the night away. They cut the cake, and threw the garter and the bouquet and were getting ready to head out to the hotel. In the morning they would be on their way to the airport. They were heading to Paris, London, and Rome for their honeymoon. It was Dakota's dream come true and Brandon knew it.

He wanted everything to be perfect, he wanted her to be happy for the rest of her life. He knew in his heart that he would do everything in his power to make sure all of their firsts were together. Just like this first trip to Europe and one day their first child together. Right now, he was looking forward to making love to his wife for the first time as Mrs. Brandon West.

CHAPTER 36

Three Weeks Later

"Our trip was amazing! It was straight out of a fairy tale. My husband thought of everything."

"I saw the pictures, it looked like heaven on earth." Kim said.

"Kim, I wish everyone would have a honeymoon like that. It's just something a girl has to have in her life."

"I agree and I can't wait for my fairytale ending. One day."

"Yes, one day it will happen. Look how long it took me."

"Girl, please. You are only 24 Dakota."

"And you are only 26 Kim, it will happen keep the faith. But for now, hold all my calls, I have got a ton of work to catch up on."

"Ok, I will. Let me know if you want all this mail or not."

"Oh, yeah bring it in and put it over there on the couch, I'll go through it soon. Thanks."

Dakota pulled up her email and began to tackle the hundreds of emails that were waiting for her. She loved the new electronic invoicing she began using before she left for her honeymoon. She had received literally thousands of dollars in payment for future bookings at her spa. This money was going to come in handy for her expansion that was getting under way this week.

Her cell rang. It was Yakima.

"Hey boo!"

"I missed your ass like air girl!"

"I missed you too hunty!"

"Ok, so I know you catching up on work and bills and shit, so let's meet up for lunch at our spot, k?"

"Of course darling, I have so much to tell you about."

"I know that's right. See you soon, my client just walked in, gotta go."

"Alright, bye."

She hung up smiling thinking about sharing all of her memories with Kima. Plus she had some gifts to give her best friend. She had gotten Yakima lots of designer gear in Europe, she knew her favorite designers and that Yakima stayed on fleek. Prada, Louis Vuitton, and Dolce and Gabbana to name a few; she couldn't wait to see her face. Dakota shopped in each destination, she damn near had a whole new wardrobe with the money her parents sent with them as a part of their wedding gift. Even Brandon was tearing the shops down, on their honeymoon.

Dakota closed her eyes for a moment and was instantly back in Paris, France, sitting outside of a quaint bistro and sipping fine wine and eating delicious hors d'oeuvres. She could smell all of the delicious scents in the air, and feel the breeze on her face; she vowed to learn French for the next trip. It was all so perfect, just as she'd envisioned it being.

Now that it was over, she was ready to work harder than ever to grow her already lucrative business, to ensure that the Wests were jet setters. She wanted to see the whole world. And she definitely wanted her children to be international globe trotters too. So, she had some work to do, break time was over.

Dakota went over to the couch and decided to tackle some of the mail. She began sorting them into piles; accounts payable, accounts receivable, marketing, personal, etc. She ran through the mail pretty quickly until she got to a large manila envelope. Her mind immediately flashed back to the photos she received from Gina, and the hairs on the back of her neck stood up on end.

She hadn't thought about Gina's crazy ass, or 'Cra-Cra' as she started calling her, since before she went on her honeymoon, three weeks ago. The last she'd seen her was when she was being dragged from her wedding reception. Now here was another envelope, obviously delivered by messenger, not mail. Dakota did not feel like no bullshit today.

She snatched the envelope open, dumped it onto the couch and stared at the contents, trying to figure out what she was looking at. It was brochures and papers. Dakota dissolved into laughter; the package was from her designer, for the new addition to her spa. Maybe Gina really was a distant memory after all she thought to herself.

All of the mail was sorted and delegated by the time she headed out to meet Yakima for lunch. She already knew what she was having for lunch, she always had the same thing at their spot; seafood Portofino. But today she was really craving the seafood.

As a matter of fact, she had eaten mostly seafood abroad, it was the main thing she wanted in each destination.

That was another reason she was going on a diet, starting next week, she had gained at least 7lbs on her trip. But she wasn't going to worry about it today, because today she was still celebrating, and she had some gifts to give out. Since she and Brandon had spent the Christmas holidays out of the country, they were eager to give their loved ones their gifts. Dakota grabbed her gift bags from the back of her truck and headed into the restaurant. She had just hung up the phone with Brandon when Yakima arrived.

They screamed and carried on as if they hadn't seen each other for years instead of weeks.

"Oh my gawd! Look at you, you're glowing!" Yakima observed.

"I know right? Girl it was all of that and then some."

"I know, I saw the pictures. You know you shoulda took me..." Yakima whined.

"I wanted to, but Brandon was like 'nah'"

"What-evs, wit his blocking ass. Anyway, what did you bring me?"

"Not too much, but I got you a little something, something."

She held the bags up and Yakima pretended to faint. Dakota sprinkled water on her face, and when she 'woke up' she ordered a bottle of wine and told the waitress to bring it stat! Yakima wasted no time tearing into her gifts, and the two laughed and caught each other up on the latest and greatest over the last three weeks that they were apart. They decided to make it a day, and neither of them went back to work.

When they finally decided to head over to Dakota's house, it had started raining. It was a lite shower, but it was steady. Dakota jumped in her truck and shivered from the cold winter rain. She put the heat up high and turned on her seat warmers, waiting to warm up a little before pulling off. She looked out her window and saw Kima on her phone, apparently warming her car up too.

She turned on her music and backed out when she saw Yakima's reverse lights. Yakima was going to follow her to her house. All they had to do was jump on the interstate and they'd be there in 10 minutes. Dakota pulled over into the far right lane to get onto the entrance ramp, but got caught by a red light. She heard a noise as she pressed the brakes a little harder than she anticipated. She looked in the rearview mirror hoping that none of her other gifts were being damaged.

She turned to get a better look but the light changed, and she decided against it. She was speeding up to merge with the interstate traffic. Her eyes glanced back and forth, between the cars ahead of her, and the side view mirror of the oncoming cars. She saw an opening and pressed on the accelerator to get up to speed with the other cars. She set the cruise-control, since she'd been drinking and didn't want to be stopped for speeding.

Looking to see where Yakima was, she checked the rearview mirror again, but instead of cars, she saw something else. A dark figure was slowly sitting up in her back seat. Dakota thought she was tripping. Trying not to panic, she turned and looked back, to assure herself that she was alone in her car. But she was not alone.

"It's all your fault, you know." Gina told her.

Dakota screamed out of shock. She couldn't focus on the road; afraid to take her eyes off of Gina.

"Bitch shut the fuck up with your scary ass! If I wanted to hurt you I would have already done it."

Dakota didn't know what to do, she couldn't think straight.

"Then why the fuck are you in my car?"

"I don't know, I just sorta ended up here while I was waiting for you to come out of the restaurant. It got really cold and then it started raining so…"

Gina's voice trailed off. She was disturbingly calm and her voice was deeper than usual.

"And I can't be out there like that, in my condition." Gina was saying.

"*Yeah in your crazy ass condition*" Dakota thought, but she didn't want to provoke her. "Have you taken your meds today Gina?" she asked pleasantly.

"Don't pretend to know or care about me, you fucking home wrecker."

"Wait, how the hell am I a home wrecker and you want my fucking husband?"

Gina began shaking her head back and forth, back and forth, like she was trying to ward off evil or some voice telling her to do wrong.

Dakota reached for her phone to call Brandon, but Gina saw her. Thinking she was reaching for a weapon, she lunged at her. Gina put Dakota in a headlock and was choking her like a wrestler.

"It's all your fault. Youuuuuu are the reason. I'm so tired of youuuuuuu." She sang in Dakota's ear.

Dakota struggled to break free, but her wind pipe was closed. She clawed at Gina's face and arms, but it had no effect on her. Gina just kept on singing her strange song in Dakota's ear, and choking her as if she thought the truck was on auto-pilot.

"If youuuu never came along, I wouldn't be singing this song…" Gina threw her head back and sang at the top of her lungs.

Dakota felt like she was looking through a tunnel, as everything around her turned grey, then there was total darkness. And as the front wheels left the road, the truck began to flip.

CHAPTER 37

Dakota lay very still. She could hear a steady beeping close by and muffled voices far away. She opened her eyes and began to squint. Her eyes hurt from the light, but she didn't know why. She didn't recognize her surroundings, but it looked like a hospital room. She strained to sit up, but felt too weak.

"Hey beautiful, you decided to wake up." Brandon said softly.

Dakota smiled at the sound of Brandon's voice. She turned towards him and tried to speak. To her surprise, no words came out. Her throat felt like it was filled with sand; grainy and dry. She looked to Brandon questioningly.

"It's ok. The doctors said that you may have trouble speaking at first, because of all the pressure applied to your windpipe. But no worries, you'll be yakking again in no time." He joked. "Be easy, it's no rush."

He leaned in and kissed her softly on the forehead, eyes, nose and her lips.

"Your parents just left to get something to eat. We were all here since last night when you were brought in by the ambulance. Yakima came but, you know how she is with hospitals, ever since her grandfather was in one, she can't take it."

Dakota nodded. She knew how close Yakima was to her grandfather and how long and drawn out his death was. They went to the hospital day and night to be with him and Yakima held on to the hope that he would leave there with them. Instead, he died in the hospital and Yakima was alone with him when he went. So Dakota understood why her friend wasn't there.

But she was still blurry on all of the events that led up to herself being there. And why couldn't she talk? What had happened to her? She remembered leaving the restaurant and seeing Yakima on the phone. It was raining and cold, so she'd let the truck warm up a bit before she left for home. She remembered wanting to call Brandon urgently, but why? And why didn't she just call him? What could have kept her from it, and how did that lead to her being in the hospital? Her thoughts were interrupted by an officer coming into her room.

"Excuse me Mrs. West, I am detective Jones. I hate to bother you, but I have some questions about the accident."

"Come in. I can't promise you that I have all the answers you want, some things are a little blurry in my memory." She whispered in a hoarse voice.

"That's ok, just answer as honestly and completely as you can. This will help us in the investigation. Can you tell me, in your own words, what happened on yesterday?"

"Ok. I went to meet my friend for lunch. We hadn't seen each other in a while, because I was away on my honeymoon, with my husband. This is my husband, Brandon."

"We met last night, baby." Brandon told her.

"Oh, alright. And um, we were catching up with each other. And decided to continue at my house. So, we left the restaurant, in the rain. Yes, I remember it was raining and pretty cold too."

Dakota smiled at having remembered something new. Brandon held her hand, and detective Jones nodded for her to continue.

"Well, I was waiting for the car to warm up, and so was Kima. She was going to follow me to my place. Anyway, we got on I-26 and then something happened. I wanted to call Brandon. I remember that. I wanted to call him but for some reason, I couldn't."

Brandon squeezed her hand and mouthed "I'm here" to her. She thought back on the situation and felt a sense of anxiety overcoming her. Her heartbeat sped up and her eyes widened as if she saw something everyone else did not. Her parents, who had returned while she was recounting the incident to the officer, came to her side to calm her.

"What is it honey? You can tell daddy." Her father told her, taking her other hand in his.

"Yes, Mrs. West, whatever you can tell us will be helpful, no matter how insignificant it may seem or how hard. You are protected from any harm now. Did you remember something new?" the detective asked.

"I couldn't breathe...I was struggling...someone was singing to me and I couldn't stop them."

"Was it a song on the radio?" Her mother asked.

"Please allow me to do the questioning ma'am, sir." Detective Jones looked at her parents for confirmation that they understood how important this was. They both nodded their consent and allowed him to continue.

"You said 'someone was singing to me', who was it? Can you see the person?"

"No. I can't see them, they're behind me...choking me! I was choking and I was struggling to get free, but she wouldn't let go."

"She. Who is she? Think back now..."

"Gina! It was Gina! She was in my truck when I got into it."

"Did you see her when you entered the vehicle?"

"No, I didn't see her until I was on the interstate. She just kept saying it was all my fault, over and over again. That's what she was singing to me when she was choking me!"

"What did she think was your fault, Mrs. West?"

Dakota looked at Brandon, and the detective followed her gaze.

"She believes that I am the only reason she doesn't have my husband's last name. She must have been stalking me to know where I was, and then waited to get me alone. She's crazy you know."

Brandon held a cup of water for her to sip. She sipped it and her throat felt better.

"So she hid in your vehicle, waited until you were on the interstate, and then attacked you. Is that correct?"

"Yes. She accused me of being a home wrecker, and when I went to get my phone to call Brandon, she attacked me. She choked me until I passed out, and woke up here."

"Do you remember anything else? Anything at all?"

Dakota thought for a moment and shook her head no.

"Thank you for answering my questions ma'am, that's all for now, but we may have more questions for you soon. Here is my card if you think of anything or have any questions for me."

"I have a question for you now. Where is she? What happened to her?"

"Ms. Hefel is at home. She was released this morning, from this hospital. However, she has a very different story than you."

"What is she saying?" Dakota asked.

"Well, she says that you followed her to the restaurant; that she woke up in your vehicle and was fighting to be freed when you crashed." He told her, watching her reaction carefully.

"She's a liar! I told you she was crazy." Dakota stated.

"So, what does that mean? Dakota is telling you what really happened." Brandon spoke up.

"That's what we need to find out. To whom, if any, charges will pressed. For what it's worth, I believe you Mrs. West, but for now, please don't leave town. I'll be in touch."

Detective Jones left. Leaving Dakota determined to prove her innocence and to be free of Gina's crazy ass forever.

"Well it's a clear cut case." Her father, Nicholas, said simply. "She is crazy as all hell, and you were the victim of her misplaced anger."

Nicholas was a fan of anything mystery. He watched CSI, read mystery novels, and watched mystery movies. He knew a thing or two about how crime solving worked; he explained the process to them.

"All the police have to do is find out whose alibi is legitimate. We all know that Dakota left her business, where her employees can verify the time she left. The waitress and Yakima can provide eye witness account of where she was, and how long she was there. Also, the time stamp on her receipt tells approximately what time she left the restaurant. That along with the time that 911 was called, all corroborate my child's account of events. This psychopath, on the other hand, was sneaking to do everything that she did. She had no witnesses that can account for the time lapse, while she lay in wait for my daughter. It doesn't take a genius to figure out that she is indeed in need of medication, and is not taking it regularly. So, all in all, I say don't worry your pretty little head about it baby girl. They will have her in custody soon enough."

"No, not soon enough." Her mother interjected. "We don't know where this crazy girl is, or who is keeping an eye on her. Hell no, she won't get another chance to hurt my baby again. I'm getting my own detective on it. Someone who will know Gina's every move and report to me."

"Who you thinking about using, ma?" Brandon asked.

"Samuel Jackson."

"The actor?"

"No, he just has the same name without the middle initial L. But he is a damn good detective and he will get the job done."

"Good. And Dakota won't leave my site until all of this is over and done with." Brandon assured them. "I hate to say it, but I think Gina may end up in an institution for a long time."

"Probably." Karen agreed. "She does need help. I feel bad for Phyllis. Joan says she did the best she could with that child after Jeff passed. And she seemed to be doing well, from the outside looking in. Graduated from law school, passed the bar, had a career; such a shame she had this illness." Karen said shaking her head.

"I wonder why she stopped taking her meds." Dakota said. "Remember at the wedding reception, her mom said for some reason she wouldn't take them lately and she's been getting worse over time. So she must have stopped recently."

"Ain't no tellin'." Brandon replied. "But she's home, now we've gotta get you well and out of here."

"Yes, I wanna go home."

CHAPTER 38

Dakota was putting away the last dish from breakfast when the doorbell rang. She went to the security control panel to view who was at the door. She was being extra careful, although her mom had a private detective following Gina day and night. It was detective Jones and before she could answer, Brandon opened the door, and let the detective inside. They talked briefly in the foyer and then came into the kitchen to talk to Dakota.

"Good morning, Mrs. West. How are you feeling?" Det. Jones asked.

"Good morning, I'm feeling much better, thank you. Have a seat."

They all sat around the island, Dakota and Brandon on one side and the detective on the other side.

"I'm sure you're both anxious to know what's going on with your case. And that's why I'm here, I have some news." He looked at the couple for a long while.

"Well are you going to share the news with us?" Brandon asked.

"Yes, of course. We have issued a warrant for Ms. Hefel's arrest. We are looking for her now."

Brandon and Dakota hugged, grateful that the ordeal was almost over.

"My mother can tell you where she is, she has a detective following Gina." Dakota offered.

"Actually, that private eye, informed us that Ms. Hefel allegedly drugged him and he couldn't move for a period of time. During which time she confessed her plan to get rid of you, Mrs. West. And after a blood test confirmed the drug in his system, the judge issued a warrant for her arrest."

Dakota was ashamed that she hadn't believed Brandon when he told her about the drug that Gina used on him. But now she was worried about where Gina was, and what she was doing.

"Where are you looking? What leads do you have?" Brandon wanted to know.

"Currently we have an A. P. B. out and a description. We want you to stay inside, Mrs. West and do not leave here unless it is absolutely necessary. Do you understand?" Det. Jones asked.

"Yes. What did the private eye say she planned to do to me?"

"Remember that she is unstable, but she was saying that you would be out of the way, so that her family could be together."

Brandon turned her face towards his.

"You ain't got nothing to worry about baby. I'm right here and I ain't gonna let shit happen to you." Brandon pulled her into his arms.

"And we have a patrol car parked across the street until she is apprehended. But if you need me, call me, or if it's an emergency dial 911 immediately."

"We will. Thanks."

Brandon walked the detective out and set the alarm. Dakota went upstairs to lay down. Too many thoughts ran through her head, for her to concentrate. She knew that Gina blamed her for the story she made up in her head. She knew Gina was mentally unstable, and she knew that Gina had put her in the hospital recently, but she couldn't believe Gina really wanted her dead. The thought hit her like a ton of bricks.

Brandon found her on the bed, and laid down behind her, in the spoon position. He hadn't said anything in front of the detective, but he had a burner in the safe, and anyone who threatened his could get it. He wouldn't hesitate to air Gina's ass out if she came over there on some murderous shit.

About an hour passed, and somehow they had dozed off. Dakota's cell rang, waking them both out of sleep. Brandon sat up behind her to see who it was. She picked up the phone displaying detective Jones' number. She put it on speaker phone.

"Hello?"

"Mrs. West, its Detective Jones. We've got Ms. Hefel in custody."

"Wow! That was pretty quick."

"Yeah we were tipped off by a merchant. She was trying to purchase a gun and didn't want to wait the required time to register the firearm, so she attempted to bribe him. I thought you'd want to know. I'll keep you updated, have a good evening." He hung up.

Dakota looked at Brandon.

"Now what?" She asked.

"What do you mean?"

"Every time we think it's over, it's always something else with this chick."

"Naw, this time, it's a wrap. Now we just go to court and hope the judge does the right thing. Either she going to jail or she going to an institution, but she's outta our life for good this time." He assured her.

Yet Dakota couldn't shake the feeling that was creeping over her. She knew logically that it was over, but her intuition told her otherwise; she prepared for the worst.

Gina lay on the bottom bunk in her cell, thinking about her plans for the future. At the hospital, they discovered her little secret, but it was cool because no one else knew. So it was still to her advantage. They had also given her medicine intravenously and now she was able to think a little clearer. It was like a fog was lifted and she could see her whole plan clearly. Not everyone had the patience that she had, it was a hard learned skill. She had learned it the hard way waiting for Brandon all of these years. And now it was going to pay off big time.

The police thought they had stopped her by arresting her, but how wrong they were. They hadn't stopped shit. In fact they had probably helped her formulate a better plan. Now she would just serve enough time to solidify her role in Brandon's life; he would need her so much more than he ever realized before.

The officers here were force feeding her meds daily. At first she resisted so much that they had to restrain her, but an inmate told her they had access to her hospital records, in order to give her the appropriate meds. So, now she looked forward to her dosage; it helped keep the fog away from her mind.

Once she was sentenced, as she knew she would be, all the parts of her plan would be in place. She figured she would get sentenced anywhere from 5 to 15 years. That would drive some people crazy, no pun intended, but not Gina. She could wait that long to have the perfect life with Brandon. Hell, she had waited damn near that long now, but now she had the missing piece to the puzzle.

With this final piece, the puzzle was complete and she could see the whole picture; and so would Brandon and Dakota. Dakota, most importantly, would see that she was not a part of the picture anymore. She would see that the bond between Gina and Brandon could never be severed or replaced. And here's the kicker, the whole time that Gina would be serving time, her ties to Brandon would, literally, be growing tighter and stronger.

Luckily, Gina had a cell by herself, and she was glad. She had been approached by some of the inmates for sex. During the day she could avoid it, but she knew what all of the crying and protesting was about late at night. She heard the pleas of the women that were being forced to perform sexual acts, and she saw the bruises on the ones that defended their territory, so to speak. Each day she prayed that she would keep her private cell. And each day she prayed that she would be sentenced to a psych ward, rather than a prison.

She imagined, in a psych ward, she would have her own room that they would lock her safely into each night. Each day she would go to the cafeteria for meals, to a therapist for treatment, and the rest of the time would be spent in the activity center playing games or watching television. Maybe she had watched one to many movies, but at least it had to be better than prison. She hadn't done anything deserving of prison, in her mind.

Soon though, her luck ran out, and she was assigned a cell mate. She had almost made it, in another week she would be sentenced. Her cell mate's name was Daphne and apparently she was not new to the game. She was just as tall as Gina and a truly big boned girl. She spoke to most of the inmates by name as the guards walked her to the cell. Gina's plan was to just keep her mouth closed and not interact with Big D, as she was called, but that plan went out the window before the guards were out of sight.

"What up bitch? Hop yo' ass up out my bunk, you up top from now on." Big D said matter-of-factly.

Gina just stared at her trying to figure out her next move.

"What the fuck? Is you deaf or what? Get yo ass the fuck up!"

Gina got up slowly, keeping eye contact with her new cell mate. She wasn't doing it to intimidate Daphne, she just didn't want to turn her head and get snuck. However, she didn't want no trouble with only a week or so to go before sentencing.

"Oh, so you can hear, huh? Now get your shit off my bunk and make it up for me."

She threw her sheets at Gina to put on the bed, but Gina let them fall on the floor instead. They stared at each other. A guard walking by, looked into the cell. Daphne smiled at the guard and then smiled at Gina.

"Everything straight in here. We ain't got no problems. Right?" she looked at Gina.

Gina turned away and started stripping her sheets off the bottom bunk. The guard eyed Daphne and then they both watched Gina, bent over the bottom bunk.

"Yo, let Officer Sanchez know where I'm at when he comes in for night shift. Can you do that for me Officer Middleton?"

"Yeah I can, if you can stay out of trouble today, D."

"Not a problem, not a problem at all." She agreed.

The guard continued on and Daphne turned her attention back to Gina as she prepared the top bunk. She walked up behind her squeezed her ass slowly, and deliberately. Gina didn't stop what she was doing, she acted as if she didn't feel a thing.

"You think you tough, newbie? I can feel your heart beating out your back, 'bout to break your fucking rib cage, but you playing it cool. I like that. We'll see how cool you are tonight after lights out tho."

Gina waited for her to walk away before climbing onto her new bunk. She was not looking forward to tonight. She made herself a promise that whatever happened, she would not cry and she would not plead. This was just another hurdle to get over, to get to her fairy tale ending.

That night, Gina was shocked when an officer came inside her cell and began undressing. Apparently it was the officer Sanchez that Daphne had asked about earlier, because she got undressed faster than he did. Gina hoped they would get caught, but it soon became obvious that the other guards knew what was going on.

"Get down here bitch and give my dude some head." Daphne ordered

She snatched the cover off of Gina and grabbed one of her legs to pull her off the bunk. Gina got up on her own. She could tell the officer wasn't going to let her off the hook, so she began to kneel down.

"Get naked and hurry up." Daphne barked at her.

She stripped down and began giving him head. Thankfully, he smelled and tasted clean. He and Big D were kissing and fondling each other while she sucked him off. Big D was behind her grinding on the back of her head; she was sandwiched between the two of them. Just when she thought she couldn't take anymore, Big D announced that it was her turn now.

She laid back on her bunk with her legs spread eagle waiting for Gina to lick her into orgasm. Gina remembered her promise to herself, not to plead. So she did what she had to do. Big D grabbed the back of her head and pushed her face up into her hairy pussy, humping like a nympho.

Then she felt Officer Sanchez mounting her from the back. He spit on his hand and rubbed it across her pussy and pushed his way into her. They had her sandwiched again, banging her from both ends. He was jabbing her pussy as fast and as hard as he could and she was trying to grind Gina's teeth out of her mouth. Finally Big D came and wanted some dick.

Gina thought she was off the hook until Big D told her what she expected her to do. She wanted Gina to eat her out while Sanchez hit it from the back. Gina started to protest, but decided against it, besides Big D had already straddled her face, and was bending over to give Sanchez access to fuck her. He slid in and Gina could feel her wetness dribble down on her face. She wanted to throw up, but instead she licked and sucked the clit that was in her mouth.

Soon they were humping and grinding like she was a vibrator and not a human being they were both laying on top of.

"Don't you cum in me, you hear me?" Big D warned.

"Ooo, don't worry, I won't"

But Gina knew he was close. His ball were hitting her mouth so much, she began licking and sucking them too. She wanted this to be over as soon as possible. Big D started cuming first and her body went stiff. She pressed herself hard against Gina's face. Gina couldn't breathe until her orgasm passed.

"I'mma get some of that ass too." He told Big D.

"Get it. Get it good." She cried out.

He wasted no time getting in her ass and pumping as hard as he could. Soon Daphne's legs gave out. All Gina could do was turn her head to the side and snatch air when she could.

"I'm cumming!" he told her.

She pulled away from him and he shot his load in Gina's face. They both laughed and went over to the sink to clean up a little. Gina just laid there humiliated. Until he left and Big D kicked her off the bunk. She washed herself quietly and got into her bunk and eventually drifted off to sleep.

This was the routine every day for the rest of the time Gina was there. They treated her like a slave. They had Gina lay face down on the bunk, with Big D laying on top of her, so that Sanchez could 'double dip' into both of them. He'd fuck Gina for a while and slide up to fuck Daphne, then back down into Gina again.

Once they stretched Gina's ass hole, repeatedly pulling it open, for 10 minutes in an attempt to fist her ass. Finally they gave up and let Big D, whose hand was smaller than Sanchez's, fist her pussy while he fucked her in the ass. And through it all, Gina never shed a tear or pleaded for them to stop. She was counting down the days. And today was the day, she would be sentenced and never have to see Big D or Sanchez ever again.

CHAPTER 39

Brandon and Dakota sat in anticipation of the judge's verdict after hearing Gina's case. The court room was packed, but it wasn't like the cases Dakota had seen on television, it was tiny and cramped. Most of the people there were reporters who were only covering the case because Gina had recently worked for the District Attorney. Aside from them, Yakima, Karen, Nicholas, Joan, and Phyllis were all there also. Phyllis looked terrible, this case was really wearing on her, and it showed.

Gina on the other hand, looked just fine. She was looking around the courtroom as if she were a spectator at an event. If Dakota hadn't experienced it first hand, she would have never believed that Gina was crazy for an instant. She looked perfectly sane.

"But most of the really crazy ones do, don't they?" she thought

"All rise for the Honorable Judge Marion." The bailiff called out.

The judge entered as everyone stood. Dakota noticed that Gina looked like she'd gained weight. She wondered what they were feeding her in jail.

"You may be seated. This court is now in session. The Honorable Judge Marion presiding." The bailiff informed them.

The judge addressed the court and then he addressed Gina, who paid him no mind. He spoke for a while and finally came to the part that Dakota was waiting to hear.

"In the case of State versus Hefel, the court finds the defendant guilty as charged on all accounts. Ms. Hefel, would you like the opportunity to say anything to this court before your sentencing?"

Gina looked at the judge solemnly and said "I got what I wanted your honor, thanks for your help."

She turned and smiled at Dakota, then grabbed her stomach and curtsied deeply, as if addressing royalty.

"Very well, Gina Hefel you are to be committed to the Regional Mental Health Institute until such time as you can be rehabilitated or 5 years, whichever comes first."

Gina stood there like he had given her a slap on the wrist; expressionless. Dakota's senses were on the edge, something wasn't right. The judge flipped through some papers and shook his head.

"Given that you are with child, when your child is born, he or she will become a ward of the state unless paternity is established and the child's father takes custody. Otherwise your parents will have the opportunity to raise the child at that time. Do you know who fathered the child Ms. Hefel?"

Dakota's heart dropped.

"Yes I do, your honor."

Gina turned and pointed at Brandon.

"State his name, for the record, Ms. Hefel." The judge instructed her.

"Brandon West, your honor."

Dakota knew something was coming but she hadn't expected this. She wasn't prepared for this at all. She wanted to cry, but she refused to break down in front of Gina. Besides she knew that was what she wanted her to do. Gina was still trying to break them apart, even as she was being sentenced to five years of lockdown; she was content as long as she broke them up.

Brandon couldn't believe his ears. His first thought was of the last time they were together and he came inside of her. He couldn't help himself, but he did give her his seed.

"What if that is my baby?" he wondered

How could he have a baby with Gina? He was supposed to have his children with the love of his life, his wife, Dakota. He looked at Dakota, and saw the deep pain in her eyes. He couldn't take the accusation there, so he looked away. His eyes fell on his mother, and he saw the disappointment there as well. Brandon didn't know how to feel or what to do.

"Mr. West would you be willing to submit DNA to determine the paternity of this unborn child?" the judge asked him point blank.

His head was reeling and he couldn't think straight. He looked at Phyllis, whose eyes begged him to take the test and save her unborn grandchild. He decided right then to take the test.

"Yes your honor. I will." He said and grabbed a hold of Dakota's hand.

"Very well. DNA testing can be done starting in the 10th week of pregnancy by the CVS procedure. Council will give you the details and give us both the results. At that time, we will reconvene to determine the welfare of the child. For now, this court is dismissed."

Everyone stood as the judge left the courtroom first. Gina smiled happily as they escorted her out of the courtroom. The family gathered around Brandon and Dakota.

"Smart move, Brandon. You take the test and prove it's not yours and that's the end of that." Nicholas patted him on the back.

"Exactly, its time Gina started to face reality." Karen agreed.

Brandon looked at Dakota, still holding her hand. She looked hurt deeply, but she squeezed his hand.

"Well," Brandon began, and cleared his throat, "there is a chance that the baby is mine."

No one said a word. All eyes were on Dakota.

"I was aware that it could be his." She looked at her husband. "We don't keep secrets from each other, anymore."

"Whatever happens, we'll be there to help you through it." Joan told them and Dakota's parents agreed.

"Thanks Ma."

The attorney came over and spoke with Brandon briefly. He gave him a packet and shook his hand. Brandon told them all that Gina was almost out of her first trimester, so he was going to submit his DNA for testing in the morning. Everyone agreed it would be better to get it over with than too wait. Brandon knew it was better to know than to worry unnecessarily, but he was really afraid.

The ride home was long and quiet. Neither knew what to say. They were both thinking the same thing. What if this was Brandon's baby? All of their careful planning had been in vain. All of the plans to enjoy their marriage before having children could go up in smoke. And Dakota wondered if she could love Gina's child.

"I'm sorry that I've put us in this situation, Coca."

"I know."

"I wish I could take it all back, but I can't."

"If wishes were horses, we all would ride." Dakota smiled at him

"Huh?"

"It's just something my grandma used to say. Forget it."

Brandon kissed her and held her for a long time.

"If it is my child, I can't turn my back, baby."

"I wouldn't expect you to."

She hugged him tighter and prayed that the test proved he was not the father.

Dakota went with Brandon to submit his DNA the next morning. It was a simple procedure. They swabbed his mouth for a few minutes and he filled out some paper work and he was finished. Now all they had to do was wait to hear the results.

They tried to go on with life as usual, but it was not easy. Dakota was snapping on her employees and short with Kima. She even flipped on Brandon for leaving his socks on the floor. Her nerves were at the breaking point. She needed to know if her husband had a baby mama or not.

CHAPTER 40

Gina sat by the large picture window of the activity room. The landscaping at the Regional Mental Health Institute was beautiful, but Gina barely noticed. She was deep in thought. She hadn't realized that the DNA testing could be done so soon, but it was just a minor thing in her mind.

She stood up to stretch. Looking around the room, her eyes landed on a familiar face. She recognized her from the old neighborhood. It was Mrs. Green, Monica and Theresa's mom. Gina stared at her for a while; she looked so old. Gina wondered why she was still here instead of an old folk's home. She turned away, and then it hit her; Monica, worked at the facility that was doing the testing.

Gina looked around the room at the available orderlies. One in particular, had a thing for Gina. She caught his eye and motioned for him to come over.

"I need to use the phone" she told him.

"What's in it for me?" he asked looking at her body.

"I'm sure we can work something out."

"Give me a minute, I'll get you a pass."

Soon, Gina was in a secluded office talking to Monica while the orderly, Chuck, fondled her breast and ass. She figured, she would need him more and more as time went on, and he wasn't too hard on the eyes. Besides he was eager to sample her goodies, and she knew she would want some sex eventually. So, she figured she'd let him get all worked up and she would piece him off whenever she needed something.

"Yes I'm sure." Gina said for the third time.

Her patience was starting to run thin with Monica. It seemed like Monica was trying to get out of helping her, but Gina needed this, big time and she wasn't getting off the hook now. "And you know what else I'm sure of? I'm sure that your mother is here at the mental hospital with me; just a weak little old bitch that couldn't possibly push her pillow off of her face. She'd just go to sleep and never wake up again, no one would suspect a thing. You get what I'm saying?"

"Yes, I get you loud and clear. I was just asking for clarity, is all,,."

"Oh ok, so to be crystal clear and completely fucking transparent…fix this. I don't care how, but It better be in my favor, or your mom will pay the price for your fuck up. Is that enough clarity for you, Monica?"

Monica was so tired of Gina, but she had to go along with her twisted plan. Who knew that Gina of all people, would end up in the same mental hospital as Monica's mother? Gina always seemed like the "Most likely to Succeed" when they were in school. Now she had Monica all tangled up in this deception. She felt bad for Brandon, because he was a good guy when they were all growing up, but she had to think of her mom's safety. So, she kept her tone even and calm.

"I got it, Gina. I know exactly how to fix this. It won't be as hard as I originally thought. All I have to do is change the report that has the results. I just hope I don't lose my job."

"Even if you do, at least you'll still have your mom." Gina chuckled. "I don't know if he's shooting blanks or what, but I've taken care of the hard part. I'm already pregnant, the father doesn't know and he never will. So, now you'll make sure Brandon is the father."

"You do know that I'm only changing the report, right? This won't make Brandon the father for real." Monica explained.

"Of course I know that dummy, I'm not crazy."

Monica had to hold her tongue. Gina was crazier than a wide-mouth mule, but she wasn't going to debate that over the phone with her. Especially since Gina was in there with her mother.

"Now, get off the phone and get to work, bitch."

Gina dropped the phone into the cradle and smiled to herself. There was never a time that she doubted her plan. Sure, there had been twists and turns along the way, and it seemed like the longest way to her goal sometimes, but she would still get what she wanted in the end. She couldn't wait to see the look on Dakota's face when the results were read.

Her thoughts were interrupted when Chuck slipped his finger into her. Her hospital attire didn't offer much resistance. She decided to let him play in her pussy a little. Surprisingly, he had some really talented fingers. Before she knew it, she had her legs draped over the arms of the desk chair, while Chuck ate and fingered her at the same time. He had her soaking wet by the time she came.

He stood up and she could see the huge bulge in his pants. It was obvious that he wanted to give her some pipe, but she wasn't about to give him some pussy for a phone call. So instead, she got up and quickly headed to the door.

"Wait, where are you going?"

"I'm finished using the phone, but the next time I need you for something, we can pick up where we left off."

She gave him a seductive look and licked her lips.

"Besides, we've been gone for a while…don't you think the other orderlies will miss us?" she asked.

He agreed. But he needed time for his dick to go down, because his erection was clear through the hospital scrubs he wore.

"But, next time we will pick up right here." He told her, placing her hand on his hardness.

Gina, gave it a little massage, then turned and walked out. She knew she had him right where she needed him. And soon she would be secure that she had Brandon as well. As long as Monica did the right thing.

Although Monica had done Gina's dirty work, she was still worried about her mother's safety. Monica picked up the phone and called the number she'd just looked up. The phone rang and a receptionist answered. Monica took a deep breath and asked to speak to Mr. Black.

"Who's calling please?"

"Monica Dent."

She was put on hold. She wondered if he would remember her, it had been a long time. She reminisced on her college days, before her mother got sick. Those were some of the best times of her life; she had the best roommate a girl could ask for.

"Hello?"

A baritone voice answered, and fresh memories flooded Monica's mind.

"Hi. Alexander?"

"Yes."

Monica didn't know exactly what to say, but she had to protect her mother, even if it might incriminate her.

"I don't know if you remember me from college, but I was Falilatu's roommate."

She paused to see what his reaction would be.

"Monica? Is that you?" he asked in amazement.

"Yes it's me. How are you?"

"I'm great. How are you?"

"I'm good."

"To what do I owe the honor?"

"Well, I actually need your legal help. I know you are one of the best lawyers in these parts, so…"

"What's going on?"

"It's a long story, but I feel that my mother may be in danger at the institution where she lives. There is a woman there that is blackmailing me and using my mother to make me do what she wants."

Alex's mind immediately thought about Gina and her trial that put her in the mental hospital.

"What is the woman's name?"

"I really just want to get my mother transferred, I don't want to cause any problems for the woman."

"All of this information stays right here with me. Can you tell me her name?"

"Her name is Gina."

Alex knew it.

"What is Gina making you do, Monica?"

"She had me to change some results of a DNA test for her, or else my mother wouldn't wake up the next day." Monica started crying.

"It's ok, don't worry Monica, I can help you. We need to sit down and talk, can you meet me this evening?"

"Yes, of course. Thank you so much Alexander."

"No problem. Let me ask you this, why did she need the results changed?"

"She's pinning her baby on another man, and she needed the results to say he was the father. I feel so bad about doing it, but Gina was threating to put a pillow over my mother's face if I didn't." she was sobbing again. "And I know the guy she's trying to fool, he's a good guy."

"Is he? What's his name?"

"Brandon."

Alex thought about how those false results might affect Dakota. Something like this could crush her spirit and change her forever. He wasn't going to let Gina hurt her like this. If she threatened to kill Monica's mother, he knew she was capable of doing the same to Dakota. He wouldn't let that happen. He couldn't take another loss like that. He would take the case.

Brandon got the call two weeks later to be in court at noon. Dakota tried to think positive and keep an open mind. She held it together until they walked Gina into the court. Gina was showing a little more than she was the last time they had seen her, even though it had only been a couple of weeks. She waved at Brandon, and Dakota lost it, and shot her the bird.

Brandon pushed her hand down and told her to calm down. He put his arm around her shoulder and that wiped the smile off of Gina's face, which made Dakota feel better.

"All rise…" the bailiff announced the entrance of the judge.

Dakota's heart beat sped up and a sweat broke out on her forehead. She was grateful when the bailiff told them to be seated. She looked around the courtroom, it wasn't nearly as full this time as last time. She guessed no one really cared who the father was, except for her and Brandon. She reached for his hand and held it. She could feel her heart beating in her chest. Her thoughts were all over the place.

She thought about how she would feel raising another woman's child. Could she love the child? What if the child looked like Gina? Would this delay her having a child even further? What if she never cheated with Alex, would this still have happened? What if this? What if that?

The judge finished what he was saying, and picked up the results. Dakota started hyperventilating. For some reason she couldn't catch her breath. The judge was saying something, but all

Dakota could hear was her own heartbeat in her ears. What was going on here?

"I'm going to miss the most important part." She thought

"In the response to the question of paternity. Brandon West has submitted the requested DNA for testing. The results of the test were conclusive and are as follows…"

The room began to spin. Dakota cupped her hand over her mouth, trying to catch her breath, but it wasn't working. She saw the judge's lips moving.

"…it is 99.999% chance that Mr. West is the father."

Dakota fainted.

She awoke to the sound of the judge's gavel pounding and Gina's shouting.

"Order! Order in the court! Bailiff remove Ms. Hefel from my courtroom."

As they dragged her from the room, Gina continued pledging her love to Brandon.

"I love you Brandon! We will be a happy family soon, don't worry. Take care of our baby until I come home!"

Dakota realized she had two choices. She could either play the victim and have a pity party, or she could embrace her new role as wife and mother. She decided to embrace it. She was going to raise this child as her own, and love it like her own. And after five years of waiting to meet and hold her child, Dakota would make sure that Gina knew what real pain was. Gina had taken the opportunity of having Brandon's first born child from her, but Dakota vowed Gina would never have its love.

"Yeah, smile now bitch, because you'll be crying soon enough. That's my child you're carrying. You are just a surrogate and after you have this baby, I'll make sure it never loves you."

MISS KP STILL ROCKING WITH THE BEST! A WIFE'S BETRAYAL IS HOT!

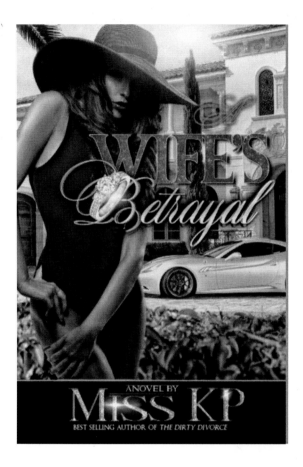

BEST-SELLING AUTHOR KENDALL BANKS DOES IT AGAIN WITH

FILTHY RICH PART 1 AND 2!

PART 3 IS ON THE WAY!

@authorkendallb

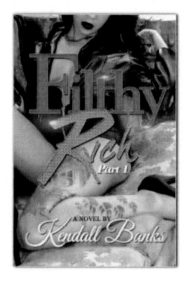

Danette Majette presents

I SHOULDA SEEN HIM COMIN' PART 1 AND 2!

Get it now...ONLY on #kindle!

HEART BREAKER II
FOR THE LOVE OF KARMA

Avery Goode's

PILLOW PRINCESS

Part 1 and 2!

VISIT LCB @LCBOOKS

WWW.LIFECHANGINGBOOKS.NET

ORDER FORM

MAIL TO:
PO Box 488
Brandywine, MD 20613
301-362-6508

Date:	Phone:

Email:	

Ship to:

Address:

City & State: Zip:

Make all money orders and cashiers checks payable to: **Life Changing Books**

Qty.	ISBN	Title	Release Date	Price
	0-9741394-2-4	Bruised by Azarel	Jul-05	$ 15.00
	0-9741394-7-5	Bruised 2: The Ultimate Revenge by Azarel	Oct-06	$ 15.00
	0-9741394-3-2	Secrets of a Housewife by J. Tremble	Feb-06	$ 15.00
	0-9741394-6-7	The Millionaire Mistress by Tiphani	Nov-06	$ 15.00
	1-934230-99-5	More Secrets More Lies by J. Tremble	Feb-07	$ 15.00
	1-934230-95-2	A Private Affair by Mike Warren	May-07	$ 15.00
	1-934230-96-0	Flexin & Sexin Volume 1	Jun-07	$ 15.00
	1-934230-89-8	Still a Mistress by Tiphani	Nov-07	$ 15.00
	1-934230-91-X	Daddy's House by Azarel	Nov-07	$ 15.00
	1-934230-88-X	Naughty Little Angel by J. Tremble	Feb-08	$ 15.00
	1-934230820	Rich Girls by Kendall Banks	Oct-08	$ 15.00
	1-934230839	Expensive Taste by Tiphani	Nov-08	$ 15.00
	1-934230782	Brooklyn Brothel by C. Stecko	Jan-09	$ 15.00
	1-934230669	Good Girl Gone bad by Danette Majette	Mar-09	$ 15.00
	1-934230804	From Hood to Hollywood by Sasha Raye	Mar-09	$ 15.00
	1-934230707	Sweet Swagger by Mike Warren	Jun-09	$ 15.00
	1-934230677	Carbon Copy by Azarel	Jul-09	$ 15.00
	1-934230723	Millionaire Mistress 3 by Tiphani	Nov-09	$ 15.00
	1-934230715	A Woman Scorned by Ericka Williams	Nov-09	$ 15.00
	1-934230685	My Man Her Son by J. Tremble	Feb-10	$ 15.00
	1-924230731	Love Heist by Jackie D.	Mar-10	$ 15.00
	1-934230812	Flexin & Sexin Volume 2	Apr-10	$ 15.00
	1-934230748	The Dirty Divorce by Miss KP	May-10	$ 15.00
	1-934230758	Chedda Boyz by CJ Hudson	Jul-10	$ 15.00
	1-934230766	Snitch by VegasClarke	Oct-10	$ 15.00
	1-934230693	Money Maker by Tonya Ridley	Oct-10	$ 15.00
	1-934230774	The Dirty Divorce Part 2 by Miss KP	Nov-10	$ 15.00
	1-934230170	The Available Wife by Carla Pennington	Jan-11	$ 15.00
	1-934230774	One Night Stand by Kendall Banks	Feb-11	$ 15.00
	1-934230278	Bitter by Danette Majette	Feb-11	$ 15.00
	1-934230299	Married to a Balla by Jackie D.	May-11	$ 15.00
	1-934230308	The Dirty Divorce Part 3 by Miss KP	Jun-11	$ 15.00
	1-934230316	Next Door Nympho By CJ Hudson	Jun-11	$ 15.00
	1-934230286	Bedroom Gangsta by J. Tremble	Sep-11	$ 15.00
	1-934230340	Another One Night Stand by Kendall Banks	Oct-11	$ 15.00
	1-934230359	The Available Wife Part 2 by Carla Pennington	Nov-11	$ 15.00
	1-934230332	Wealthy & Wicked by Chris Renee	Jan-12	$ 15.00
	1-934230375	Life After a Balla by Jackie D.	Mar-12	$ 15.00
	1-934230251	V.I.P. by Azarel	Apr-12	$ 15.00
	1-934230383	Welfare Grind by Kendall Banks	May-12	$ 15.00
	1-934230413	Still Grindin' by Kendall Banks	Sep-12	$ 15.00
	1-934230391	Paparazzi by Miss KP	Oct-13	$ 15.00
	1-93423043X	Cashin' Out by Jai Nicole	Nov-12	$ 15.00
	1-934230634	Welfare Grind Part 3 by Kendall Banks	Mar-13	$15.00
	1-934230642	Game Over by Winter Ramos	Apr-13	$15.99
			Total for Books	$

	Shipping Charges (add $4.95 for 1-4 books 1-3m)	$
	Total Enclosed (add lines)	$

* Prison Orders- Please allow up to three (3) weeks for delivery.

Please Note: We are not held responsible for returned prison orders. Make sure the facility will receive books before ordering.

*Shipping and Handling of 5-10 books is $6.95, please contact us if your order is more than 10 books. (301)362-6508